Once Bitten
Twice Shy

Once Bitten Twice Shy

MARISA FERRARO

OPENBOOK CREATIVE

Published in 2015 in Australia by Marisa Ferraro

oncebittentwiceshy.com.au

Text copyright © Marisa Ferraro 2015

Book Production: OpenBook Creative

Cover Design: Anne-Marie Reeves

Consulting editor: Bree DeRoche

Copyedited by: AuthorSupportServices.com

Australia Cataloguing-in-Publication entry

Author: Ferraro, Marisa, author.

Title: Once Bitten Twice Shy: when love doesn't conquer all

ISBN: 9781925680096 (paperback)

Subjects: Man-woman relationships—Fiction. Love stories.

Dewey Number: A823.4

To the greatest guy in my world. My father. You were a beacon of light with your encouragement, strength and your heart that was filled with love.

To all women who love—may your hearts always be open and abundant.

To Joanne—who taught me about men.

To Carol—who taught me self-love.

I

The sun peered through the curtains brightly enough to wake Maxine from her slumber. She rolled over and squinted at the clock–nine a.m.

"Already?" she moaned. She lay in her usual waking position, like a starfish splayed across her queen-sized bed. She stretched and looked at the gown hanging on her wardrobe door, instantly reminding her that it was Sally's wedding day. It had been just over a month since Shamus broke up with her. Thirty-three days, eleven hours and twelve minutes, to be precise. She needed a wedding like she needed a dip in a piranha-infested plunge pool. She looked around her bedroom–tissues, macaroons and self-help books had taken over of late. She was still trying to understand how men do what they do ... how a person you adore can tell you they love you at breakfast, then tell Tanya from the Accounts Department the same thing by lunchtime. What the fuck?

Jesus, Shamus.

She'd thought she was on her way to having it all. Yet now she was having to face that fact that she most certainly did not. She was back to square one. And just to add salt to the wound, she had to go and face a couple that *did* have it all, and were walking down the aisle at noon to prove it. To say it sucked was putting it mildly. Sucked for *her*, not for *Sally*, of course. She was happy for Sally. But she really didn't want to start the day feeling this way. She couldn't stop the thoughts racing through her head: What if Shamus was here with me now? What if we were getting ready for the wedding together? What if it was *us* getting married!? What if …? What if …? What if …? Funny how life can pan out sometimes—one woman's Cinderella moment is another's Dante's inferno.

Enough! She had to slam the brakes on her self-indulgent thought-train. She had a wedding to go to, like it or not. She looked down at her brand-new Jimmy Choo heels, still in the box, right next to the bed, and smiled. Although she felt like shit, she didn't have to *look* like it—she could strut her stuff in designer labels. Was there any other way? Maxine was addicted to frocking up and Jimmy Choo was her drug of choice. Her mood lighten as she thought about finally getting to break out those strappy badboys.

She rolled over and came face to face with the last remaining macaroon in the packet on her pillow… sad, pathetic, lonely. Like her. She brushed it aside, half-heartedly. It was time to get up, frock up, bling up and face the day. Time to forget about Shamus The Shit, who fucked off with Tanya The Tramp. No more time-wasting over him, as he certainly didn't waste time getting over her. *I'm better than that,* she told herself.

Maxine—or 'M' to her friends—was a social butterfly. Give her an occasion to mingle, drink Hendricks, with cucumber of course, and have a laugh, and she was there. Social interactions were her strong suit. Definitely not your shy girl, she had no trouble striking up a conversation with anyone. Shattered heart or not, Sally's wedding would be no exception. Good friends, good company, music and laughs were on the menu. Maybe it's what she needed after thirty-three days, eleven hours and... sixteen minutes.

M found herself musing about weddings. As the years had gone by, she'd witnessed her share of them as her friends took the big leap, one by one. She was excited for Sally. And she enjoyed weddings – they always made her wonder what married life might be like ... but at this phase of her life, she wondered if it would ever happen for her. Was it supposed to be every woman's destiny? M considered herself kind of on the fence about it. A hopeless romantic at heart, she was also a realist. She had a strong and vivid personality, but, at the same time, a vulnerable soul filled with compassion and love. Does a girl really need to have a 'ring on it?' Is it wrong if she never does? In the whole grand scheme of things, does it really matter?

Her twenties had been filled with parties and big nights out with friends, and with boys here and there. She'd done some travelling and worked hard in between trips to save up for the next holiday. She recalled a conversation with her friend, Elisha, years ago before university graduation. As they were primping in the mirror, getting dressed for their big end-of-year presentation, Elisha had asked, "Hey, Max, what do you think we'll be doing ten years from now?"

Maxine, running a brush through her hair, had turned and looked at Elisha and said casually, "We'll be happily married with two-point-five kids. Or," she added with a cheeky wink, "we'll be sexy, sophisticated single women-about-town with a stack of gossip-worthy experiences to brag to our boring married friends about."

Chuckling in retrospect, M wondered who would have thought the latter would turn out to be the case. She certainly hadn't. She sat on her bed and thought about how during her twenties she'd felt bulletproof. She, Elisha and Caroline would go out straight after class on Fridays at uni, bringing their sequined tops, leather jackets (and of course the ever-important straightening iron, which Caroline kept in the boot of her car 'just in case') to the girls' locker room to get changed. After an hour of touching up and hair spraying they would be ready to hit the town, bar-hopping and arriving home in the wee hours, only to do it all over again the next night. M smiled as she wondered how they'd done it for all those years. She couldn't do it now. Recovery would take three days at least.

"Enjoy your youth–it will be fleeting," her aunt had once said.

To the seventeen-year-old M, the concept of being old–say, like, *thirty*–had been inconceivably far ahead. "I've got ages, Aunty Rose," she'd replied.

Yet Aunty Rose was spot on. The years did go by quickly and so much had happened. However, experience did teach a thing or two, she'd discovered. What seemed the be-all-and-end-all in your twenties isn't the case at all at thirty. Back then she'd wanted to get into fashion, so she'd begun her bachelor's degree in design. But as she matured, she knew something was missing–it was a choice based more on fantasy than reality; champagne catwalks and gem-encrusted Manolo Blahniks—and she became confident enough in herself to question her choices, to acknowledge her true strengths and to let go of the girlish whimsy. The question became what she really liked, what challenged her intellect and sparked her creativity, and it drew her to advertising. She had discovered a flair and a passion for lateral thinking, the ability to know what made people tick and the ways to get a buyer's attention. Now her career was set, and she could honestly say she loved it.

The jury was still out on men, however. M had always lived under the common female assumption that men matured later than women. So did that mean that a thirty-or-forty-something man *always* knew how to treat a woman—the chivalry and courting? She'd once fancied a guy in first-year uni and found out he fancied her, too. She'd given her number to one of his friends to pass on to him. It took a week of text-flirts, concluding with a coffee date, for her to finally discover that it was the *friend* texting her, not the guy she'd fancied, as he'd been too shy to approach her. At twenty that might have seemed cute, but if a man in his thirties or forties did that to her today, she'd probably run for the hills. The same goes for any forty year old who constantly checked in with his mum. He might have his mortgage paid off, but if Mummy still did his cooking and his washing, then clearly 'Mummy's Boy' hadn't quite left home, so to speak.

Still, M liked to think of herself as someone who always gave people the benefit of the doubt. Maybe it was stupid or naïve of her—case in point, Shamus The Shit. It took him months to reel her in (originally she'd pegged him as not her type: a dashing dynamo from the Legal Department with a Brad Pitt smile—too handsome, too charming ... too risky), but he gained her trust and when she fell for him, she fell in a big way. For her, it was bliss. He could do nothing wrong. It was *Shamus this, Shamus that* ... *Shamus, Shamus, Shamus.*

Yet, in like a blink of an eye, she'd turned into a macaroon-eating, vodka-swilling single girl reading books on men, sex, love and chemistry and how to unleash the power within. She wanted her Vogue days back. Yet, she thought, do men and women ever really figure each other out? Freud couldn't even answer that one.

Finally dragging herself out of bed, M put one foot in front of the other and walked to her wardrobe and swung open the doors. There, her shoe collection lay before her and she couldn't help but smile. With macaroons as her recent bedfellows, one could easily put on a kilo or two. But shoes don't end up on the hips and tummy. They always looked amazing.

M gazed abstractedly at the gorgeous dress in the wardrobe and thought about how during the past decade she hadn't really had a care in the world. Carefree, without much responsibility, it had all been about discovery–what she liked and didn't like, which jobs she chased as she climbed the career ladder and became more financially stable, what made her happy. Balance was the key for her. She'd found it eight years ago at Louis Advertising, the firm that had become like her second home. Her job let her express a different part of herself, and she very much needed that outlet because she tended to hide her deepest feelings. Yes, she was a good communicator and even a social butterfly, but when dealing with matters of the heart, she was, conversely, a bit of a recluse, not wanting to express too much too soon, or explore too deeply.

Was this because she thought men always had an agenda? Hadn't her own history taught her once bitten, twice shy?

M occasionally felt herself repressing hurtful memories. She hated Shamus for taking away the future she wanted. She was still angry. But she also believed in karma. He was going to regret it some day. His loss. Would a few bad experiences make her think romance would always be like that? Was the thought of having a doting partner who adored her, with a nice home to call their own, just an illusion? Did it always have to be just about fun and the thrill of the catch for singles? The answers to thoughts like these eluded her. She knew, though, that closing herself off would be a hindrance to future suitors. All she really wanted was true sincerity. She was a sincere person filled with passion, and she expressed this inner fire in many ways—her work, her home, fashion, cooking and especially close relationships with those she held dear. She loved her friends and was always there for them, and they mutually inspired each other.

At work, M's creativity and commitment had moved her up the corporate ladder as her dedication came to fruition. She was proud of this. She knew things took time, and her patience and persistence had paid off, as she found her niche. But now it seemed an entire decade had passed by in a flash, and Sally's wedding today brought it all into sharp focus. She'd hit her third decade and it seemed life was going by in the blink of an eye, as it brought more responsibility into her life. She had a mortgage. She worked longer hours. She'd seen relationships begin and end. It was really a whole new ball game. She believed that, like a fine wine, people got better with age, and she trusted that as she grew older, she was becoming wiser too; learning as she went along, which was a good feeling. If only men came with a manual! Apart from her thirty-three days of enforced singledom, she was in a pretty good place in her life. She had a great network of people around her and was doing the things she loved.

She *had* had a man who adored her ... but unfortunately he came with Tanya from Accounts, let's not forget. With her deceased relationship hanging around her neck like a dead albatross, she had to go and witness the magic of matrimony under a stained-glass window of the Virgin Mary in a few hours, no doubt with Ed Sheeran cooing in the background about loving each other until they're septuagenarians. A flat tyre or a sprained ankle would be ideal right about now. But she'd suck it up. The truth way, as jaded and heartbroken as she'd recently become, she had a somewhat nagging feeling that something more was out here. Was all that happened with Shamus a sign? Was something else meant to be? Perhaps it was. Maybe in some way it was the age thing that also bugged her—the idea that women should reach certain goals, most notably marriage, by a certain age, and have children. She quickly dismissed this Jane Austen line of thinking in favour of Germaine Greer, however. Never underestimate the power of a woman, she thought to herself. We can do and be whatever we want to do.

Newly single, she was determined to start fresh—take life by the balls ... even though she couldn't completely let go of the fear of ending up with an ass in her face again. Did she feel the way she did because she saw all her friends getting married and she was now sans boyfriend? M looked at those friends and their spouses with admiration. Their deep connection, friendly loving banter and open communication all made, in M's eyes, a great example of how she wanted her own future relationship with a hypothetical spouse to look. But when would that happen? And if she'd already hit thirty and it still hadn't arrived … then when?

M thought about her first boyfriend, Michael, and wondered what he was doing these days. At the time, she'd thought *he* was The One. As it turned out, he wasn't. Maybe their break-up had been fate, even though at the time she hadn't thought like that. All she though about at the time was the pain and the hurt, and how nobody else could ever possibly be as wonderful. But she'd stopped trying to compare. Experience had taught her that you never feel the same for one guy as you did for another—everyone is so different, there are so many tiny factors, so many variables. And, luckily, experience had also taught her that every new person brings something into your life. Even Shamus The Shit. And what exactly did she learn from that experience? Don't be fooled by blue-eyed lawyers in slim-fit Armani suits? Probably good advice for women everywhere.

Nevertheless, looking back on Michael, the so-called 'great love' of her youth, she smiled, understanding, in retrospect, that it was never meant to be. Rather, it was a special moment in time; simply part of the tapestry of the bigger picture of her life. This gave her confidence that she would find another great love in this lifetime. Perhaps the next one would be *The One* . The One, if there *is* such thing as The One. Life changes and so do people, and so does what they want. Shamus The Shit cemented that belief in her. M found it comforting to know that her great love for *this* moment of her life was still out there. He just hadn't found her yet. And when he did, he'd completely rock her world. She deserved it, for God's sake.

M glanced at the clock. Shit, time to get a move on. She dashed to the kitchen to make coffee. Every time she walked into her beloved kitchen, she sighed with pride. It was an open-plan room, which had looked worn down and ready for the discard heap when she first moved in, with a seventies-style Laminex benches and old timber cupboards. She'd immediately had a vision of what she could do with it and had designed the new kitchen herself, transforming it into a contemporary dream, with granite bench tops, frosted splashbacks and the latest chic electric stovetop. She'd also re-done the lounge, finding various pieces–from an Art Deco glass coffee table to a large chrome lamp that lit up the room with an ambient hue. Eight weeks after moving in, M had the kitchen and lounge area she'd always dreamed of. Her home was definitely her castle, and she was as proud of the work she'd done on it as she was of her best advertising campaigns. She loved expressing her style and personality through her personal interior decorating.

She glanced out the window. Not a cloud in the sky–a perfect day for a wedding. M and Sally had been inseparable since school, sharing every special moment with each other–graduation, holidays, first cars, first boyfriends and, now, another milestone– marriage. Even though, as careers took off, they didn't see each other as much as they wanted to, they both knew that, at the drop of a hat, they would do anything for each other. It was a nice feeling, yet surreal, like watching a sister grow up and fly the coop. M felt proud and happy, as if she were going through this rite of passage along with Sally. But, again, that self-indulgent thought popped into her head: would she follow suit herself?

Maybe you have to create your own journey. Yes, destiny plays a big part, but you have to contribute to it yourself. She sipped her steaming coffee and nibbled a piece of toast, M thought about how everything happens for a reason; our journey is written—who we are, what we do, what we will experience in our lives. Sorrow, heartbreak, happy times, the people we meet. The older she got, the more she believed it. Was there really someone for everyone? M was never the type to be on the lookout. Life was meant to take you by surprise. Good and bad. Love and also loss. Shamus had been a surprise. He accidentally spilled his macchiato on her Dior bag in the building's elevator. He apologised, asked if he could buy her lunch and the rest, they say, is history. It was also a surprise when he came home in a state of agitation thirty-three days ago and told that he was in love with someone else and that it was "a force bigger" than him, and that her name is *Tanya*. Cue the horror and dramatics. There'd been whispers at work that the gorgeous Brad Pitt-esque lawyer from the Legal Department had found his 'Angelina Jolie' in Accounts. Oh my god, it suddenly occurred to M, does that make me the 'Aniston'? She was already getting all the 'Poor M' looks. People became either team Shamus or team M. At least, that's what she'd imagined.

M took another sip of her coffee, snapping herself out of her self-pity. It will get better than this! Surely. She knew she wasn't the first girl to be jilted, and certainly wouldn't be the last. You little turd, Shamus! M knew he'd look back one day and regret his choice. *I'll still be hot and happening and you will be an overweight couch potato and Tanya The Tramp will leave you for a hotter man!* she cackled bitchily, but it was a cathartic release.

Her internal rant over, M finished her coffee and toast and made her way back to the bedroom, bypassing the gown, for now, and slipping into some jeans. She was the designated driver today and had to be at Elisha's for their hair appointment, after which she, Elisha and Kathy would all head to the church together. Looking forward to a pampered morning of hair and nails, she left the house carrying her dress and shoes to change into at Elisha's.

On the way, M stopped off for a 'real' coffee at her favourite café, Jimmy's, a well-known coffee shop in her area. Jimmy's had been there for well over twenty years, though, oddly, the owner, a Greek man in his sixties, was actually called Jerry. Whom Jimmy had been, she'd never know. Jerry was there every morning, and he greeted M with his customary big smile.

"Hello, beautiful Max."

"Morning, Jerry. The usual, please."

"What's on for you today, love?" Jerry asked, as he made her coffee.

"Oh, big one today. It's my friend's wedding. So it's a quick coffee and go."

"Oh, beautiful, love. You enjoy, hey?" Jerry beamed as he passed her the coffee.

M paused outside in the sunshine for a moment and she took her first sip as she spotted a familiar bohemia woman in her seventies approaching. M saw her on a regular basis at Jimmy's, getting her morning caffeine fix, like M.

With her wild salt-and-pepper hair flailing in the breeze, the old lady was clad in a colourful gypsy dress and large stone rings on every finger, and, as always, was pushing a purple trolley bag. M was fascinated by her and always tried to sneak little glimpses of her from behind her sunglasses. She looked like a woman who'd lived not one, but fifty lives, and had some stories to tell, if you let her. Most mornings they would flash each other a polite smile, yet today, unexpectedly, the woman spoke.

"Hello, love. How are you today?" she said, in a heavy Greek accent.

"Good, thank you," smiled M, feeling a little awkward. As fascinated as she was, M wasn't sure she wanted to get locked into a conversation with the crazy gypsy lady and today, of all days, it seemed the old lady was eager to strike up a conversation as she stood staring expectantly at M. Maybe she was lonely. M felt bad, but she had no time. She smiled and waved as she raced off to the car, due for her hair appointment at Elisha's.

"Where are my chicken fillets?!" Kathy yelled from the kitchen, as M walked in the door to all the pre-wedding hubbub.

"Open your eyes," Elisha called back, while putting on her mascara in front of the air-conditioner.

"Does my bum look big in this?" asked Kathy, walking through the doorway and posing.

"No, honey, you look hot. Hot, baby, hot," Elisha replied with conviction, glancing up.

"You can always count on your girlfriends to tell you the truth," said Kathy. "I don't know why women ask men that question. It just makes them roll their eyes and lie." They laughed.

"Oh, hi M, amazingly you're only 15 minutes late," Elisha teased, spotting her at last.

"Better late than never," replied M with a smile, kissing the girls on the cheek.

The girls got busy applying makeup and chatting away. As the hairdresser sculpted, pinned and sprayed, the girls manicured each other. Finally, the dresses were unsheathed of their drycleaner wrappers and the girls zipped in, ready to pile into M's black Alfa Romeo and set off for the church for Sally's big day.

2

It was a beautiful occasion for them all to be reunited. They hadn't seen as much of Sally as they used to, due to Sally's job taking her places and her father living away in rural suburbia. To M, nevertheless, no matter how much time they'd spent apart recently, they all definitely qualified as BFFs, as they'd all been through a lot together over the years. They had a special bond, and M felt there was something to be said about 'the sisterhood'– like the time Kathy had had a bad flu and M and Elisha had helped her with her housework, made her food and nursed her back to health. Or the several occasions when M had had a bad date and one or another of the girls had made the 'emergency' phone call to bail her out. Or when Elisha had been dealing with difficult family issues, Kathy and M would take her out for the night or take turns hosting and having a girls' nights in.

It went without saying that whenever they needed each other, they were there. Elisha and M often joked that their friendship had lasted longer than most marriages, as they'd both had long-term relationships that had ended. This made the bond between them even closer, as they had supported each other during these extremely difficult times in each other's lives.

It seemed to M that men's friendships had a different kind of dynamic. She believed that women were more nurturing and unconditional, and she felt glad for this. Women hugged, cried and supported each other. *We are biochemically made that way and men are just different*, M thought. *We have deeper ways of showing friendship.* Women instinctively knew that even though life might move on and they would be older and have different commitments, they would be together through thick and thin, and most women chose to keep it that way.

Ready at last, M and the girls made their way to the church. The antique statues on the lawn and the cobblestone path leading up to the front doors made it look like a church from the Renaissance. The finely crafted golden statue of the Virgin Mary shone brightly, lending an air of beauty and grace. This could easily be a church just off one of the main streets in Florence– except that there were no handsome policemen guarding the church doors. God bless Italy and its men.

As they approached the vestibule, M spotted their other bestie, Laura, in a gorgeous frock, over in the corner having a cigarette.

"It's not a good look, I know," Laura said as the girls walked over to greet her. "I'm keeping it as far away from me as I can. I don't want a smoke stain on a Cavalli dress."

"You're all ass, no class," joked Kathy.

"Shut up, bitch. I've got a *nice* ass … well at least my husband thinks so!" Laura replied with a smile. They laughed and all made their way into the church. James, Laura's husband, quickly ran in moments later, as it had taken him a while to find parking.

"Laura," he said as their eyes met. She waved at him to come and sit with them. He walked over and got his seat.

"Ladies, how are we?" he said to them all.

"Always good, James," Elisha said.

As they quietly took their seats, the girls looked around to see who else they knew and what everyone was wearing.

"Christ, look at that chick," Laura rolled her eyes at a woman in a miniskirt across the aisle. "Any shorter ... I mean, *really*."

"It's a shame Caroline couldn't make it," M said. "Fancy having two weddings on the same day. Talk about a clash."

"Oh, I'm sure she is enjoying her time away in the Caribbean," replied Kathy. "If you had a wedding in St Barts, wouldn't you go?"

"Hell, yeah," M said, raising an eyebrow for emphasis, suddenly thinking about how a little tropical escape was just what she needed herself.

Kathy nodded at a middle-aged woman just entering the nave. "Check this lady out. That jacket looks like the curtains we had at the beach house in 1985," she giggled.

"What are you, the fashion police?" M asked. The priest heard them chattering and gave them a look of judgement.

"Can you girls cut it out? The priest is giving us a greasy," James said in a theatrical undertone, grinning.

"Hey, how old do you think the priest is?" Elisha asked.

"He looks young," M replied after a brief analysis. "Like maybe in his early thirties."

"I always wonder whether priests shag heaps before they get their calling from God," Elisha whispered.

"Oh my God, Elisha, you're talking about a priest–in *church!*" Laura said, looking a tad shocked. The other girls struggled to contain their laughter.

"Well, she has a point," Kathy observed. "He is a man first and foremost. Being a priest is a career, like being a plumber or an accountant … or a barista."

"You're comparing being a priest to being a *barista?*" M asked, rolling her eyes in amusement at her friend. "The priesthood is a way of life!"

"Sorry, Frauline Maria," laughed Kathy. "I just have this thing, you know. I mean, he *is* young. What drives them? Who chooses to just *stop* having sex?"

"He's cute, too. *I'd* go there," said Elisha.

Laughing, the girls tried once again to contain their volume, as an older lady turned to look at them with a frown.

"Seriously, the service hasn't even started. Surely we can talk a little," M protested.

"Elisha, honey, that is all very *Thorn Birds* of you, but please don't start fantasising about a priest," Laura said.

"There is nothing wrong with fantasies," Elisha replied with mock hauteur. "You aren't actually doing anything; it's only imagination. And imagination is healthy!"

A hush fell as the service finally began. M looked at the groom. Paul appeared nervous, justifiably so, as he awaited his lady, and such a significant moment. He was a good man, M knew, looking at him with pride. Sally was doing well by marrying him.

Glancing at the groomsmen, M suddenly felt a little buzz in her gut as she caught a glimpse of the last one. She'd seen him before, he'd been around over the years, although she couldn't recall his name. She knew from other occasions that he seemed nice, although they hadn't ever really exchanged more than a "hello". She'd never given him a second thought before ... so why the flutter now?

She leaned to Kathy and asked softly, "Hey, what's the name of the second groomsman? I know it's a weird name. Do you remember?"

"I think its Bagadi, but the boys call him Adi, for short. I think it's a Hebrew name or something ... not sure. He looks pretty good in that tux, hey? Wonder what his story is."

M looked at him again. *He is a pretty good looking bloke ... I'm a free agent now so I will perv away*, she thought cheekily to herself.

M dismissed more chatter as the priest asked everyone to stand and the service commenced. Sally looked a picture of perfection in an off-white, strapless gown with an embroidered train, as she walked down the aisle on her father's arm, with a radiant smile. If a girl ever wanted her fifteen minutes of fame, this would be it. Many guests snapped amateur photos to commemorate the moment, while the professional photographer took shots from various angles. As Sally walked past, she looked at M and the girls, and beamed at them with a dazzling smile.

The blushing bride finally at the front of the church, by the priest and her handsome groom, her face was filled with emotion, as was and Paul's, which was clearly visible to the room as they gazed lovingly at each other.

It was a traditional Catholic service—so many of the readings referenced the Bible—as the priest spoke of the sacrament of marriage, and about love, compassion, commitment and compromise. M was very attentive to what he was saying, thinking about how it all fitted together and how two souls connected spiritually to become one. The priest's words were lovely to hear, and it was even more lovely to see her friend enter such a deep connection with Paul. Still, a part of her couldn't help but wonder, even with all the blessings and a couple's willingness to love and commit, whether anyone could *really* live happily ever after. She hoped so, for her friend's sake ... and, in a tiny corner of her mind that didn't bear too close examination at the moment, for her own sake too.

She looked again at Adi. *Damn, he's fine*, she thought. She'd never noticed how tall he was before, how broad shouldered; nor that smile. She just stared at him, transfixed. Why? She suddenly felt desperate for a macaroon. Why the lust all at once? She had to concentrate on the wedding ceremony. No time for sexual fantasies.

M was moved by the exchange of vows and rings. This was her favourite part of a wedding. Sally was surprisingly calm and at ease as she uttered her oath. Paul was actually the more emotional one (who said men didn't get emotional?), his voice cracking audibly as he looked into Sally's eyes and spoke his vows. They were pronounced husband and wife, and loud cheers and clapping erupted in the church as their kiss sealed the deal. M could see Sally's mother wiping her eyes in the front row and her father looking on with pride. Paul's elderly mother also wore a beaming smile.

After the service, Laura lingered with her husband to chat with people while M and the other girls made their way down to the reception centre together. They had heard through the grapevine that this wasn't going to be your average reception, and sure enough it was quite a bit more opulent than they were used to. *Of course, it always helps when the man you are marrying has a hefty bank balance*, M thought, smiling to herself at her friend's good fortune.

"Ladies, you look like kids tasting candy for the first time," Elisha said as they stepped into the lavishly decorated, lush green reception-centre gardens.

"Wow, look at this place!" Kathy exclaimed.

Perfectly manicured hedges framed roses that bloomed so large and so brightly that it seemed as though they stood in a postcard, like Royal Ascot meets Versailles. It was a stunning view. The girls treated themselves to a leisurely stroll through the gardens before heading inside to the reception.

"This place is amazing—go Sally! She really went all out," said Elisha.

"Tell me about it. I'd love to get married here," replied Kathy.

Many guests were making their way around the gardens, taking in the spectacular views and having photos taken.

"Girls, let's get a photo here. It will be so nice," M suggested.

Elisha asked one of the other guests nearby if he would kindly take a shot for them. As he took the camera, she glanced at his left hand. M noticed the wave of disappointment cross her face when she saw there was a ring on it, and laughed.

"Any excuse for you," she said to Elisha with a smirk.

"Oh well, one can only try," Elisha replied with a wink.

"Hey girls, wait up!" waved Laura, walking quickly over with James. "I see a photo op—count me in!"

"Ladies, you all look lovely," James said, smiling.

"Thank you, J," Kathy replied.

"Okay, girls: one … two … three!" said the man taking the photo. James snapped one with his camera, too. With that, they had yet another addition to their book of memories. They made their way inside to the foyer.

Many guests mingled, drinking the Bollinger champagne offered on trays by the attentive staff. The décor lent the venue the appearance of an eighteenth-century ballroom—something Marie Antoinette might have dined in.

"Is it just me, or do you feel like you have just stepped back in time?" Elisha asked, echoing M's thoughts.

"Sweetie, would you like some champagne?" James asked Laura.

"Sure, thanks so much," she replied, kissing him on the lips.

As James headed in search of drinks, Elisha asked, "You two, honestly … how do you still manage all the lovey-dovey stuff after all these years?"

"We just do. I guess it still feels like high school. I still see him in the same way. I adore him." Laura had such a happy aura about her, you could just about believe it was teenage-style first love as she gazed after her husband. You could see it in her eyes.

"Well, I think it's great. I hope I find someone like that someday," M said, looking at her friend with pride, yet her expression on her face said otherwise. Laura saw this immediately and hugged her.

"You will, honey. You will. You are a special girl. You're our girl," Laura said.

M looked around the room, admiring the people, along with the décor. Most of the men were dressed in black tie and many women were dressed in long gowns with sparkling diamonds–clearly not your run-of-the-mill wedding. That was the thing with Sally, she never did things by half: straight marks in Year 12; graduated with honours; business analyst with a highly paid job at one of the world's top companies; trips to Europe every year; scored a man in finance with a holiday house in Italy, a housekeeper and a personal chef. Maybe some women do get it all. *Hell, why not, if you can do it?* M thought. And what woman wouldn't want to pull out all the stops for her big day?

"Maxine!"

M turned around to see an old high school girlfriend, Tracy McMullen, approaching with a wide smile. Tracy, their class captain, who twelve years ago had been the perfect blonde skinny girl that all the boys went for. She'd always had the latest of everything because Mummy and Daddy would buy it for her. Between that and her classic good looks, if any girl made you feel inadequate, it was Tracy. And judging by her appearance now, that had not changed a bit. She looked stunning.

"Tracy, my God, how are you? What a surprise to see you here!"

"I know! It was sweet of Sally to invite me – we only just got back in touch over the past few years through Facebook.

Although we were good friends back in school, of course. So, what's new with you? Married with children?"

The inevitable question. Heaven forbid it doesn't get asked. M faked a smile.

"Oh ... not at the moment. Life has been so busy and exciting that I haven't gotten around to it yet." She thought that sounded like a dignified response.

"Oh, darling, don't worry. Take your time. I got married to my first and only boyfriend, had two kids and then he left me for someone ten years younger. Now I live in a flat and I'm going to court to get the child support payments he owes. Hasn't paid a cent. He can buy his pissy little girlfriend lingerie, but can't pay for his kids. Can you believe it? If I had my chance again, I would have taken my time and not rushed. Trust me, Maxine, you'd rather be alone then have problems with your other half, or be stuck in something that's not working."

"Oh, Tracy, I'm sorry," said M, realising life wasn't so perfect after all for the girl she thought had it all. What might be perceived as rosy for the person outside looking in might actually not be true at all from inside—not even for someone whose life seemed so ideal. "You'll be okay, though. Karma comes around, so don't you worry. His girlfriend will get sick of him as he gets older. You just think of yourself and the kids. Fuck him. He will realise in time what he's lost, you'll see," M said, hoping to make Tracy feel better.

"Thanks, Max. You know, the main thing is being happy," Tracy said, sipping her champagne and looking thoughtful. "And that's something that was hard to achieve with him, no matter how hard I tried. He wanted a Barbie Doll, not a wife. It's a struggle now, but I'm better for it. And the kids are fine, so that's all that counts at the end of the day."

"You're amazing, Tracy. Good luck with it all," said M warmly. "It was nice to see you and talk to you again. Enjoy the night." They hugged, and as Tracy walked away and M made her way to the list to see what her table number was, she found herself amazed all over again at how people and situations change. Do the things that happen to us make us change or do we just evolve naturally? Are we products of our environment? Is it all cause and effect?

She exchanged smiles in passing with a few other people from high school. It would be somewhat of a reunion for them all tonight. There were Laura and James, already being seated, Elisha at the bar and Kathy talking to another school friend. Just as she was about to check her table, she heard her name again.

"Oh, Maxine, darling, I haven't seen you in such a long time!"

It was Mrs Whitaker, the retired alterations lady who had been well known in the community ever since she had immigrated from Poland back in 1956. Mrs Whitaker was like everyone's favourite aunty. All the local kids had grown up with her. She'd done alterations until she finally retired two years ago.

"Hi, Mrs Whitaker, how are you?" M said, kissing her powdery cheek. Here was a woman she was truly happy to see and whom she admired greatly. Mrs Whitaker had escaped from war-torn Europe and raised four kids in a tiny flat while working all her life. M liked her tenacity and courage, and aspired to be like her.

"Good, love. You are as beautiful as ever," Mrs Whitaker said. "Always smiling, you bubbly girl. Got yourself a fella, darling?"

There it was again. Twice in thirty minutes. Not bad. A slight dagger in the heart but nothing champagne couldn't soothe.

"Not yet, Mrs W, it's not a race," she spat out. She'd been trying to sound funny but it came out a little more defensively than she intended. *Oops.* "Better the right one than the wrong one," she added, trying to lighten her tone. Is that all people think about when they see a single girl, even in this day and age? What happened to "How's work? How was your holiday? Nice shoes"? There's a million other questions one could ask. Why is it always that one?! She was so distracted that she almost missed Mrs Whitaker's reply.

"Of course, darling. You enjoy and let the master do his work. Remember, getting married is the easy part. It's *staying* married that's hard. Forever is a long time to promise someone. You are a beautiful girl. Always remember that."

M gave her a hug. "Nice to see you, Mrs Whitaker. Take care." And then it was off to the singles table, to which she discovered she'd been assigned. Of course.

There was a certain stigma attached to being placed at the singles table, but M never let that bother her. For some, it was a big deal not to be partnered off–a reminder that you didn't have a 'plus one' and were still on the lookout for that perfect person. Or that *not-so*-perfect person. But for her, it was any excuse for a meet-and-greet. In fact, M considered the singles table to be the best one. There was plenty of chatter, banter, drinking, laughter, getting to know others, and perhaps making a friend or finding a lover. She thought it should be dubbed the 'social network' table. It had its own style, and she fancied that it even spoke on behalf of all those who shared it. *Yes, it's true we haven't as yet found The One*, she imagined it saying (with a theatrical sigh at that last part), *but we take our freedom and run with it, rather than worrying needlessly. We live our lives on our own terms!* In short, M reckoned that the singles table was a friend, not a foe, and now that she was back there she was going to make the most of it and not wallow.

As the day turned into night, the usual formalities played out—the cutting of the cake, the first dance, speeches, and lots of champagne and dancing. M and the other single girls got on the dance floor as though it were a nightclub, making things memorable and fun. She spotted the handsome groomsman a few times—*what's his name again? Aiden? Addi? Adi? Adi!*—in his crisp white shirt that really showed off his gorgeous tanned complexion. How did his shirt stay so crisp when everyone else, as this point in the evening and all the dancing, the heat and champagne, was looking a tad bedraggled? *Mr White Shirt*, she giggled to herself. *Damn, he is cute!*

Every time she saw Sally dancing with her 'husband', he made her a little emotional and so happy for them. It was beautiful to see the look in their eyes as they gazed at each other—this was real love. M had a hunch, a feeling that they were a perfect match.

The girls finally got a few moments with their friend after the main course had finished.

"Hey girls, thanks for coming," Sally said as she and Paul walked over to their table. Sally hugged them all, one by one.

"Thank you for inviting us. You look amazing," Kathy said.

"Congratulations, Sal. This is a beautiful wedding," Laura said as she kissed her friend.

"Congrats to you both," said James as he shook Paul's hand and kissed Sally on the cheek.

Sally sighed, sounding both happy and tired. "It's been a long day … and it's not quite over yet."

"Enjoy it, darling," M told her. "It goes so fast, doesn't it?"

"I know … all the preparation and stress … for one day. Then that's it done."

"I'm looking forward to relaxing," Paul added.

"Yes, 'relaxing'. Is that what the kids are calling it?" M said with a grin. Paul laughed.

"Come on, let's get a quick group shot," Sally said, as she grabbed the passing photographer.

They all chatted for a few more minutes, then Sally and Paul were off to say hello to friends at another table. With 250 guests, M knew she was lucky to have spent even that much time with them.

James looked at Laura and said, "Do you remember our big day, babe? It doesn't feel like all that much time has passed, hey? What a great day it was, and so much fun." He smiled and reached for his wife's hand.

"I know, it feels like yesterday for me—unforgettable," Laura smiled back. M knew from many previous conversations how lucky Laura felt to be married to such a wonderful and adoring man. Here was her proof that 'happily ever after' really was possible.

As the night continued and the dance floor filled again and again with swaying people, M's indulged in a little reckless self-pity, envisioning herself having her own first dance with her man. She'd thought it would be Shamus ... but then she quickly forced herself to knock it off, as jumping on that train of thought would only lead to Depressionville. She figured that with all things in life it was only a matter of timing.

She made her way to the ladies' room to freshen up her lippy. As she fixed her dress and her hair, she listened to two girls bragging about their past conquests. She smiled and had a little chuckle. As she walked out of the ladies' room, her long gown got caught on her heel and she immediately lost balance and began to fall, when—in mid-air—a pair of strong arms caught her, saving her from an embarrassing tumble to the wine-soaked carpet.

"Are you okay?" It was Mr White Shirt himself, still looking crisp and handsome and a little heartbreaking with a huge pearly white smile beaming down at her.

Oh God, she instantly thought to herself, *how mortifying! I hope he doesn't think I'm pissed! I almost went ass over tit!*

"Here, let me help you," he smiled. Was that a smirk on his face? M felt a fresh flush of humiliation. She couldn't help but notice, though, that he kept his arms around her, even though she had regained her footing. Her heart was beating one hundred miles an hour.

"Thank you ... oh my God, I'm such a loser!" she laughed. "This dress and these heels are a lethal combination," she stressed, hoping he wasn't putting it down to the Bollinger.

"Don't worry. These things happen. As long as you are okay?" he said.

"Yes, I'm fine. I guess that makes you my Batman, hey?" she said. *Oh, you fuckwit, M!* she thought to herself. What a response. Of all the things to say. *Batman.* Really?

"Are you having a good night?" he proceeded to ask.

"Yeah, it's been great. It's so lovely here. And you?" she replied.

"It's been a fun night so far. May I say, you look lovely in that dress. You stand out in the crowd. Even though it made you fall," he added with a smile.

She looked into his eyes, transfixed. She was smitten. Was he feeling it too? They just stood there for a moment and paused, not really knowing what else to say. *I'm so glad I fell*, she thought to herself.

"Well, I guess we'd better get back to it," she said, feeling awkward and breaking the pause.

"Yeah, of course."

"Thanks for your help," she said.

He smiled and walked away as she watched him. *Nice ass!*

As the wedding drew to a close, the girls met up and made their way to M's car. Elisha said in a sombre tone, "And another one bites the dust. Another single girl has flown the coop and become a 'we', not an 'I'".

"She is still one of us ... just not like before," Kathy said.

"I think we should never lose the 'I'," M said. "You're an 'I' before you ever become a 'we', so we should never lose that. It's important to never lose yourself, even when you're with someone. Your partner should be a part of you, not all of you." There was a short silence as the girls pondered this.

"You know what, Dr M? You're absolutely right," Kathy said.

When M got home, she sat on her bed and reflected on the night. Eating a piece of wedding cake she'd snagged on the way out the door—caramel-swirl chocolate mud cake!—she wondered, do we all secretly want that princess moment deep down? Part of her said, *don't worry, it will happen!* While the other part of her snapped back, *Oh shut the hell up!* There were too many rules when it came to romance, especially marriage—it all had to happen at the right age, under certain circumstances, with someone who ticked all the socially acceptable boxes. But who makes those rules? We run our own race, right?

Still, she wondered what happened to a person after they said "I do". A single girl can only assume or wonder, she thought; you never really know until you're living it for yourself. It's the life you make *after* the princess moment that counts. So many people get caught up in 'the day' and all the planning that they lose sight of the fundamental thing: spending the rest of your life with that person—highs and lows … gastro bouts and morning breath … for better or for worse. True, there were perks to being single, perks of which M and her girlfriends were living proof. She counted down the list for herself: no one to tell you what to do; no one to answer to; total freedom in life; go where you want and do what you want. Single or not, M was certain of one thing— you have to embrace what you've got and take what life gives you. She knew that as much as she had loved her life with Shamus, for some reason the Universe had decided it was not meant to be. She had another destiny.

Yet at times, especially like these, that one inevitable question would pop up for her as it did, she was sure, for most single women: *When will I find The One?* Even as she indulged in the thought, she cringed to herself. She wasn't *that* girl–the one who puts her entire life on hold waiting to be rescued by her prince charming. She was successful, financially self-reliant, fulfilled. No rescuing required. Although flashes of pessimism would occasionally creep in, M was always one to see the light in the dark. Man or no man, she had an amazing life and was filled with high hopes for the future–*her* future, whatever it held.

She went to sleep and dreamed, with a smear of caramel-swirl chocolate on her pyjamas.

3

If there was one thing that became a ritual for the girls, it was their chats about the happenings of the week over drinks on Saturday nights. This ritual was echoed by many girls the world over, thanks to a certain show about four single girls living in Manhattan drinking Cosmopolitans.

Tonight they were at The Barkley, a swanky, happening bar on the rooftop of one of the city's most popular, five-star hotels, and M was already onto her third Japanese Slipper, while Laura got stuck into the Canadian Club. It was where one went for the best-known cocktails, to see potential eye candy, mingle and, if you were lucky, spot an A-list celebrity. The Barkley was generally filled with thirty-to-forty-something alpha males, some business financiers and real estate moguls. The women were always dressed to the nines, some of whom had also had a little plastic enhancement. Basically, The Barkley brought together anyone who was anyone.

The view from the roof was breathtaking. The girls sat in the lounge area while they watched the city and its bright lights. The conversation, inevitably, turned to men.

"He just watches sport all day. I can't get a conversation in. I feel like I cease to exist when footy season is on," Laura moaned.

"Isn't sport like a 'can't live without' thing for a man?" asked Elisha.

"How mundane," responded Laura. "Don't you want to watch something else or try something new? Every channel does an update, so why do you have to see it on every channel? They just say the same thing. It's like eating dry toast every day. Don't you eventually want Nutella, or butter and jam, or peanut butter?"

"Sweetie, you *married* one of them," M replied. They all laughed.

She took what was nearly the last sip of her third Japanese Slipper. She felt relaxed and at ease. They continued their repartee as they looked around the room at all the eye candy. Even though so much time has passed, their get-togethers were always fun and full of laughs. Life with 'the sisterhood' was certainly never boring. Her girlfriends had been so great and she really enjoyed their nights out. It had been her saving grace since Shamus The Shit had flown the coup. "You know, I'm actually starting to enjoy some alone time … no dramas, you know. It's nice to have peace," she said, starring in her glass. They girls looked at her with empathy and smiled.

"You are doing fine, babe. You keep doing what you are doing. You are fabulous and don't you forget it, honey," Elisha said.

When M was almost at the end of a drink, she had a habit of eating the cherry seductively. This was made even more fun when a guy would hold the cherry and feed it to her. She would look around the room, find someone who caught her eye and ask him nicely to pop her cherry. It was her ice-breaker, which at times even lead to some playful banter. M looked around the room for a candidate, but then had a sudden case of stage fright, which must have shown on her face.

"Why don't you pop your own cherry tonight, M?" Kathy asked.

"You can't always count on a man, babe. Sometimes it's worth popping your own," Laura agreed, smiling as she sipped her own drink and lit up yet another cigarette.

"Are you seriously telling me that?" M asked, blushing and surprised.

"That's right, honey. Don't always expect a man to fill you up. You will be disappointed, believe me," Kathy replied.

"Oh, honey ... I'm aware of that," M replied.

"I have a dare for you, dear friend," began Elisha. "How about, if tonight you don't find a guy to put the cherry in your mouth, you go home later and do your own thing?" she said with a smirk.

"Are you fucking serious?" M exclaimed.

Kathy and Laura both put their glasses down and exclaimed, "Yes!"

"You girls are off your rockers. I have nothing to fear as I will *definitely* find a guy to pop my cherry!"

"Good luck, girlfriend!" Kathy laughed.

I can handle it, she thought. What was the big deal anyway? She shook her head and smiled. Come to think of it, after the emotional toll Shamus The Shit took on her, perhaps it could be a good thing. Maybe that's what she needed. Hell, it had been a while. Why the hell not? He definitely wasn't mourning her, so why should she?

"What am I going to do with you girls?"

A fourth Japanese Slipper arrived and M nursed her drink as her friends got up to dance. From the corner of her eye, she spotted a tall man coming toward her. With all the lights and people in front of her, she struggled to make sense of what she was seeing, but as he got closer, she realised who it was and her eyes lit up like a Christmas tree.

"Hey, Maxine, how are you?" He leaned over and kissed her on the cheek and she blushed.

"I'm good, thanks, Jack. Oh my God, this is such a surprise! I haven't seen you in ages." She hugged him tightly.

They knew each other from school–he was a few years below her. She still remembered him in his uniform. Now here he was–older, but as cute as ever. Cheeky blue eyes, blond hair and a Tom Cruise Maverick smile. Little Jack had grown up to be quite the handsome man. They'd bumped into each other a few times since school, but not for years. Perhaps it was the Japanese Slippers talking, but tonight she was thrilled to see him again after so long. He looked poised, confident and happy, with not an arrogant bone in his body. She felt at ease with him at once as the caught up on each other's lives.

As the girls danced, their banter flowed, until the inevitable question arrived. "So why aren't you hooked up and married yet?" he asked.

Of course you had to ask that question, M thought.

"Well, it's not my time, darling. I have other plans for the moment. Do I have to be married?"

"No, I'm not saying that. You don't have to be anything–none of us does. But how can a beautiful girl like you still be available? Are guys that dumb?" Jack laughed.

She paused for a moment, thinking of what to say. She hated comments like that, because she never had an answer.

"Probably," she finally replied. "What about you? Where's your missus?"

"Nope, not me yet. I think it's one of the most important questions you can ask, so I have to be one hundred per cent sure when I do. It's hard."

"It sure is," she agreed heartily. They both chuckled.

As they chatted, M realised how much she was enjoying his company. She was surprised at how their energy flowed. She learned that Jack was a business partner in a company he had worked for since leaving school. He'd studied interstate for a few years, commuting home on holidays. He had travelled a bit so he spoke highly of the places he had been and talked about where he would like to go next. *A man with a plan and a good head on his shoulders*, M thought to herself. *Nice.*

"So how is your house going? Still in the same place?" Jack asked, sipping his single malt, neat.

"Yeah, same place. It's funny, over the past year my pay has slowly gone into fixing the place up, whereas before, I would dedicate my disposable income to shoes. Now that the house is sorted, I can go back and feed my addiction," she smirked.

"Ah, yes, you women and your shoes. I will never understand. I literally own three pairs of shoes: work shoes, runners and thongs," Jack laughed. M was mesmerised by his smile. If this was a spell, she wanted to be bewitched.

"Well, we girls gotta have something, right? You boys have your toys. We have ours. I get the same kind of euphoria a man would give me, but since I don't have one right now, I can enjoy what shoes bring me," M laughed and her eyes glowed.

"I'm sure a man can give you more than that. You can't really compare."

"True, but you never really know when that will happen."

"Well, you make it happen. A woman like you …" Jack stopped speaking and they looked straight at each other. The connection was palpable–intense and strong. She definitely felt a flutter … several, actually.

The girls came back from the dance floor and Jack's gaze swivelled to them.

"How are you, ladies?"

"Good, Jack, how are you?" Elisha asked, as the girls took their seats.

"Really well, thanks. It's been a while, hey?" he said, smiling at them all.

"Too right. I thought you'd disappeared for a while there," Kathy said jokingly.

"Nah. Under the radar, yes, but disappear? Never," Jack laughed.

"Ever the quiet achiever," M remarked with a grin on her face.

"You can talk," he replied back in a teasing tone.

"What do you mean by that?" M asked with a flirty grin.

It was weird—she was definitely feeling a rush of sexual energy. She liked it. It was fun. And she wasn't the only one to notice it. Kathy had her radar on and it was clear to M that she'd noticed the vibe between the pair, although she kept her thoughts to herself. Not like Kathy, but for some reason this was an exception to the rule.

M and Jack kept talking, drinking and losing all sense of time. She found him to be very funny and quite flirty, and this brought on certain butterfly-like feelings inside. The 'high school crush' kind. She was actually quite turned on. How could this be? She'd known him since he was in Year 7! But there it was.

As the clock rolled into the wee hours of another Saturday night, the other girls left the venue separately and M and Jack found themselves hailing a cab, as they were both fairly drunk and lived in the same direction. There was no denying, she didn't want the night to end; she actually found herself praying for something to happen. Then she realised she could take matters into her own hands and see where things may lead.

"Who would have thought in a million years that you would be sleeping on my couch?" she said with a laugh twenty minutes later as they walked into her house.

"Yeah, I know, life is funny, hey?" he replied.

Jack began to undress in her living room as she prepared the blanket and pillow for him. She heard a zipper as she adjusted the couch and turned around. There he was—Jack in all his glory. A boy she'd known since school, now a handsome man in nothing but his underwear, about to lie down on her couch. M made some mental notes: *Good body; nice ass; Dolce & Gabbana trunks. Oh my God, hello Christmas! He is not the boy from school any more. He is a man, and quite attractive.* Internal sigh. *Go to bed, Maxine, now!*

As she grabbed an extra pillow from the other chair, she felt Jack move closer. He grabbed her from behind and started kissing her neck. "I think you are an incredibly beautiful woman, Maxine," he whispered in her ear, holding her hips tightly.

No reply was necessary. She leaned into his kiss. She wasn't sure if it was the effect of the alcohol, but she didn't care at that point. It had been too long since she'd just gone for something without all the thinking and evaluation that she would usually do. Tonight she simply wanted the attention and affection, and she went for it without thought.

Their kissing became intense, passionate, as she melted in his strong embrace. His lips were so soft, his body so hard and masculine. She kissed him as though her life depended on it. They fell to the couch, pieces of her clothing coming off one by one. She felt his manly presence and was taken in by all of him. He touched her in all the right places. He did all she wanted him to do, and she in turn did the same. Odd how a boy she'd seen grow into a man was suddenly her lover. She gave in completely to temptation and let go of all inhibitions as he entered her, fulfilling her senses. They fell to the floor as they rocked together, on and on.

Complete fulfilment was not to be had yet, however, as Jack teasingly pulled away. He grabbed her hair with force, pulling her head back as he kissed her neck from top to bottom. Making his way down to her chest, he began to stroke her nipples, then suck them hard. She let out a euphoric sigh. This was one of her prime erogenous zones and she loved it. Jack made his way down and down until he reached the fruits of her womanhood, his tongue working magic. He could do no wrong. Her climax was intense and as she released her final pang of euphoria, in a single move he flipped her over and entered her again, pounding hard, while she found it impossible to restrain her guttural cries, merging with his as he groaned like a wild beast and reached his peak.

In a sweaty heap, they finally collapsed and she felt like a million dollars as they fell asleep in each other's arms on the couch. M had a grin on her face like the cat who just stole the cream. The heartbreak and rejection of being dumped by Shamus The Shit was finally over. She'd been officially fucked back to life. She felt ecstatic.

M awoke with a sore head, the alcohol having taken its toll. She looked at Jack sleeping, a brawny hunk of a man. Yet she could still see traces of the boy she'd once know in his sweet slumbering face. A gorgeous Man Boy. He'd done all the right things at the right time. *Christ, life is funny*, she thought to herself as she got up and made her way to the coffee machine. She felt empowered, elated. She remembered that old saying: the way to get over someone was to get under someone else. Well, for her it kind of worked!

"Wow, that coffee smells good. What a way to wake up."

She turned and there he was, wide awake with his cute smile. He dressed as she poured him a mug of the fresh brew. She felt simultaneously at ease and a little reserved.

"That was great last night, hey?" he said.

"Yes. Yes, it was," she smiled at him shyly, feeling like a little girl.

"You're not embarrassed about what happened, are you? We're adults now. You don't see me like you used to, do you?"

"No, not embarrassed. Stunned and surprised, yes. And no, you're certainly not the boy I knew. You're a man. A *good* man. It's funny, though, don't you think? We've known each other since we were kids. Now we've had *sex.*"

"Yeah, it is. You're incredibly desirable, Max. On many levels. Don't ever forget that. Enjoy it. Don't let a man ever make you feel anything but sexy, worthy and special. You're one of a kind. It was as true back in school as it is now."

M didn't expect Man Boy to spin such deep philosophy and express such feelings after a night of passion. She was perplexed, but appreciated it a great deal, as she felt how sincere he was.

"Jack, that's so nice of you to say. I … It's been a while since I have felt that way. It means a lot. Really." She looked directly into his eyes as she spoke.

"Well, it's true. Believe it," he replied.

After coffee, he gave his thanks and left. A wave of disappointment fell over her, as she actually wanted him to stay longer. *Is this how it's always going to be?* she wondered as she fixed up the couch. *Is this the kind of sex I want to be having? Passion, but no TLC, no spooning?* She felt odd, with the high of the night followed by this little lull. She was still pinching herself that the whole thing had even happened. She blushed. It had been damn good. It had been a night of intense passion and lust, but she knew in her heart that that was all it was. It wasn't the sex that was the problem, she reflected—it was that the deep-down feelings and the nurturing were equally important to her. Sure, a shag-a-thon is fabulous. But at the end of the day, one can't help but think, *is that all there is?*

She did enjoy what had happened, but another part felt that this was not how it was meant to be. A man whom she allowed to sleep with her—even in the heat of the moment—should feel good to be with, and not just sexually speaking. A man should look deeply at her, engage with her and connect with her, even after … *especially* after. M knew that men were not all wired to do the hugs and spooning. It's what most women craved. But what's wrong with that? As she got ready for her day, she remembered how it had been for her and Shamus. When she *was* held and when she *did* connect with the other person on all levels, not just sexually. She had loved it. It was respectful, kind and thoughtful. Maybe all guys aren't the same.

As she relayed the events of the night before, she made her way to the bathroom for a quick cleaning session. She got out her rubber gloves and frantically began to scrub the sink, tiles and toilet. Domestic duties were oddly enough the one think that distracted her and brought her some sort of calm. Her home was her castle, after all, and she wanted it to sparkle with perfection. She sighed as she was interrupted by the telephone.

"Hello?"

"So what happened with you two?" shot Kathy's voice, as straight to the point as you can get. M heard the rustle of paper in the background. Kathy was doing her Sunday morning ritual—coffee and paper on the couch in her pyjamas.

"What do you mean?" M replied, trying to sound casual. The last thing she wanted was to 'fess up to her friends about her naughty little one-nighter and have them load it up with substance that she knew was simply was not there.

"Come on, girlfriend! You could have cut the sexual tension with a knife. You two looked pretty full-on, and we left before you." Kathy sounded like a crime-scene investigator.

"We had fun at the club," M said, noncommittally, not wanting to lie to her friend, but also refusing to divulge any of the truth either. "It was nice to catch up with him after so long, but ... he's a kid. You can put away your CSI suit." M's confident tone was, luckily enough, convincing enough for Kathy to give up and change the subject. M was firm that her rendezvous with 'little Jack' was never to be known by her friends.

Still, M found herself thinking of Jack the whole day. It was funny how a certain chain of events could make you feel a particular way. She felt a sense of calm and a sudden boost of confidence at the same time. She actually felt ... good. This sudden attention by someone she never dreamed of in a million years was a definite self-esteem enhancer. She'd thought that only the latest-season Jimmy Choo pumps could do that for her, but it turned out that secret sex was far, far better ... and easier on the purse strings.

She wanted to continue the flirt, see how long this high could last. Could they meet up again? Could it be something deeper? Should she text or call? Why was this always the dilemma after meeting someone? It always boils down to that one thing—the 'after' call. Who does it first: the girl or the guy? It doesn't have to be the guy all the time, does it? And why is it always midweek by the time you hear from him? Is it because they want to keep you hanging for a bit until they make contact?

There are no rules, M thought to herself assertively. *You can do as you wish. If you want to say 'hi', say 'hi'. No big deal.* And with that positive thought, she picked up the phone and texted:

> Hi there, how are you? Thanks again for a great time last night. Would love to catch up with you again soon. Take care,
> M xx

If he wrote back, he wrote—one can only try. Remember, you're never a failure, but rather courageous for trying. Expecting nothing, M rose to walk back to the kitchen when the unthinkable happened—a reply. "Oh my God," she said out loud in her surprise. "Guys *never* text back straight away. Well, not for me, anyway." She clicked her phone's display and read:

> Hey there, I'm well, hope you are too. It was a great night and I'd love to catch up soon. Let me know when. J xx

Well, that was something to look forward to. M had a feeling that good things were to come. Jack's message made her feel warm inside.

She was to meet the girls for lunch that day, and she knew full well the topic would be discussed again. Sure enough, as expected, the girls debriefed her during their catch up. They had decided to meet at Le Bouche, the popular French patisserie that boasted the city's best pastries and macaroons. Everyone seemed to have the same idea; the place was busy. People were getting takeaway orders, and some were reading the paper or working. As it was a drizzly day, they decided to book the back room with its cosy antique couches and an open fire to get some private time with each other. It had a very European feel to it–the old lounges, the wrought iron tables and dimmer lights.

After M had finished squirming around the topic of her and Jack the night before–convincing the girls that nothing happened while carefully bypassing actually lying to her homegirls (not an easy feat!)–they got onto the topic of dating in general.

"You know what it was like when we were going out in our day?" Laura began. "It was boy meets girl, boy likes girl and asks her out. No texts or emails. You would actually speak to each other. There was a connection. You'd go steady, *blah, blah, blah* … you know the rest. That's how it should be."

"You're either really naïve or you have no idea what it's really like out there, now that you're married," Elisha protested. "It's not like that any more. There has never been such a huge gap between men and women–so many grey areas and blurred lines. It's like a game, even when you get older. Some men still beat around the bush. And some women have too many expectations and read into things. No wonder no one understands each other!"

"I can't understand how they can go from one to the next … to the next," said M. "Take Shelley and Chris, for example. They weren't broken up for very long, and after what–a few months?–he's already in another serious relationship. How is that possible? Do men move on that quickly, like they emotionally detach in an instant? Can it be that easy for them? It should be for us too. Fuck 'em."

"Women take longer to move on and to mend a broken heart. Men just make it look so effortless," Elisha replied. "I'm sure they hurt too. They aren't robots. They're also human."

"You're too nice," M said. "Or too naïve. I can't decide."

"I think some men can't be alone," Laura said, as she lit up a smoke. "They want a companion around. They want to be taken care of and looked after. Maybe those are the guys you always see in relationships. It's because they're too dependent or can't hold their own—like babies."

Laura's theory was followed by a long silence as it got the girls thinking. *Maybe she is right*, M thought. Could it be that simple? Is it just that we have our communication all mixed and we make things bigger than they really are? Why was it that some dates seemed to go with the flow, yet others felt so daunting? There were so many expectations and conditions placed on men and women that it was hard to know what was right. She knew some men felt they had to do certain things or behave in certain ways in order to get a girl to be interested. And women definitely tended to analyse everything. A touch, a message, a kiss, a date—what did they mean? It was like a switch in the brain flipped, already concocting some fairytale scenario to describe each minor detail, where maybe it was better just to see things simply for what they were.

Maybe this is our big downfall as women, M thought. *We place all these expectations on men and then we're disappointed when they are not met.* M knew she had this not-so-great tendency, and she knew she wasn't alone in all the over-thinking and the 'what ifs'. All the women she knew did this to some degree. She broke the silence first. "I think that when a woman reaches a certain age, she starts to see things differently. It's not just about the date or the fun any more. We actually envision what the guy would be like as a lifelong partner. We want to meet someone who fits the bill on all levels—not acting or coming across as desperate. But that thought of whether he is the right one is never far from our minds."

"All I know is that I hate complicated. Give me simple and I'm yours," Elisha stated.

"Since when is it ever easy?" Kathy said. "I think it's luck, too. But, then again, you should never give up hope. You just have to keep going, even when it seems fruitless."

"Thank you, Miss Optimism," Laura chuckled. "Girls, I say just live and enjoy. Take it as it comes and don't let it bring you down. No man has that right. Love yourself always, and all will come to you. God's will, ladies. God's will." As their one representative of the state of wedlock, Laura's optimism for love was catching.

M jumped into the conversation again. "Girls, different strokes for different folks. It's different for every guy and every girl and the situation that you are in. You can never judge and you never know what's ahead. Que sera, sera, my friends … que sera, sera."

"I think we just have this instinct where we dream a lot," Kathy added. "Men just see what is, which is great, but we want the dream. We jump to second base in a flash. It sucks sometimes. It sure wasn't like this in our twenties, I can tell you that much. I have less tolerance now. It's like, okay, you want me? Yes or no, because I don't want to waste time with someone who really doesn't want me."

Kathy was firm in her view because she'd been screwed over not once, but twice by the same guy, Dave. They'd been dating and she was desperately in love with him. She didn't really know what direction they were going in, so one day, she laid all her cards on the table, asking him if he wanted to pursue something more serious or not. Dave said yes, and they went full steam ahead … only for him to get cold feet six months down the track. Kathy was shattered beyond belief, as she had invested all of herself based on his word about their relationship. She grudgingly went back onto the singles scene at the urging of the other girls, and had slowly begun making her way into life again when Dave came running back four months later, begging for her forgiveness and to take him back, as he'd realised he had made a terrible mistake. Against her friends' warnings, she'd taken him back because she believed in second chances. She said she trusted him. One year later, he left her for another woman. That time, it took Kathy over a year to pick up the pieces of her life and her heart. From that time on, she'd sworn that she would never compromise herself and put a man first, as she'd done with Dave. M feared that she would always have that resistance in her attitude toward men. She let them in, but ever so slowly and only so much. She never lost herself or let herself be consumed by passion.

After coffee, the girls went home. That night, while assuming her starfish position in bed, M thought back to their conversation and the world of dating and how one event had placed her back on the market of singleton. She was definitely not a shy girl–she was all for chatting and meeting people. She could recall many occasions when her friends watched in amusement as she dished out the goods to a waiter or some guy at a bar. Friendly banter was what she did best. She was comfortable and at ease in a crowd, and her friends loved her for that. She knew she probably underestimated just how courageous she was—not really scared to try. However, underneath all the laughs and her somewhat tough stance on men, she was a sensitive girl—maybe a little bit shy, even—who was protective of her privacy and feelings. She knew she was scared to open up. Especially after her betrayal. How do you forgive that? Opening up again, she felt, would always be a gradual thing for her, like peeling off layers, one at a time. She gave, but not too much, even though she yearned to give it all. Even after all that transpired, she still believed in love. With Shamus she gave a lot of herself, and was now left with battle scars. *Never again*, she thought. Sex seemed to be easy. It was love that you pay the highest price for. It comes at a cost.

She knew that one day, someday, she would have to open up and be vulnerable—to really let someone in. It would take a certain someone else to get her to do that, as she wouldn't open up to just anyone. She would really have to care very deeply for that person. M was a passionate woman who did things from her heart. She was also a sincere person, honest and true. If she were to let someone in, it would have to be based on honesty and a trust that was built over time. Could she open up again? Who would break her wall? At this point she really didn't care.

She switched off her lamp and rolled over. "Que sera, sera," she sang softly, as she drifted into slumber.

4

"Oh God, oh God!" M cried out in delight. He pleasured her in all the right ways. She could feel his heart beat as he held her in his arms, stroking her. Being with him felt comfortable. She felt safe, happy—not a care in the world. He gazed into her eyes.

"M, you are a beautiful woman. You're a great girl. I would love to be with you." He stroked her hair.

"That's sweet. I really would love to be with you too," she replied before kissing him passionately. Her heart beat in sync with his. She felt a wave of calm and sheer happiness wash over her. This was where she wanted to be. This was where she belonged.

A loud alarm bell shattered the spell, startling M awake. She felt strange—the dream had been so vivid, so real. The man holding her in such a close embrace had been ... Mr White Shirt. *What the hell? That Adi guy!* she thought to herself, still stunned at how real it felt. She was taken aback. It was so unexpected. Some dreams feel a million miles away as soon as you wake up, and some feel like they actually happened. This was the latter type. She got up and made a strong coffee, still reeling. *Wow. Since when do I dream of Adi?* she wondered.

She didn't want to think about it all day, though. Every year the girls got together on this inevitably hot and balmy weekend to go to the St Kilda Festival, Melbourne's annual carnival down by the city foreshore. It was a big event, and as they had missed the previous year, they had organised well in advance to go this time. The heat was strong and the humidity seemed to be borderline uncomfortable, like the tropics. M knew a cold beer would definitely be in order—maybe two or three.

She parked about five blocks from the water and walked down, noticing droves of people doing the same thing. She enjoyed the diversity as she headed to the waterfront—young families, teenagers, grungers, ethnic folk, singletons. After all, who doesn't love a carnival? She noticed all the bars and restaurants setting up for the big day. Each had its own flair and style. Lounges and DJ booths stood near the front. Tables were organised in lines where people could sit. Streamers, colours and lights were everywhere. All made for an interesting line-up and made the strip come alive.

She heard Spanish music, dance music and buskers on the street playing their instruments. There was even a touch of Sinatra. On the corner where she was to meet the girls there was also a huge jumping castle and face painting for the children to keep them entertained and amused. They sky was blue and bright and it was a perfect day for an outing with the girls. As she walked among the crowd she saw a familiar face and body structure. She stopped cold. She recognised that t-shirt. She bought for him herself last year when they holidayed in Fiji.

Shamus The Shit.

It was the first time she had seen him since the breakup. *You shit, Shamus … you bloody shit.* Her eyes darted left to Tanya The Tramp, looking tall, blonde and modelesque. That bitch. There they were—the golden couple. M's thoughts instantly went into a pity spiral. *What does she have over me? Thighs? Did I not get on the stairmaster enough? Maybe her lasagne is better than mine?*

Stop, M, stop! she said to herself. She kept walking, *fast*, with her head down low to avoid any contact. She prayed to God to never seem them again. In that moment, she felt empty, remembering how they were happy for a while … and how now he was happy with someone else.

She sat on a stoop of a neighbouring house. She just needed a moment to gather herself and her thoughts. She took a deep breath and focused. *Why should one woman make me feel bad?* she thought. Do we bring our insecurities out on ourselves? Do guys do this crap too? She thought of all the great things she had in her life but it was her self-esteem that needed a Red Bull. *He is the past, the best is yet to come*, she said to herself. The sun warmed her body and she suddenly felt calmer. She thought for a moment about fate. *Maybe this was a blessing? Maybe, if we'd gotten married down the track, he would have cheated then? Did I dodge a bullet?* She got up and continued to make her way to meet her friends – the people that loved her.

They met in one of the trendy cafés they had frequented many times before. The funky sound of music blaring from bar to bar made it feel like they were on an island holiday, not at home.

They seated themselves at an outside table, which they were happy about, as they got to people-watch. This was one of their favourite pastimes.

"This is pumping. Let's order some wine!" said Elisha, eager to start the day.

"I can't believe how packed it is," said Kathy. "This is fantastic!"

They ordered a nice bottle of white and also a big jug of water. M looked around in her brand new Bvlgari sunglasses, enjoying how she could look directly at a person and they couldn't tell. She spotted a familiar face coming toward her and looked straight at him as he approached.

"Oh my God," M murmured under her breath. It was groomsman number one, from Sally's wedding. Not White Shirt, but the other guy—Frankie, his name was. She was surprised at his tight Diesel top and nicely cut jeans. *Bloody hell, what's with Sally's groomsmen – he looks pretty good too*, she thought. As he got closer he spotted her too—his smile switching on like torchlight—and came over to their table.

"I thought that was you! How are you, Frankie?" M said, as they kissed each other on the cheek. He smiled and blushed, pulling back with obvious reserve. *Maybe he's just shy because the other girls are here*, she thought.

"I'm good, thanks. How are you doing?" he replied, with that sparkling smile. "And how are you, ladies?" he asked the table at large.

"Not bad, thanks, Frankie. Just trying to stay cool with some wine," Kathy replied. The other girls said hello, then turned back to each other as M and Frankie begin to chat.

"Gee whizz, he is pretty rip," she heard Elisha whisper. "Under a suit and jacket you can never really judge, but, fuck me, he has some body. I wouldn't mind me some of that!"

M hoped Frankie was far enough away not to hear such pointed girl talk. He stood back a little and kept his hands in his pockets, like a little boy on his first day of school. This was the Frankie that M knew from previous social occasions: friendly and chatty, but also, clearly, somewhat uncomfortable in his mannerisms—and reserved around women, especially. This always stymied M, who actually found him cute and had a bit of a secret crush on him. He was quite a handsome guy who could get any girl he wanted if he cared to, but for as long as M and the others had known him, he had always been traditional and old-school in his approach.

Maybe that was what would scared women away? Otherwise M couldn't figure out why he remained unattached. In a way, it was kind of nice to be with a guy who showed a decent amount of chivalry and didn't just race in and jump on a girl. But, on the other hand, he needed to relax and go with the flow. It frustrated M, who repressed the urge to smack the shy Frankie to bits. Yet, given the chance, she would probably sleep with him anyway.

The conversation lapsed as it became clear that he was uncomfortable and wanted to leave. "Have a great day, girls. I gotta run, but hey, enjoy," Frankie said. He kissed M on the cheek again, waved goodbye and walked away. She couldn't keep her eyes off him ... or his butt. Over the years, M and Frankie had always exchanged banter and a little bit of flirtation. It was all harmless fun, but M had always wondered what he would be like as a boyfriend or a lover. She wondered why he would never seriously entertain the thought of them having coffee together, or dinner or a movie—she had dropped some not-so-subtle hints over the years—or even the two of them as a couple. But it was probably for the best, she reflected. Although she was attracted to him, she found him to be a bit shy, not willing to take chances or try anything; even a tad cold, when she thought about it. The slightest closeness would make him uncomfortable, and he'd blush or pull back, as he had today. The girls, having seen this behaviour a number of times, had dubbed him Father Frank. So formal in his mannerisms most of the time that he seemed almost frigid. M had met priests who seemed more at ease around women than Frankie. As lovely as he was, he was one of those guys who thought too much of the future, of the 'what ifs' and 'whys', almost as though he feared chance itself.

M had occasionally wondered whether she could help him change, but she knew you can never change someone, most especially a stubborn man. She'd realised some time ago that Frankie was a fun, but fruitless fantasy. She wanted an outgoing man, not a shy guy. She was a vibrant, funny and social person, and Father Frank was the total opposite.

"Your loss, kid," she said out loud to the air as he disappeared through the crowd. "You will never know what could have been." Frankie would remain a friend, but romantically speaking, M's door was open for something better—or so she hoped.

"How good do you think he is in bed?" Elisha asked out of the blue.

The girls looked stunned.

"Hello? Since when do you want to know that about Father Frank?" said Kathy.

"Oh, come on, girls. Think about it," Elisha returned. "A ripped body like that? What do you think?"

After a pause M replied, "I'm of two minds. He acts all shy and 'don't touch me', but that could be a diversion. I think he has his own way of pulling girls in. Maybe he is a quiet achiever and a total animal in bed who would make you scream and come like ten times. Either that, or he is just a dead fish. I actually can't decide."

The girls broke out into gales of laughter.

"Oh, let's stop it. We are being bitches," said Kathy.

The carnival turned into a later night than expected, especially for a 'school night'. M knew that the next morning she had a meeting with her boss and needed to get home for a good night's sleep in preparation. She didn't know what Mr Ferguson wanted, but he didn't go in for random chitchat, so she knew that whatever it was, it was important. She said goodbye, left the girls to their own devices and headed for home.

People of all kinds were still everywhere. She thought about what a mixed bag the city was as she walked to her car. Getting closer, she saw a white piece of paper on her windscreen. "Oh, no, don't tell me it's a fucking fine!" she exclaimed. She picked it up—ah, relief. It was a handwritten note. She opened it and read: *Nice to see you, Maxine. I hope this is the right car. Maybe we can have coffee sometime? Frankie. X*

"Well, I'll be darned. Father Frank wants a coffee," she said to herself as she slipped behind the wheel, musing at how he could be so standoffish for so long, then seemingly out of the blue, ask her out. *And they wonder why women analyse everything,* she thought to herself. *We have to, because we don't fucking GET them!* But she was flattered, nevertheless. She grinned to herself all the way home and was a happy smiling starfish in bed that night.

5

"Maxine, can you come into my office, please?"

Mr Ferguson was her boss and mentor, but he was more like a father figure to M. Over the years they had developed a great relationship, both professionally and personally. He'd taken her under his wing and trained her as she made her way into the advertising world. Most of all, he believed in her and encouraged her, which was a comfort when she wasn't sure of herself. Mr Ferguson was smart, charismatic and kind. He ran the show, but M trusted him.

She went in. His office was large, with a side table and a small bar, a lounge near it and a panoramic view of the city. Everyone in the firm loved going into his office; it was like the kind you'd see in a Hollywood movie, only real. M was curious about this meeting. Sometimes he would just ask her to come in and touch base on how the day was progressing and to take a ten-minute break with him, but even these apparently casual get-togethers had a purpose. He was still mentoring her. However, she knew there was to be a merger with another company. Was this about that? Mr Ferguson was in his usual position, standing behind his desk looking out at the city and flicking his Parker pen. He always dressed immaculately, as any high-powered man would. Today was no exception. His Hugo Boss suit was accompanied by an Armani tie and a Rolex watch. She walked over to him with anticipation and curiosity.

"Take a seat, Maxine. How are you doing?" he asked with a smile.

"Good, thank you. Still trying to get a handle on the Phillips account, but it's underway ... waiting for a few emails. You know how it is."

"Yes. Yes, I do. Sometimes it feels like the days roll into one." His hands were busy at the bar. "Lemon in your mineral water?"

"Yes, please. Thank you."

He passed her the drink.

"How are you finding this project? Are you overwhelmed or are things going well?"

"No, it's not overwhelming," she responded. "Luckily the team is all on board and working together without drama. There is a bit to do, but it's not choking me."

"I hope it's not all work and no play for you," said Mr Ferguson. "I know the hours you put in when deadlines are due. I hope still have time for a social life?"

M set her glass down, not really knowing what he was implying or where he was going with this. "Well, no, it's not all work and no play. I definitely have an active social life–great friends, good times."

"And a serious partner?" he said looking at her closely.

M froze. Was he saying this out of concern or being nosy? Or–God forbid–was he coming on to her? Please, God, no! Over time, they had discussed lots of things about life and philosophy and work … but never love. M was suddenly uncomfortable. It wasn't what she wanted now anyway.

"Um, not at the moment," she said. "But I have a fulfilling life." *What the fuck?* she thought to herself.

"Oh good, I'm glad to hear it. I hope you don't mind that I ask you," he said, looking slightly embarrassed. "Anyhow. The reason I called you in here is that I have good news and a bit of bad news. I'll give you the bad news first. The company is downsizing. Middle management is mostly effected, which means us. We don't know who or what as yet. We have just been informed ourselves. We will know for sure in a month or two. It does suck as we will be in a spot of limbo for a bit but we have to carry on and do what we do. No one wants to think their job is on the line. I don't want you to worry. Please keep this to yourself for now as I don't want to alarm other staff until we have the right information," he said.

"Okay, well thanks for letting me know," said M calmly, while feeling the opposite internally. *Unemployment threat?! Peachy. I'm going to need more that self-help and macaroons for this one. That's if I can still afford to buy them!* "I won't say anything. I'm just a little shocked. Good news would be good now, please," she said with a smirk.

"Okay, good news. I was just on the phone with Europe. You know the annual convention is coming up. But I'm totally swamped with trying to get this merger deal off the ground.

This year they are holding the convention in Prague, of all places, which sounds exciting. I wish I could go, but I just can't. So I want you to go to the convention for me. Attend the meetings and the workshops and report it all back to me. All expenses paid, of course. That is, if there's nothing holding you back here?"

M was stunned. "You ... you want *me* to go? Really?"

"Yes, Maxine. You have proven yourself with your dedication and hard work this past year. I have watched you, and I'm proud of your work and your competence. I'm confident you will do a good job representing us." Mr Ferguson raised his glass in salute. "See something different. Explore. Make it work *and* pleasure. Maxine, this is your time."

"Mr Ferguson, this means a lot to me ... thank you so much!" M stammered, still shocked by the sudden turn of events.

"Stacey has all the details," he told her. "Go and see her now, and she will give you all you need. Well done, Maxine. You deserve it." They shook hands and she left his office, still in shock.

As the news sank in, M felt over the moon. She wanted this feeling to last forever, but at the same time she had to remain realistic that this could be the first and the last work trip. All that hard work was finally paying off, at least for the moment, and she felt a rush of excitement at the prospect for Europe as she called the girls during her break to organise a celebratory after-work drink.

Although, she couldn't help but have a tight knot in her stomach though. *Surely another door can't slam on my face. I can grasp being single, but out of a job—hell no! I need a plan B*, she thought.

She arranged the get-together at KeïKeï, a chic Japanese bar—restaurant renowned for its lychee martinis. Luckily all the girls were free, and there was nothing like teppanyaki to spice up an otherwise dull weeknight.

"That's fantastic, babe!" Elisha enthused as she embraced M.

"Imagine all the shopping and the men and the great food," said Laura.

"Yeah, I know. That's what I'm looking forward to. The first three days are going to be full-on so there will be no time to chill, but I'm looking forward to the three days I have to explore and enjoy the city afterwards."

"Lucky bitch, I wish I was going," Elisha said, grinning to take the sting out of her words. "Hey, maybe we should all go for a girly escape one day."

"You may have a plan there, sister," Laura said. "Hey, M, make sure you nab yourself a nice European man. A lot can happen in three days, girlfriend. Once you go Euro, you don't go back, they say."

"Don't you mean black? Once you go *black*," said M.

"Ooh, even better!" replied Laura.

They all burst into laughter, and the banter continued.

"I wish my boss would make *me* go on a work trip to Europe," said Elisha. "Bastard. It's like the world is his oyster and we're just the production line. I think I need a new job."

"Out with the old and in with the new, I say," said M.

"Like guys, you mean?" said Laura.

More laughter.

"Darling, if you aren't happy where you are," said M, seriously, "talk to your boss and tell him how you feel or start looking for something different. There's no time like the present."

"Speaking of which," Elisha said, changing the subject and lightening the tone, "let's put that European holiday on a bucket list of things we should do before we hit forty-five."

M smiled and nodded, thinking about how much she adored her friends. Even though other commitments now filled their time, they were still as thick as thieves, managing to get together to laugh, joke and just be. And 'girl time' was sacrosanct to them. No one interfered with girl time. Not for the first time, M thought of their friendship as a collective bank account. You had to invest in it long term to get the full benefits and reap the rewards.

As their lychee martinis arrived, they all raised their glasses.

"Cheers!"

"To Maxine and her grand adventure!"

"To a great life!"

The week passed with the excitement of planning, and on Saturday morning M went out for her coffee and newspaper early as she wanted to get a jump on the day. She had plenty of things to buy before her trip.

Saturday at the local shops was as bustling as always with busy cafés, people jogging and dogs being walked. Cars lined up in the supermarket car park, angling for spots. People strolled with their takeaway lattes. It was a lovely, quaint neighbourhood, and M loved her Saturday mornings here. Usually she would walk to avoid having to find a parking place, but because she had a few things to buy, she drove and luckily found a good spot. After coffee and the paper she was ready to hit the shops and get all the things she needed for the trip.

"Hey, stranger!" she heard.

M turned … and her heart skipped a beat.

Adi was wearing *Top Gun*-style aviator sunglasses and a dark blue shirt over pale jeans. He had her at the aviators. He approached her with his Tom Cruise smile and she was slowly going weak at the knees. Very few men have that look, that walk, that aura. But damn Mr Adi White Shirt was a fine specimen. Well, at least her hormones thought so. *Va-va-voom.*

"Hey, you. What's up?" she said, trying to sound casual, yet was smirking away like a large Tiffany box had just landed in her lap.

"I thought it was you," he said, as he came up and kissed her on the cheek. "How are you?"

"I'm great. How are you going?" she replied with a smile.

"Great here, too. It's been a while, huh?"

"It has."

"What you been up to?"

"Busy with work." She swallowed heavily and her mouth began to dry. They gazed into each others eyes like star-crossed lovers. She couldn't even find her words. Her gut was tightening.

"It's flat out for me, too. This major project is on. You know, the usual crap," he said. There was a short pause, then he continued. "Can I compliment you again on how nice you looked at the wedding. You were the prettiest woman there."

M felt her cheeks on fire and smiled. "Oh, gee, thanks so much. You're sweet," she said.

"I like to tell it how it is. I hope you don't mind?" he asked.

"Well, if we are heading that way, you scrub up alright too," she said and they both broke into nervous, flirty laughter.

"Well, we've certainly broken the ice, haven't we?" he said.

"Should we shag now or shag later?" M said in an adrenaline-induced splurge of confidence.

Adi laughed again.

Nothing like reeling off an Austin Powers quote to get away with a cheeky sexual entendre in broad daylights. Certainly beats the Batman comment!

"You're a real character, Maxine," he said.

"Call me M," she replied.

"M for *mmmmm*," purred Adi, followed by more nervous, flirtations laughter from them both, their eyes glued to each other.

After what seemed like an eternity, M blurted, "I'm leaving for a conference in ten days," trying to break the tension. Another moment of all that eye-gazing and she feared she'd be humping his leg.

"Really? I'm going away too, for a wedding, then I'm meeting a friend afterwards to travel for a few days. I leave in a week. Let's have a coffee before we go, maybe," he suggested. She was flattered by his gesture.

"Sure, sounds good," said M, trying to sound cool while the butterflies in her stomach did back flips.

After they exchanged dates and numbers and said goodbye, M thought, *Oh my God, Adi and coffee!* But then she had to remind herself to take it down a notch. The thought of having coffee with Adi and his aviators and tight t-shirt and Tom Cruise smile was something that made her vibrate to the core–and his stare and mannerisms felt like he was sharing the electric vibe–but could she be mistaken? *Oh, but how nice it would be if he was my Maverick?*

she thought to herself, as 'Take My Breath Away' was suddenly playing in her imagination and she saw herself and Adi riding off in the sunset on a motorbike. She sighed. Its nice to dream.

Regardless of his intentions, M was pleased about the semi-date, even if it was just a mate-date, as this would give her the chance to get to know him better. She had always found him attractive, but never really knew him properly. To her, he was just a pretty boy who girls would drool over from afar. She wanted to see the personality and the character behind the face and the body. Who was Adi, really? Just another pretty face or a real man? M wasn't one to judge a book by its cover because she knew how deceiving looks could be. She had dated a number of good looking men in her time who had turned out to be total tossers, shallow and arrogant. But maybe Adi was actually a great guy who happened to have equally great looks? Can you really get the complete package? A girl can dream.

M was still in la-la land, thinking about him as she strolled past Jimmy's and was seduced by the intoxicating aroma of Arabica beans and decided it was time for another coffee. Really it was just an excuse to sit in the sunshine as she savoured each second of her unexpected interlude with Adi. She sipped while looking at the sky and the tussling row of elms that fell in line across the strip, which brought character and charm to the street. She didn't plan on telling her girlfriends about the encounter with him and their potential coffee date, as she wasn't entirely sure if it would transpire and she knew the girls would just create hype and anticipation when there wasn't anything to talk about ... *yet*, anyway.

Still in her daze, sipping creamy froth out of her mug, she heard a sweet little Greek accent, "Hello, dear. Nice day."

There she was again, in blinding colour. Personally, M would never mix bright yellow with red ... and purple Converse shoes ... and rings on every finger. But she wasn't an old Greek gypsy. M squinted slightly, surprised, mainly by her vibrant colour scheme, then smiled.

The old lady took this as an invitation and pulled up and sat next to her.

M didn't really feel like making small talk–she was locked in fantasies about Adi–but she didn't want to be rude so she just rolled with it. "It sure is," she replied with a dreamy smile. She sipped her coffee, hoping the old lady didn't feeling like a full-on conversation.

"You having a good day, dear?" said the lady, staring deeply at her.

This made M feel a little uneasy. *Why is she looking at me like that?* "Yes, it is. Just bumped into a friend. Doing the usual daily routine ... You know how it is," M replied, sipping the last of her coffee, planning to make a quick departure. Her eyes we getting sore just looking at her.

"I'm Soula," she said. "Don't mind the outfits," she continued, as though reading her mind. "When my husband passed away eight years ago everyone wore black, black, black. I did the total opposite. Colour. Colour makes you feel good even when sometimes things are no good. I say stuff black. Black is good for the twenty-year-old girls that go to those clubs and dances. Black makes old people more old. Not me."

"I'm Maxine ... but call M," she said.

Soula looked at M and they both smiled. She noticed that M's coffee cup was finished and she picked it up, staring into it with a curious face—much to M's astonishment.

"In my village in Greece I begun to read cups when I was eighteen. I had a gift. All that I saw came true in people's lives. I have ... how you say ... a *sense*. The word got out and many people would ask me to do this. I have been doing it ever since. You don't mind if I look at yours, do you?" Soula asked.

M thought for a moment. With all the relationship curve balls she had been thrown, plus the possible upheaval at work, what did she have to lose by listening to a gypsy read her future? Even if it was complete tripe, at least she's be no more in the dark that she always was! "Sure, why not. Some more excitement for the day," M replied.

Soula stared at the cup and looked at it pensively, concentrating, then spoke. "Your one true love will come as two, but before he's yours, he'll be untrue ... That's all I can tell you darling. He is coming. So no more worries about the boys, huh," she beamed.

"Wow, thanks. Come as two? Interesting," M replied, now a bit curious, despite her rational voice telling her it was nothing but the ramblings of an old lady with a touch of the crazies.

"No charge for you, darling," Soula winked.

M let out a little laugh, picturing Soula asking for money when M had never even asked for the reading – Soula had offered. "Well, thank you, Soula. I have to go now. Things to do," M said. She walked away pondering what Soula had said, wondering what it all meant, while simultaneously dismissing it, knowing she had to take it with a grain of salt. She had never had a tarot card reading or any sort of clairvoyant reading before. Was there ever any real substance to these things? She put it out of her head.

As the day wore on she couldn't help but reflect on the chances of bumping into Adi. It wasn't even his neighbourhood. What a coincidence! She went to bed that night with Cirque de Soleil performing in her stomach.

As the days rolled by and her departure date drew near, Adi didn't called. Maybe he was too busy. He'd said so, hadn't he? Besides, she reasoned to herself, she was so stretched for time that *she* didn't really have time for a coffee date herself. Perhaps they could catch up on her return. Besides which, she was too excited to give it too much thought. A new adventure was on the horizon. Work and play–what a combo.

As the conference approached, M realised she was actually quite nervous about the whole thing. She was usually the one who doted on and praised others, giving her all to her peers, friends and family, but her thoughts were tied up with the big event. If she did well at the conference, she would definitely be recognised for it. At times she knew she underestimated her potential–or so her friends always told her. Only now, as her career really appeared to be beginning to bloom, she was finally able to start believing it. 'You reap what you sow'–as the saying goes. 'You get out what you put in.' It's the Law of Attraction. Now that these things appeared to be manifesting, she had to pinch herself. She knew, of course, that her future with the company was unknown, due to the restructuring, yet there was no point focusing on *that*. What would be would be. She loved her job. She didn't want to lose it. She knew her energy was better spent on focusing on this incredible opportunity she'd been given to attend the conference and potentially boost her career. *And, if nothing else, it's an exotic adventure*, she thought to herself.

She had been busy answering emails and cleaning up last-minute details before the big trip when Stacey stopped by her office.

"Maxine, are you almost ready to leave for the day?"

"Yes, almost there. Bloody hell, it feels like I'm leaving for a month, not a week! I'm getting excited, though. Except I think I'm more confused about what shoes to take than about the trip itself."

Stacey laughed. "Now, here is all your paperwork and your schedule. This is your cab charge and the name of the company that will be driving you to and from, once you get there. These are your tickets and all your international contact numbers. Enjoy, and good luck."

"Thanks so much, Stacey. It will be a good experience, I know."

M wrapped things up for the day, walked out of her office and sighed. Once home, she flung open her wardrobe to begin packing. *What does a businesswoman bring on a business trip?* she thought to herself, feeling very grown up. Shoes, bags, clothes. It was only six days, but there were dinners and business meetings involved. Different and classy attire, each day was essential. She wasn't sure how businesswomen dressed in Europe, how it differed from home. Did they dress up or down? Were they more casual and relaxed in their clothing or dressier? She wouldn't worry about it too much, she decided. After all, she'd have lots of time for shopping.

Shoes were not a worry though. M had a vast array. If there was one collection of possessions she was proud of, it was her shoes. Actually, most of her spare cash was invested in them. As she stared down at her collection, she finally made the difficult decision to bring just three pairs–her loafers for walking the city (you needed comfort when you were a tourist); heels for dinners and functions (her favourite black pumps from the trip to France five years ago were oldies but goodies–if she could get by walking the Left Bank in Paris, she could do it in Prague); and her open slingbacks (just *because*).

That night, attempting an early sleep, she found it hard to settle, as she was filled with confliction feelings–nervousness and excitement. Despite her uncertain future with Louis Advertising, some instinct told her everything would be okay, that her career was on track and that she was onto something good.

However, it was Adi's delicious smile that she fell asleep to.

6

M's eyes were stuck together like glue.

"Excuse me, Madame, we are about to land. I need you to put your seat up."

M looked at the stewardess, then around in a blur. Had she really slept through the whole flight? She quickly collected herself–fixed her hair and squirted some body spray. She felt like she'd been living in a tuna can for that last twenty hours, despite the opulence of Business Class.

As M disembarked, her anxiety swelled, but it was overshadowed by a feeling of exhilaration. All she had wanted professionally was now coming true. M noted how clean and spacious the Václav Havel Airport was. There were many people swarming around, even though it was late at night. As she waited for her bags, she noticed lots of coffee stands and little bars. The smell of roasted beans ignited her senses–it had been a long flight in that tin can and it was nice to have something in her nostrils other than the smell of air-conditioning and strange gasses emanating from other people's bodies. She got a latte and a pastry.

Outside she hailed a taxi and she took in her first breath of the fresh European night air. As they drove, she looked at the beautiful city that surrounded her. All the bright lights and the people–she still couldn't believe that she was in Prague. The city was quaint and illuminated everywhere she looked. All the lights brought character to the place. As they passed street after street, intersection after intersection, she realised just how big the city was, the largest, of course, in the Czech Republic. She was in awe, like a child unwrapping shiny presents at Christmas time.

The cab driver, who spoke English well, chatted to M about how Prague boasted more than ten major museums and galleries. The city was divided by the Vltava River, she knew, with the Charles Bridge connecting the two halves. As they crossed it, she saw an entire row of statues and Baroque-style monuments, mostly depicting saints and patron saints. Giddy with excitement, M whipped out her iPhone as the cab drove them through the night and she unabashedly did the tourist *click, click, click* at everything that moved, knowing full well that the images would probably turn out as nothing more than blurry streamers of shooting light, but not caring. She had to capture it all. She felt she had stepped back in time.

Her hotel was a stone's throw from the busy, historical Wenceslas Square and entering the foyer, she realised she was in love already. The foyer was quiet, with not many people around, as it was now after midnight. The huge ornate ceiling had a shimmering Edwardian chandelier hanging down, like a cluster of jewels.

Once checked in, she showered and hopped into her king-size bed. As usual, she became a splayed starfish, stretching her limbs across the cool thick linen. She exhaled deeply as she released the airplane-seat knots in her neck and shoulders. She'd made it. Yet her serenity was short-lived as the *ding-ding-ding* of incoming text messages startled her and she fumbled for her phone. Her backlog of messages from home were now arriving that she'd switched the Airport Mode off.

Message one:

> Hey, girlfriend, hope all is well. Meet a nice European man for me and drink lots of vino. Luv ya, Kathy

Message two:

> Bon voyage, M. Have lots of sex. Nab yourself a European or a black man. Either one or both. Honey, once you go there, you won't go back. Well, so I heard! LOL! Laura

Message three:

> Hi Maxine—hope you have a safe flight. Sorry I didn't get a chance to catch up with you. Let me know when you are home. XOXO

Adi!

She didn't expect that one. She smiled like the Cheshire Cat. With that, she fell asleep and had an inappropriate dream, her grin still stretched from ear to ear.

The first morning of the convention found M both excited and nervous. She put on her black dress and her pumps and heaved a big sigh. The convention was only four blocks away from the hotel, in a large exhibition room. From the outside it seemed like a huge run-down old warehouse made from brick and steel pillars, but the inside was another story. Painted murals and mosaic figures made up a big feature wall in the entryway, while the interior was graced by marble statues and large chandeliers, the size of cars.

She walked in feeling like a fish out of water, and also like she had stepped back in time. Different companies from around the world were there–marketing analysts and companies launching new concepts and products. People were setting up booths at the side of the main room. She checked in to get her name badge and her papers, still feeling a little odd. It was her first time at one of these and she wanted to make a good impression and also learn as much as possible. She didn't know where to look. She knew she'd definitely see some handsome men out there. How was she going to concentrate with all that eye candy?

As she left the registration line with her itinerary, she noticed a very handsome, immaculately dressed man of about forty looking at her. He had short dark hair, speckled with a little salt and pepper around the sides, and was wearing an Armani suit and emerald silk tie. His chiselled features and olive skin made her think he must be Italian, or something equally as exotic. Most striking were his crystal green eyes, which seemed to radiate like kryptonite, set off by the green of his tie. They were certainly draining M of her power, making her a little weak at the knees. *Mmmm, I really am in Europe*, she thought. *He can park his Gucci loafers under my bed any day.*

Her heart skipped a beat as he smiled and started walking towards her.

"Hello, I couldn't help but see that you seem a little confused, like I am, so I thought I'd join you. My name is Antonio," he said, in his melodic accent, as he extended his hand to her. *Bingo*, M thought. *Hot Italiano.*

"Hello, I'm Maxine. Yes, I'm a little thrown off by all the commotion, so I guess I'm glad you're confused too." She smiled warmly, trying to control the curvature of her lips to exude both formal professionalism and playful flirtation.

"I'm from Rossi and La Rocca, from Milan," he said.

"I'm representing Louis Advertising, Asia Pacific. This is my first time here. Well, obviously," she added. She was very happy to bump into a fellow newbie–and a handsome one at that–and thrilled with his European panache: that he'd had the confidence and grace to approach her and introduce himself. This was not something she was used to encountering a lot of back home. She welcomed it and wished all men were just as amenable.

"Well, let's see how we go today," he said. They both laughed and walked together into the seated section where the program was about to begin.

During the breaks, she and Antonio got to talking about what he did for a living and his hobbies. He introduced her to other employees from his headquarters in Milan. She was amazed at how different their approach to everything was. Antonio said that they worked from nine a.m. until noon. Then they took a three-hour break before starting again, and wrapping up for the day at six or seven p.m. She noticed how they were so relaxed and casual about everything. *These Italians have it worked out*, she thought. It brought up one of life's big motifs: work to live, not live to work. She admired that; in her world it was a very different ball game. Most people got so lost in the everyday grind of life that they forgot to stop and breathe. Then they wondered how the weeks and months went by so quickly. M was the type of person who would stop and take in the moment when she had a chance, but she knew she was guilty of forgetting to do that on many occasions.

As the conference went on, she got to know many of the international delegates and learned more about her industry and networking. That was really what it was all about. She saw how firms incorporated new ideas and concepts; how advertising was changing and what was to be expected for the future; how people perceived things; how consumer spending and living had impacted life; and the power of consumer psychology. Not surprisingly, she learned that she loved networking. She'd always found her way in a crowded room. She was a communicator and a joker, a real people person, and all of this was right up her ally. Mr Ferguson had known that, and she planned to make him proud.

She wined and dined with some of the heavyweights of advertising, diving in head first, no longer feeling like that fish out of water. She felt confident and it showed. She spoke with a few different delegates and took in the whole moment. She felt confident. It was like a meet and greet. Antonio was the head of advertising at his own firm, and she learned a lot from him as well. Some people have a talent and an aura of confidence about them, and Antonio was one of them. She was taken in by all of him. The intelligence, the charm, the wit and of course his sexy northern Italian accent. She now understood how a woman could lose herself just by listening to an Italian man. She loved the attention he gave her. *Thank you, Mr Ferguson*, she thought to herself as she recalled his advice about combining work and pleasure.

She and Antonio organised to meet for breakfast the morning after the conference ended. He wanted to check out some places that had been recommended to him and said he'd enjoy her company. She obliged without hesitation. Antonio picked her up at nine-thirty and took her to a very popular café in the centre of town. She saw how the locals lived and went about their day-to-day life. They sat with their espressos and read the paper—no rush to get to work, no stress, just a chance to sit and be still for the moment. It was a pleasure to watch. A glistering, summer morning, they sat outside with a view of the main square.

"It's nice to relax now that the conference is over," she said. "It was a lot to take in, for such a short amount of time. I have twenty hours on the way home to structure the report," she laughed.

"Yes, but it is all for the good of future advertising and creativity in all departments," he replied. "Anyway, bella Maxine," he continued with a big grin, "work is now finished. Now it is time to enjoy. Tell me, do you have a husband missing you back home?"

There it was again, the question dreaded by all singletons. M struggled as always for an answer. She wished she had some confident generic reply that exuded wit and poise, and didn't make her sound as tragic as she always felt it did. Honestly, it should be illegal to ask that question. "Well," she stumbled, suddenly self-conscious, "I guess it's not my time. Sometimes you think your life is going one way but then it goes another. I guess that's life, hey?" She took a tense gulp of her coffee.

"How could a beautiful girl like you still be on the market? Are they all idiots where you are from?"

You wouldn't need to ask that question if you'd met Shamus The Shit, she thought. M laughed nervously, hoping he'd change the topic of her romantic vacuum.

"Well," he said, intuiting her discomposure, "I can tell you for sure that if you lived here, you would be snapped up in a flash because any man with half a brain wouldn't let a woman like you go. I'm sure there is at least one intelligent man back home."

"When I find him, I'll let you know," M responded with a chuckle. Try as she did to make a joke of it and brush it off with indifference, inside she felt that familiar ache of longing and frustration. Why is it that some men couldn't see what they had in front of them? What exactly *did* a man want in a woman? After a short pause, she smiled. "I guess I could move to Europe, hey, Antonio?" she suggested.

"That sounds wonderful, *cara*," he replied.

They spent the whole day together, walking and eating … walking and eating some more. She had never felt so gastronomically satisfied. He was such pleasant company–not sleazy or arrogant, and no hints about sleeping with her (although she certainly wouldn't be opposed to his sexy Italian *dolci baci* between the sheets). But, in truth, his kindness and company were what she needed most, and in that department, he spoiled her rotten.

As the day drew to a close, they walked back to the hotel. In the foyer he turned and took her hands and looked her deep in the eyes, which both electrified her and took her a little off guard after spending the day grouping him into the friend category. *Is he going to kiss me?* she thought, as jitters plagued her stomach.

Will this complicate things? I'm about to fly 16,000 kilometres away. Yet, she had to admit to herself, there was nothing complicated about the thought of being kissed by a handsome Italiano. And, frankly, a little bit of pash action would be the cherry on the cake–or tiramisu!–of an amazing trip. *Baciami*, she suddenly heard the voice in her head whisper. *Kiss me, Antonio.*

"Maxine," he said, "it has been a pleasure to have your company. You are a smart, funny, charming and articulate woman. I wish you all the best. It will all come to you in good time. Maybe I will see you at the next conference … Or maybe you can come and visit me in Italy? I would love to show you where I'm from. It's a beautiful place in the northern region, called Santa Croce. From my family property you can see the Adriatic Sea."

"Thank you, that sounds wonderful, Antonio. Thank you for everything. You are a lovely person. I've really enjoyed your company," M replied, beaming. What an offer!

Then he leaned forward and kissed her. Her body weakened as his soft lips touched hers, and he whispered in her ear. "*Il tuo destino è scritto nelle stelle. Il tuo destino ti troverà.*"

"What does that mean?" she asked curiously.

"It means that your destiny is written in the stars. Your destiny will find you," he replied softly.

The words dripped from his lips like melted chocolate and it took all her willpower not to grab him and drag him to her room. But she practised restraint. Laura would kill her for this missed opportunity, but she reasoned that the moment was already perfect.

Your destiny is written in the stars. Your destiny will find you. That beautiful whisper would be purring in her ears forever.

"Good night, *bella mia*," Antonio said and walked away.

It was a moment that she would never forget, and, admittedly, she was a little relieved that Antonio hadn't become a holiday conquest. They'd acted above that, adults simply enjoying each other's company, exchanging sweet words and possibilities, and that felt more sensual and enduring than a one-night tussle between the sheets. A part of her wished it could always be like that, with no expectations or worries. She'd learned one thing for sure—Italian men were much more mature and emotionally advanced than the men she'd always encountered back home. It was the way they treated a woman, she reflected. It was different. It made her feel different. The woman is the focus, while the man makes her feel wanted and needed. It felt more real and sincere. They certainly didn't lack confidence, as they were not shy about asking a girl out, but they were masculine in a charming—not sleazy—way. They knew what a woman wanted and needed. She wished she could take Antonio home to give lectures to the Australian men she knew on how to treat a woman. Shamus should be front row and center to get a proper education. What a difference it would make. All of a sudden she was craving a macaroon. Actually a whole packet.

As she exited the elevator and walked down the hallway musing about the events of the day, she saw a man trying to open the door in the room adjacent to hers. From afar, he looked familiar. As she got closer, her heart started pounding like a jackhammer.

"Adi?" she whispered.

7

"Holy cow! What are you doing here?" she said to Adi, in a state of astonishment.

"Oh my God, Maxine!" He looked at her in shock. "What the hell? What are *you* doing here?"

"I'm here on that conference I told you about."

"What? *Here?*" he sputtered.

"Yeah. Actually, it just finished. Now I have a few days to myself. What about you? I thought you were going to a wedding?"

"I was. In London,"

"*London?*" she said, clearly stunned. "I can't believe your wedding was in London. I had no idea you were flying to Europe. I thought you were going to Adelaide or something." M felt like she had just died and gone to heaven.

"Yeah, the wedding was yesterday," he said. "I didn't realise your conference was in *Prague. I thought you* were going to Adelaide or something," he laughed.

"This is just too freaky. So how is that that you're now in here?"

"I was supposed to meet up with a friend but he cancelled. I've always wanted to see Prague–so here I am." He paused and shook his head in disbelief, eyeing her up and down. "Hello, serendipity," he said.

"I'm speechless," M laughed.

"Of all the hotels in all the towns in all the world, you had to walk into mine," Adi said, smirking through his Bogart impression.

"Play it again, Sam," said M, and they both laughed. They were on a roll. "Jeez, you'll stop at nothing for our coffee catch up, eh?" joked M.

"Yep, you got me," he laughed, "that's exactly why I flew to *Prague*!"

Her smile in response was as wide as the Pacific Ocean. "Well, it's late," she finally said. "But if you don't have other plans, would you like to meet tomorrow morning for breakfast?"

"Sounds great," he said. "How's nine? We can meet in the foyer."

"Perfect. I'll see you then," she smiled.

In her own room, M threw herself on the bed to calm down and process the whole thing. She reached for her phone and googled 'serendipity'. "The occurrence and development of events by chance in a happy or beneficial way," she read aloud. "Well, I'll be dammed. Antonio's stars of destiny have kicked in already."

Sleep was futile. She tossed and turned for hours. How could this be? The events of the last few months had suddenly become a distant memory as her rush of feelings came soaring to new heights. Suddenly all worries of unemployment and being single went out the window. Well, at least for now. She was going to live in the moment, enjoy it and go with it. Maybe the gods were repaying her after what Shamus The Shit did to her.

She fell asleep, eventually … grinning from ear to ear.

The sun peered through the blinds, as a warm glow of exhilaration flooded through her entire being. *Adi is in Prague!* She still couldn't believe the magnitude of the coincidence. The left side of her brain was quick to point out that there *are* no coincidences. *Go, brain.*

She lathered herself from head to toe in the shower, massaging a gorgeous frangipani body wash into her skin, then picked out a soft yellow sundress she was suddenly thankful she'd packed. Meticulously she applied her makeup, aiming for minimal and flawless, aware that too much would have her face melting in the heat. The breezy look completed with her Jimmy Choo flats, she was ready for their breakfast date. As she dashed out the door, her phone beeped, but she ignored it. From now until the end of her trip, she decided suddenly, she was just going to relax. These were her few days in another world. It felt surreal to M. She'd never had this kind of opportunity before, of work and play, and to have randomly bumped into Adi was the cream on top. How on earth had it happened?

They found a sidewalk café in the Old Town Square and laughed and talked in the sunshine as they nibbled their sweet pastries and sipped their coffees, taking in the air and the atmosphere. After breakfast, they wandered the alleyways and took photos of the baroque buildings, now and then stopping to look in shops and try on some European fashions. They slowly made their way to Havel's Market where they were seduced by the delicious smells and decided to eat lunch at a bustling pub–a feast of baked pork, dumplings and sauerkraut-style cabbaged, washed down with mugs of frosty beer. M noticed how at ease she felt just chatting with Adi. She was always bubbly, the person who spoke to the mailman, the butcher, the sales assistant, the valet attendant–any excuse to be friendly. But this was a different feeling–less forced and more real. It just flowed. It was nice, and she was surprised that he was such good company. She noticed that even though he was quite chatty himself, he seemed a little preoccupied, like there was something else going on in his mind. Had something happened at the wedding? Had he meet a bridesmaid? M decided to brush it off and enjoy their time together.

They relaxed for a while under the shade of a big elm tree in the city gardens. It looked like a European Central Park. Reclining in the sunshine, they discussed life, relationships, friends back home, work. It was the first time they'd really had the chance to get to know each other personally.

"So, Maxine," he asked, "what's your story–no Mr Maxine?"

M was expecting the dreaded question, although this time she kind of welcomed it as she hoped it meant Adi was fishing because he was interested in her. Nevertheless, her stomach went tight like a knot. Even from someone as charming as Adi, this question made her want to hide in a hole, as though lacking a significant other by thirty was something to be ashamed of.

"No man at the moment. I guess it's all timing," she laughed breezily. Or at least trying to sound that way. "There was someone

... well ... he ... I guess I'm in the process of making a new path for myself, on multiple levels. My company is downsizing so we are in limbo. Restructuring. This trip just might be my last hurrah professionally for a while. But that's life, eh?"

Adi said nothing, just sat in wide-eyed attentiveness as he listened, taking in her words. It was strangely calming and M heard herself starting to rattle off more than she intended.

"Actually," she added, "to tell you the truth, my ex ran off with the payroll officer in the Accounts Department." *Oh God*, she instantly thought, *why did I tell him that?* "But, hey, all in all, I'm alive and I'm in Prague ... and spending this lovely day with you!" She knew she'd said too much and was instantly self-conscious. It was something about the look in his eye that made her feel like she could *talk*, real words, not just superficial banter.

"Firstly," he said at last, "fuck your ex. He wouldn't know a good women if it hit him on the head."

This made M smile. *True*, she thought to herself.

"Secondly," he continued, "I wouldn't worry about your work. You are smart, beautiful and articulate. Any employer would be lucky to have you."

Good woman? Smart? Beautiful? Articulate? M was aglow. "And you?" she said. "Tell me about Adi."

"I'm in the process of making a new path for myself as well, I guess. Finance and banking is good, don't get me wrong, but I have new avenues I want to take it." He seemed hesitant, withholding.

"And Mrs Adi?" M said cheekily, relaxing into the conversation, feeling her confidence begin to build again.

"Mrs Adi?" he laughed nervously.

Did he just twitch? M thought.

"Well … there is no missus. Life can be complicated. I think it's all timing, as well. And the connection. Sometimes things are harder than what you think they will be and things just take time to figure out. Nevertheless, they say things fall into place when they are meant to. So I'm just hoping for that too," he added.

M nodded in agreement.

"I couldn't be with someone just for the hell of it–there has to be something more there," he explained, then stopped to pause for a moment, perhaps considering if he should say more. "Sometimes you think your journey is going one way but all of a sudden it takes a new turn," he continued. "It must be for a reason. Love can bring happiness, but it can also bring hurt. We just have to go with the flow, hey? Otherwise we'll never know."

Was he eluding that he had some relationship messiness? Had he had some trouble in the past? How could someone so cute have issues with women? She would have thought they'd be lining up at the door for him.

"I don't know sometimes. Maybe our paths are written," M said, thinking about what Antonio had told her. "What we do and say, who we meet, where we go–it's all mapped out for us. But there's still something exciting about the unknown." She was liking the fact that she understood him. It seemed he was quite intelligent when it came to matters of the heart.

They strolled through the cobblestone streets and took in the monuments and architecture, as they traded facts about their favourite things like food, music, hobbies and clothes. They had a surprising amount in common.

"So football is a big thing for you?" she asked.

"Oh, yeah, for sure. I go as much as I can. It's a fun thing to do with the boys, I think."

"Yep, a few beers with the mates. My girlfriends and I go when we can, too."

"Maybe we can all go as a group one day—like for a blockbuster, when two big teams play together," he suggested.

Wow, had Adi actually just instigated something on a bigger scale? A full-on outing—with their friends? Perhaps this really was turning into something more than just coffee.

"Sure, that sounds like fun," she said.

They stopped for photos and ice-cream near the river, just before the Charles Bridge. They sat at a table in the main square and people-watched. M hadn't felt this serene and happy in a long time. The hours rolled by, and before she knew it they were heading back to the hotel and making plans to go out for the night. It was obvious that neither wanted their day together to end.

As she headed to her room to change, M thought about the gorgeous red dress she'd bought earlier and was excited to have an opportunity to wear it. M always took pride in what she wore and how she looked—it was probably ingrained from her background in fashion—although she sometimes wondered why she bothered to go to such effort, especially considering how comfortable she already felt with this guy.

However, as always when she started to feel like this about a guy, the two sides of her brain were screaming out contradictory advice. Her right-brain was saying, *Go for it, honey! Have some fun! Live a little! This is it!*

Her left-brain, on the other hand, was a little more cynical: *Yes, he's a man you are comfortable with. But he'll break your heart if you open it. Friendship. That's the way to go.*

It was very difficult to argue with either half of one's brain when applying mascara, she concluded with amusement. She thought about it, though. When you're in a relationship, it can be hard for a girl to get to know or establish a separate, purely platonic relationship with a guy. But now being single, M realised that she didn't have to hold back or reserve herself from anything. And that included Adi. She was going to use this chance encounter and allow herself to be open to new possibilities. No strategising or countermoves, just genuine connection–whether that lead to a romantic or platonic relationship, although admittedly she was leaning towards the romance. Either way, she was ready for something real.

They met in the foyer. His eyes glowed, transfixed, when he saw her and he smiled. M noticed this immediately. Was he attracted to her too? Was his stomach doing backflips like hers? She felt eighteen again, heading out on a first date.

"Wow, you look lovely … as always," he said by way of greeting. "That colour really suits you."

"Thanks. You scrub up all right, too," she laughed. Adi was draped in the Diesel clothing that he'd purchased that day. She was most impressed. Definitely a very stylish version of Mr Darcy.

They walked to a cosy little restaurant they'd spotted earlier. Ah, European cities, with their food, wine and views! As they walked in, they soaked up the delicious aromas, as well as the atmosphere. M wanted to pinch herself yet again, so she'd believe she was really here. They were seated by the window and ordered straight away, after the waiter reeled off the specials, seemly excited to have a chance to practise his English. He then returned with a bottle of wine and a big basket of freshly baked crusty bread. Adi poured two glasses of vino as M drizzled olive oil onto a chunk of bread and took a big bite. She actually had an appetite, which was strange. Usually she could barely eat on first dates, because of nerves. But she felt refreshingly at ease.

"I must say, I'm really loving how you appreciate your food," he remarked. "So many women get so weird about eating and being *seen* eating, but I love that you don't. You just enjoy yourself naturally. It's a good way to be."

He likes my appetite–tick, she thought. "Thanks. I truly feel grateful for things like good food. They're so simple yet so important. We may not often get to eat bread this good at home. So when I'm away and I eat, or drink, or see something really nice, I savour it. Live in the moment," she said, looking at him over her glass as she sipped her wine, trying to gauge his reaction to this bit of philosophy. "We forget all the time because the days are so busy, but being away allows us to stop and take a moment to notice things again."

"Wow, that's really beautiful," he said.

She loved that he really seemed to get her. *Double tick.*

"So true," he said as he sipped his wine. "It's nice to relax and unwind. Forget about what's going on in real life for a change."

There it was again—or was it her imagination?—the hint of a life more complicated that Adi was alluding to. For a second, she considered asking him what he meant, but then thought better of it. Time to put her usual niggles aside and instead just live in the moment. *When in Prague ...*

After their fabulous meal of fried cheese, hearty beef goulash and dumplings filled with cream for dessert, they decided to head to a bar down the street for a nightcap. It was buzzing with people and had some chill-out-session sounds pulsing in the background. As they sat and ordered gin and tonics, Adi said, "Thanks, Max, this has been really nice."

"It's been great for me, too," she replied, secretly thrilled he was feeling so familiar with that her to shorten her name. "If I hadn't bumped into you I would be alone. Thanks for finding me ... or accidentally choosing the same hotel," she joked.

"Things have been hard for me lately on a personal level, so I'm glad for the chance to get away. And spending time with you has been an added bonus. Good timing, I think. I really needed it."

"My pleasure," M told him, although definitely noticing the mention of his troubles at home this time. "Whatever you're going through, just take things one day at a time. Face things with courage, dignity and strength. Whatever happens, know that you are going to be okay. Sometimes we have to go through tough crap in order to grow stronger." She reached across the table and held his hand as a gesture of support, and he squeezed her hand in response. She didn't know what words of wisdom she had just spun but it was enough for her to look in his eyes and just melt away. They connected. Not just by hand gesture but by feeling. He looked in her eyes with yearning and hope.

"Thanks so much, Max. I'm amazed at your perspective. You're so intelligent, yet so compassionate. You aren't like most women I've met." He looked at her and smiled.

She felt his appreciation. She was happy. *Intelligent? Compassionate? Tick! Tick!*

After their nightcap, they headed back to the hotel. As Adi walked M to her door they exchanged another big bear hug and kisses on the cheek. M looked into his eyes. They sparkled in the night glare. There was a magnetic pull, drawing them together. She felt it and, by his expression, so did he. She couldn't contain it any longer. She wasn't sure if it was the gin and tonic or her hormones, but she swooned like a Bollywood starlet and they kissed passionately, as he pinned her up against the door. She broke away to look him in the eye and they both knew what was going to happen. She unlocked her door and they stepped inside. He closed the door immediately and begun to unzip her dress from behind. Her heart raced. It couldn't be just lust. There was something in her core saying it was so much more ... *hoping* it was more. But, at the same time, she didn't care. All she wanted was him. All of him. They fell onto the bed and she began to take his shirt off. Piece after piece was flung onto the floor until they were naked, never breaking from their passionate embrace.

Kissing her neck, he made his way down to her chest, caressing her nipples, as he whispered in her ear. "I want you."

That's all she needed to hear. She couldn't remember feeling this way. It was different to anything she'd felt before. Not even Shamus The Shit had this effect, even when he was still just 'Shamus'. Maybe because this was all new to her.

They made love, their eyes staying locked, their kisses never-ending. She never thought sex with someone she'd known for such a short time could ignite such passion in her. He was just what she needed. Maybe she was still vulnerable from her split or perhaps it was a connection she had longed for. She didn't know how someone could have that effect so quickly. Was it possible? Was it real? M never thought it could be possible before, but this felt real. She didn't want this moment to end. She felt safe, happy, relaxed. If she could pause time, she would. If there was a moment that could erase all the crap from the last couple months, it was this one–Adi would be the one to do it. This is where she was meant to be. And she didn't want to leave. He kissed her delicate skin from top to toe, like she was the only thing that mattered in that time, in that moment. He made her feel beautiful, sensual. Like a women. Just his touch ignited her nerve endings. She felt his manliness on her … then in her. She felt his heart beat as she held him tight while he thrusted. He grabbed her hand and intertwined his fingers in hers. He kept going until she let out her euphoric sigh. He smiled as he looked in her eyes. He then motioned for her to lay on her stomach. She lay like a starfish as he slid inside of her. As his intense thrusting increased, he let out a moan of ecstasy.

And just like that, M and Adi's coincidental meeting in Prague came to a peak of pure bliss. Never in a million years would M have predicted this.

They awoke in an embrace. He smiled at her. "How are you?" he asked, with a grin on his face.

"Good," she purred, returning his smile. "How are you?"

"Really good," he replied, as he swept her hair from her face. They looked at each other with a smile, still emanating in the glow of what had transpired the night before.

"That was quite something," he said.

"Yes ... yes, it was. I'm surprised. It's been a nice, unexpected surprise," M said.

"I couldn't agree more. I'm glad that I bumped into you ..."

"I bet you are!" laughed M.

"Oh," laughed Adi, "pun intended, I guess! Seriously, though, thank you for being comfortable with me. To want to be with me," Adi said as he caressed her face.

She smiled at him, feeling comfortable, happy and safe. "Likewise. This was something I never imagined. But now, I believe that anything is possible," M replied as she gently kissed his lips. The softness and smell of his skin consumed her as their limbs locked around each other and their bodies began to move, as though independent of their conscious thoughts. Suddenly they were in a tangled embrace as passion consumed them once again and they lost all awareness of time and space.

Sometime later, in a sweaty hold, Adi finally spoke. "Are we still good for that bike ride today," he laughed.

"Absolutely!" she replied. "It will be fun."

"I know something that would be more fun," said Adi, his fingers trailing down the nape of her neck. "But if I don't get out of your bed now, I don't think I'll ever be able to," he sighed.

"And I think we might starve to death!" They both laughed at this. "I'll going back to my room to shower and change," he said, as they reluctantly unlocked their brace position.

As Adi reached for his jeans, M examined his buttocks in the light of day and grinned. "Okay, me too–see you soon," M replied, watching him closely as he dressed, doing an internal checklist:

Nice butt–tick.

Excellent love making–tick.

Shamus The Shit … who dat?

As soon as he shut the door, she stretched out on the bed. *Oh god, oh god, oh god!* she thought to herself as she finally had some headspace to take it all in and pondered about how the last twenty-four hours had swept her away. *Is this the real thing? Or is it a holiday fling? Does he have feelings for me? Or was it just the heat of the moment?*

Stop! the rational M instantly demanded. *Stop overloading this.* Yes. She had to break the old patterns. Every love affair wasn't necessarily *the grand love affair*–her future husband, father of her children, her soul mate. She reminded herself to stay in the moment. Enjoy it. This was the best thing to do for now. Safer.

The only thing she *was* sure of, though, was that it was pretty fucking amazing … the sex, the chemistry, the connection. But, for right now, she needed live it for *now*. Who knew what the future held.

Twenty minutes later, she was barely out of the shower when she heard a knock. "Oh my God! Just, uh …" she opened he door, still in her bath towel. "I'm so sorry, I'm not quite ready," she said, checking out his lean frame dressed in his sexy slim-fit denim jeans. He looked so good, it was disconcerting. She still couldn't believe the twist of fate in randomly meeting up, not to mention the previous night…

"Don't stress, crazy," he laughed. "I'll wait here."

She left him standing in the hallway while she quickly threw on a dress and got herself ready in a matter of minutes. As she re-emerged, he looked at her and smiled, with a concerned look on his face. "Um … you look gorgeous. But I don't think a dress would be wise on a Vespa."

"Oh," she smirked awkwardly, acknowledging. "You're right. Thanks for the tip. I'll be one second, I promise," she replied, closing the door on him again. She quickly fished her shorts and a singlet top out of her suitcase and threw them on, slightly flustered. She grabbed her bag and sunnies, then opened the door and greeted him again–take two!–and they set off for the bike hire place.

As Adi did the organising at the front desk, M texted Elisha. She hadn't communicated with the girls for days, so she quickly typed:

> Hey, babe, Maxine is going on a Vespa ride through Prague with a very handsome man. I wish I could pause time. Must go … gorgeous man awaits. M x

Just as she clicked 'send', Adi walked toward her with the helmets and keys. Damn, he looked good! She was looking forward to straddling him on the back of the bike all afternoon. "Thank God I don't care about my hair today," she said, as she climbed aboard.

"You'll be fine. I'll lead the way," he said, swinging into the saddle in front of her. Yes, it was only a Vespa, but she couldn't help but feeling all *Sons of Anarchy*. He, of course, had other plans. "Hold on tight," he said. "I plan to be Valentino Rossi."

"I hope you know what you're doing!" she chided. They laughed, and away they went.

M's pulse pounded as she held onto his torso, tightly, feeling his sixpack through his t-shirt. She couldn't help herself from subtly fingering the ridges of abs, as she tried in vain to contain the shag flashbacks from the night before!

They made their way at a moderate speed through Wenceslas Square and out the other side, at which point he accelerated a bit and headed toward the riverbank. Her heart accelerated as well. As the summer wind blew her hair back, she suddenly felt all *Roman Holiday*—a kooky Audrey Hepburn on the back of Gregory Peck's bike as she played hooky from her princess duties, escaping her life, if only for a day. What a rush! Total bliss. She felt like the luckiest girl in the world.

The right side of her brain was full of its usual chatter. *Enjoy it, honey. Ride like the wind. It's a holiday. Squeeze him harder. You're on holiday, girl. Celebrate.*

The left side was, once again, more conservative, if not bitter. *While this is lovely, darling, just enjoy the moment. Be Audrey Hepburn, but then come back to reality. He is just a boy taking you for a ride. Taking. You. For. A. Ride. Nothing more. Enjoy it and have fun while it lasts.*

It made sense. She wondered to herself why women always seem to want something more than what simply is. Yes, we enjoy the moment, but we also have this innate ability to make something out of nothing in our minds. To romantacise everything. Or, at least, make things more than we should. Men don't do that. Why do we do this?

Case in point: a short play, let's call it *Girl on Vespa With Nice Boy*:

WOMAN (internal monologue): This is so nice. Very *Roman Holiday*. Oh my God, he *organised* it. How sweet of him! He must like me! Why would he want to bike ride with me if he didn't think I was nice? What if this is the start of something? What if he really likes me? What if he wants to do this back home? What if he wants to do *more* than this back home?

MAN (internal monologue): Riding a Vespa with a girl. It's fun.

That's pretty much the drill, M thought. What a difference. Women's mental perceptions grow like weeds and can stick like ticks. It takes so much effort to retrain them and yank them out! We are well considered when buying the perfect pair of shoes, but when it comes to men, we allow ourselves to jump aboard the crazy train. Are we programmed this way, or just gluttons for punishment? Maybe we do all wish for the magical moment that will take our breath away–for that one man who will steal our heart and sweep us off our feet. Yet why *shouldn't* we crave it? After all, it is a beautiful feeling.

"Are you enjoying my abs back there?" Adi asked teasingly over his shoulder.

"Settle down, Mr Egomaniac," she said playfully, while thinking, *Oops, busted fingering his abs*. She decided to be cheeky and gave his waist a firm squeeze. "Actually, yes, nice abs," she said into his ear, as he chuckled in response.

She watched all the houses and people as they zoomed by. It was nice to be out in the open instead of in a cab. She sighed as he sped up just that little bit faster, and envisioned them riding away together. Yes, it was a silly daydream. But, hell, why not? She imagined him grabbing her and kissing her passionately. If this was the definition of escapism, she didn't want to return to captivityism.

After the thrill of riding though the cobblestone streets and the outskirts of the city, they decided to devote a bit of work to one of those interests they had in common–shopping. She'd always had a keen eye, and he was surprisingly keen when it came to shopping as well. So off they went to pick up some European designs and some bargains.

Hot guy + hot sex + likes to shop–Tick! Tick! Tick!

She'd never met a guy who loved shopping before, except for her friend Don, but he was a stylist so it was his job. But it was nice to shop with a guy, as opposed to her girlfriends. He had a different perspective and the experience gave her a different feeling. Even though she was nurturing her *major* crush on him, she was hoping that this could maybe someday eventuate into something bigger.

They shopped and talked, shopped some more, then fit in a stopover at a bar for crusty bread and dips and mugs of local frosty beer–a Prague staple, it seemed. M felt an overall sense of peace. For her time had stood still these past two days, with nothing mattering but the moment, and this feeling of euphoria being at the side of a really good man. If the saying 'behind every good man there is a good woman' was true, then hell, why couldn't she just enjoy that feeling for a while before she flew back home?

"Phew! I'm walked out and shopped out," she said sitting down inside the bar.

"You did well–three pairs of shoes and two dresses," he said, looking over at her bags.

"So did you, mister. You're just as bad as me! I noticed that you were very particular about certain things, too."

"Yeah, I guess I am. I'm a funny shopper. My ex hated shopping with me. I am what I am, though … I used to tell her to do her own thing and then meet me later. But she never really had a good sense of style."

Ouch. Bitching about the ex? M wasn't sure quite what to say. He had never really mentioned the 'ex factor' until now. Maybe it was just the way he'd said it, but she was a little taken aback by his delivery.

"Well … we're all different, I guess," she replied, awkwardly.

They planned to relax for a bit, when they got back their respective rooms at the hotel, before meeting up later for their last night in Prague. They both flew out the following morning.

M collapsed on her bed in her favourite starfish position and had begun checking her text messages when her phone rang.

"Hi Maxine, it's Stacey from the office."

"Oh, hi Stacey, is everything okay?" she replied.

"Actually, it's about your travel itinerary. The travel agents just phoned to let me know that there are airline strikes in Prague–you may have heard?"

"Strikes?" M cut in abruptly. "No, I hadn't."

"Yeah, pay disputes and so forth. It's a three-day strike so you won't be able to leave for at least another three days. I'll phone or email once I'm updated and I find out what day I can rebook your flight for. In the meantime, I've extended your booking at the hotel," said Stacey. "But I am so sorry. It looks like, for now, you're stranded in Prague."

"Oh!" said M, in disbelief. "Well, thanks for letting me know," she replied and the said their goodbyes. M lay back on her bed. She didn't know what to feel. While she knew she should be put out–she had work to do, reports to compile, meetings to arrange, real life to get back to–she couldn't suppress a swelling sense of reckless jubilation. If there were airline strikes, did that mean that Adi was stuck too? Was this another case of destiny finding her? Talk about expecting the unexpected.

Just then, there was a knock at her door and M opened it.

"Have you heard about the strike?" said Adi. "I just got a text from the airline. I'm stuck here for three days."

"Well, that makes two of us. I just got a call from the office," M replied.

"So," Adi suddenly grinned, "you're stuck here too? Looks like we are stuck here together, Max."

"How about that," smiled M.

"How about that indeed," smirked Adi. "I guess we'll just have to find things to fill our time."

"Monopoly?" M said cheekily.

"I was thinking truth or dare," winked Adi.

"Truth, then: Adi, did you cause the airline strikes just to keep me here?"

"Yes," he laughed in reply. "And for my next trick, I'm going to make your underwear disappear ..."

He leaned in closer and once again his intoxicating musky aroma consumed her and they were instantly in a tangled embrace, as zips and buttons were frantically undone and clothing was peeled away. Their bodies took over, as though they couldn't get enough of each other. Her heart raced. She really wanted this. Him. It. Everything about him. She was intoxicated by his smell, his touch and his body. He had her in his grasp. She gave in to it all, feeling that the way he touched her, caressed her, treated her, it was different. It was real. She thought about the word Adi had used when they'd first run into each other two days ago—'serendipity'. She hadn't given the concept much thought before, but she appreciated how it had dealt her a nice card. Maybe he really was her *destino*.

They made love tirelessly, as the light outside the window turned to dusk, then to night. It was an erotic fantasy fulfilled. She wanted this, a delicious Mickey Rourke *9½ Weeks* fantasy. But she also wanted her Mr Darcy too. Could she have both?

After their lovemaking they lay, as before, in a locked embrace. She could feel his comfort with her, and his contentment, as she felt it too, to just *be* there, be fully present.

"Hey, why don't we do something fancy, like a posh dinner tonight," he suggested. Let's treat ourselves while we can."

"Definitely. And I saw a sign that there's a carnival happening down by the river tonight," she said. "Why don't we go down afterward and see what's around."

"Sounds like a plan. Maybe some dancing?"

Twenty kisses later and he went back to his room so they could both shower and get ready. Now here she was, preparing for another night together–she'd thought it was going to be the last, but really it was just the beginning. She was thankful for all the shopping she'd done.

In their new designer duds, they hailed a cab and drove off to a fancy restaurant recommended by the hotel's concierge. M looked forward to one of those unforgettable fine-dining experiences you can boast about upon returning home, and as soon as they entered the place she realised that's exactly what they would get. The dining room was stylish and modern, but they chose to be seated at the lovely outdoor terrace made of cobblestone and draped in fairy lights. It was beside the river, so the view was stunning. It was a clear night and the lights of the Charles Bridge twinkled as they were reflected off the water. It felt surreal.

"I can't believe how all of this has transpired. I mean … it's been such an amazing twist of fate. A magical twist of fate. Even with the airline thing too, I guess," she mused, gazing out at the river. She didn't want to look straight in his eyes, as she knew it sounded kind of corny and lovey-dovey. But she wanted to express how she felt. Bliss.

"I agree. It has been really nice, and at the risk of sounding trite," he paused, looking at her, "I think you are a beautiful woman."

Wow, M thought. *Jackpot!* "Well, thank you," she laughed. "And by the way, there is nothing wrong with sounding trite."

"It's so nice to relax and be here," he continued. "I'm looking forward to the extra days on this holiday, but I'm glad to have had the opportunity to get to know you. Maybe back home we would never have had this chance. I'm having a lot of fun."

"Likewise," she agreed. "I mean, things get so busy back home that we may not have made the time to get together. So this is a good thing for sure." She sipped her wine, her heart beginning to beat a little faster. Her stomach fluttered. How could her feelings be so strong so quickly? Maybe this *was* more than just an affair to remember. She needed to stop obsessing about it though. She couldn't let it consume her, especially not when they got back to 'real life'. For now, she knew she should just live in the moment. She would do her best to push all serious thoughts out of her head and just concentrate on her delicious dinner and her delicious lover sitting right across from her.

They lingered over the food, finished their bottle of wine, paid for the meal and made their way down to the riverside carnival. As they headed toward the embankment, they saw loads of people sitting in various marquees and bars. Music came from everywhere. Food stalls were interspersed with arts and crafts stalls. Even though they had just eaten at a very swanky restaurant, they couldn't help but salivate at the sight of all the delicious pastries.

After wandering for a while, they chose an open bar next to a performing stage near the river and sat down, deciding to order a classic Czech aperitif – Becherovka.

"How refreshing this is," M remarked. "It doesn't even taste alcoholic."

One drink turned into two … then three. They began to realise that European bartenders were very generous with their portion sizes. The drinks did indeed begin to feel alcoholic.

Eight burlesque dancers came out onto the nearby stage and began performing. Dressed in black lace, fishnets and feathers with pearl jewellery, it was classy sleaze. It felt like Prague's version of the Moulin Rouge. She was quite envious of the dancers' sculpted bodies. Her mind drifted lazily as she imagined herself performing in such a way for Adi. What would he do? Would he like it? Would he want her? Could she pull it off if she had the chance?

"Are you okay? Enjoying the show?" grinned Adi.

M was jolted back to earth. She wondered if she was blushing.

"Yes, this is great. It's not every day that I see women strip and dance for me on the street," she replied coyly. Seeing his answering grin, she continued. "Actually, I lied. Back home I train girls to become strippers. That's my after-five job … pays well." She smirked playfully as he laughed out loud. Hell, she didn't even care at that point. She was drunk, horny and enjoying her flirtation with this handsome man–not a care in the world. She couldn't wait to get him back to the hotel again.

"Okay, fabulous Miss M. I think we should call it a night," he said, as though reading her mind, leaving some money on the bar. "Come on. Let's walk back–I think the cool air will do us some good."

Good idea, she thought to herself, *I need to sober up a bit before I get you between the sheets.* She reeled a bit as he helped her out of her seat and she made a mental note: Aperitifs in Prague may taste like lolly water but they are, in fact, potent stuff.

The walk had been a good call–the fresh air was invigorating. Adi held onto M's arm as they strolled past historical monuments (wait–did that old king *really* have two heads?) and she loved it. Not only for the much-appreciated support, but because it reminded her that for a little bit longer she could still be Audrey Hepburn being romanced by Gregory Peck. It was *her* holiday, so draping herself on him with abandon was still allowed.

As he held her outside her hotel-room door, M's heart beat faster than Louis Hamilton's car in a grand prix grid. Adi's eyes shone as he looked at her. He leaned over and kissed her lips. She grabbed his shirt and pulled him closer, her nerve endings melted. They kissed passionately, softly, as he held her face between his hands.

"Your addictive, Maxine," he whispered.

"Might as well face it, you're addicted to love … addicted to love," she sang and laughed in his ear.

He laughed too and grabbed her around the waist as he fumbled with the key and they stumbled in, landing on the bed.

M awoke early with a blazing headache and immediately began drinking copious amounts of water. Her mind was filled with memories of the previous night. *Oh God, was I really singing Robert Palmer?* she reflection to herself. At least they'd started making love before she'd thought to start dancing like an 'Addicted to Love' girl and give Adi his own private burlesque show.

She stared at him, still fast asleep, and smiled, wondering how she'd been swept up in this whirlwind. Never in her wildest dreams had she anticipated it. It was too good to be true. *If something seems too good to be true, it probably is*, said the annoying little voice in her head. *But*, she quickly rebutted, *couldn't there be exceptions to every rule?* He was kind, smart, handsome, funny and seemed to really want to be with her. But was it just the thrill of the holiday for him—no strings attached? She had a gut feeling there was more to him. Whatever it was, she didn't want this time to end. Yet she knew that it would. Soon they'd be back home and she wasn't sure what shape their relationship would take or if, in fact, you could call it a relationship at all.

The ding of a text message coming through to her phone jolted her back to reality. She quietly went to her bag and looked. It was Stacey with an update on her flight. Apparently it was confirmed that all flights would resume in forty-eight hours. Talk about reality.

"Hey, sugar, what are you doing?" said Adi, surprising her with his husky voice, stirring from his slumber.

She turned to him. Buffed torso, messy bed hair, dreamy eyes. Just seeing him first thing in the morning was a delight.

"Oh, hey … I hope I didn't wake you? I just got an email. Flights resume in two days. I'm assuming you will get an update at some point today too," she replied.

"Really? I was kind of hoping they'd be on strike forever," he said with a wink. "Well, seriously though, I guess that's good news. We do need to get back to real life, hey? There are things I need to sort out at home."

She noticed that he looked concerned as he said this. He did mention that he had a few things on that needed attention, but he never mentioned specifics. He looked at her, smiling, but his eyes looked sad, like he didn't want it to end either. As though on cue, his phone dinged and he checked the message.

"It's official. My flight is back on schedule too, leaving for Melbourne at five p.m. the night after tomorrow. What time does yours leave?" he asked.

"Ten a.m. that morning," she replied, barely able to control the little wave of disappointment that came over her. The same flight would have been nice.

He reached out his arms to her. "Let's enjoy the next forty-eight hours, hey?"

She smiled and crawled back in bed beside him.

The next few days went by in a blur. Eating decadent food, walking the cobblestone streets, talking about every topic under the sun ... and making love, with reckless abandon. Perhaps it was the level of 'real life' detachment–being away from her regular life, routine, responsibilities, the scrutiny of friends–but she opened up to him, physically, sexually, in a way she never had before and never realised was possible. It was as though they existed in their own private universe, where nothing else mattered.

M packed the last of her toiletries and clothes as Adi watched her from bed. Even though Adi had his own room, he had spent the majority of time in hers. She zipped up her suitcase, her heart filled with sadness, not really knowing what to say in these final moments. She never had an encounter like this before in her life–with so much intensity and passion. It was amazing to reach the age of thirty, she reflected, without having experienced anything like this before, as though all other romantic experiences in her life had been nothing but shadows.

Finished with the packing, she sat on the bed and watched at Adi as he made them both an espresso from the small coffee machine provided. He had a clearly subdued look on his face.

"Listen, I just wanted to thank you for this time we have had," said M, searching for the right thing to say. "It's been fun and such a laugh. I really love your company. You're an awesome person and I'm glad I had the chance to get to know you better. I'll never forget this."

There it was. She'd said the words. Acknowledged their time together. Carefully resisted saying too much, like, *What next? Where do we go from here? What should we name our first-born son?!* even though she desperately wanted to. She was proud of her restraint—yet she also knew it was a not-so-masked invitation for him to declare his feelings for her. However, as he looked back at her with his shining eyes, he paused for what seemed like an eternity, as her unspoken question remained unanswered. She'd thrown the ball into his court, and he was leaving it dangling in mid-air.

Finally he spoke. "Thank you for everything, too. You're amazing. I'll never forget this either."

That's it? she thought, as her euphemistic ball came crashing to the ground.

Then he leaned over and kissed her passionately on the lips.

Ball back in mid-air!

In a rush, she melted into his soft skin and the subtle smell of sweet coffee on his breath, as her stomach fluttered like the butterfly enclosure at the Melbourne Zoo. Yet the moment was short lived—the telephone rang and the kiss abruptly ended. Her taxi was waiting downstairs.

He walked her down to the foyer with her luggage and helped her to the waiting cab. They embraced and she couldn't resist breathing in deeply the smell of his skin on his nape. It was like a drug. She climbed in the car and watched him watch her drive away until he was just a small dot far down at the end of the street. She sighed. She knew life was full of unforgettable moments. This was one of them. And what an insane whirlwind the last six days with Adi had been! It was a completely unanticipated moment in utterly unforseen circumstances. A mind-bogglingly unexpected turn of synchronistic events. Her right-brain told her there was more to come, while her left-brain—ever the party-pooper—*tutt-tutted* and told her it was nothing more than a fling.

All she knew for sure was: fling or not, she was hooked.

8

"Welcome back, bitch!" yelled Elisha as she pounced on M, hugging her.

"Hey you! Welcome home, girlfriend," Kathy said in delight to see her dear friend.

Knowing she'd be battling jetlag, M had texted the girls from Prague and told them to meet her at home so they could order pizza, drink some wine and defrag the past week from the comfort of the couch. A cold night back it Melbourne, having a cosy night in with the open fire seemed heavenly.

M twisted the top off a bottle of Oyster Bay, as Kathy and Elisha got comfy on the couch, eager to hear all about her adventure.

"Where's Laura?" said M.

"I'm not sure," Elisha replied. "She should be on her way. I wonder what's taking her so long. She's never usually late."

"Has she called?" M asked.

"No. Let's wait ten minutes, then we'll ring. So, anyway, how was the trip? Tell us. Tell us all!"

M knew she was going to have to mention the goings on that had taken place–she'd never be able to hide her glow from the girls – but she didn't know exactly what to make of it all herself yet. To be honest, she was still on cloud nine. She wanted to wait, just so she could get her head around it first, process it all, and then get back to reality. But reality was impatient. "The city was lovely–so much to see," she said, attempting a casual tone of voice. "I shopped a bit, of course. It was a really nice time, both professionally and … um, personally."

"What do you mean, 'personally'?" asked Elisha wickedly. "Did you sow some wild oats with a hot European guy?"

"No, not exactly … but the most incredibly coincidental thing *did* happen. I bumped into Sally and Paul's groomsman in Prague … you know that guy Adi?" M took a sip of her wine and braced herself for what she knew was coming.

"Oh. My. God. No *way*, M!" squealed Kathy.

"You gotta be fuckin' kidding me!" Elisha exclaimed.

M smiled.

"How on earth did *that* happen?" Kathy asked.

"I know, I know, pretty freaky, eh?" M responded mildly.

"Aaaaand? … What *happened?*" Elisha asked, her eyes sparkling.

"Well, we couldn't believe our luck, or coincidence, or whatever you want to call it. We organised to meet for breakfast and then we totally hit it off, really enjoyed each others company. We spent a few of days hanging out doing touristy things and eating great food. I got to know him. He's a really lovely guy."

"And then what happened?!" shrieked Elisha, scooting in closer on the couch.

"We hung out. Road a Vespa. Ate good food. It was nice," she said, once again skirting the fine line between not wanting to lie to her friends and also not wanting to tell the truth. She just couldn't handle a romantic dissection at this point in time, not until she knew herself what was going on. *Please, please, please don't ask more questions*, M thought frantically, *because if you probe me at all I might burst open like the Hoover Dam and everything will come gushing out!*

"A lovely guy, romantic city, an airline strike that had you grounded together ... and?" Elisha pressed curiously.

"I was there for work, remember?" M replied, again subtly dodging the question, yet hoping that they weren't noticing that fact.

The girls just stared at her inquisitively, the pause hanging in the air.

Finally M blurted out, desperate to change the subject, "So, what's been happening here?"

"Oh God, where do I start?" Elisha said.

Phew, thought M, *we're moving on.*

"Jackson has been texting flat out. I tell you, this whole 'will he, won't he' thing is really starting to bother me. I don't understand it. It's like he has this radar. He doesn't touch base for a week or two, then all of a sudden he senses he's starting to lose me and he is flat out again. I keep telling him I ain't just a booty call. That's not me–he knows that. Is it just because he's confused, or does he want to keep me on the side until something better comes along?"

"Fuck him, I reckon," said Kathy. She was always direct and firm–to the point of cut-throat–something the others loved about her. "Men are so one-dimensional. They think a certain way and can't deal with two things at once. They don't see the reality that's right in front of them. They also aren't mind readers. You have to tell him how you feel, honey. We have to step up and be real with them. Otherwise it goes over their heads. He's playing the game, so you either play with him or cut him off. But I think, fuck the game playing. You're worth more, babe."

"It's like he knows you are waiting in the wings for him. Give him something to think about," M suggested. "Date someone else and make sure he finds out about it from his inner circle. That will drive him nuts."

"You know what, girls? You are absolutely right. What is it with men and their games?" Elisha asked, rolling her eyes.

"Hell knows," Kathy replied, topping up everyone's wine. "Maybe it's a power thing? Curiosity? They are on a totally different level," she laughed. "Nothing surprises me any more, honestly. They have something good right in front of them but they can't see. It's like they're looking through frosted glass. So then they go elsewhere. Some women know how to play the game, manipulate them back. And we good girls get left behind. It's the power of the *you-know-what*," Kathy added, pointing down to her pelvic area.

Maybe it was the jetlag, or the wine on an empty stomach, but M had hitched a ride on a passing cloud. She had mentally clocked out of the conversation and was indulging in sweet memories of Adi, his touch, his kiss, his smell … his abs. She could close her eyes and imagine his lips on hers … his firm body pressed against her … his–

"Earth to Maxine!" Elisha laughed. "Are you falling asleep?"

M snapped back into the present. "Sorry, guys, I guess it's the jetlag knocking me about." *Nice save*, she thought.

Suddenly all their phones beeped at the same time. They checked their messages and read:

> Hey guys, so sorry but I can't make it. Got some shit happening at home I have to deal with. Talk to you all soon. Have a good night, Laura.

"Some shit happening? I wonder what could have happened?" M said.

"I'm not sure. I hope she's okay. This is unusual for her. She never misses anything," Elisha said. "Or at least lets us know beforehand—not at the last minute. Maybe James is sick or something."

Though they were concerned, the girls knew Laura would let them know if it was an emergency, so they'd let it go for now, agreeing they would get in touch with her first thing the next day.

"Okay … time for pizza!" M announced. "This wine is going to my head!"

The following morning, M sat in her kitchen over her steaming coffee when destiny called. Literally. She looked at her phone.

It was him.

She was embarrassingly excited, and also totally taken by surprise. *He called!*, squealed the hysterical teenage girl inside of her.

"Hello?" she said, faux chilled.

"Hi, Max, it's me."

"Welcome back! How are you going?"

"I'm great. It's good to be back."

"How was your flight?"

"Not bad, but too many layovers! That's the price you pay for a cheap ticket."

M thought about her own champagne-and-caviar, deep-seat-reclining, zero-layover flight. "Well, yes, darling, we can't all fly Business Class!" she teased.

"True, I guess you have to have *some* plebs to eat if the plane crashes in the Andes," he bounced back at her. They laughed.

The banter flowed playfully and M was once again struck by how easily she could talk to him. How natural it felt. Finally, Adi asked if they could have dinner and exchange photos and they arranged to meet at M's place the following night.

As M hung up, she felt exhilarated, then, right on cue, her right-brain and left-brain rose to the surface and had another predictable round of emotional ping-pong in her head.

A dinner date already? He only just got back, right-brain served. *He clearly can't wait to see you! And that flirtatious banter!*

Settle down, left-brain instantly hit back. *The holiday romance is done and dusted and now life will go back to normal. He said he wants to 'exchange photos'. He wants to be friends and friends only. That was 'friendly' banter. Don't imagine you'll be rekindling Prague in your living room.*

M knew the voice was right. She just didn't know *which* voice! And this internal match of neurotic ping-pong was making her feel like a thirteen year old lying in a daisy patch, obsessing over her first crush. *He loves me ... he loves me not ... he loves me ... he thinks I'm hot!* Clearly, she was still trying to wrap her head around what had happened in Prague. Yet there was no denying that she was absolutely smitten.

For now, though, she had to put those thoughts aside. She still hadn't heard from Laura—she wasn't returning her calls or texts, which was so unlike her—and M was getting concerned. M had always looked up to her like a big sister, admiring her for her assertiveness and strength. To M, Laura had the perfect life. A great job, a wonderful husband who doted on her, a beautiful home, holidays in Europe every year. What more could a woman want?

M couldn't stand the silence any longer. She drove to Laura's house, parked on the road and walked up through the perfectly manicured lawn. The sound of the doorbell rang through the house, followed by total silent. It felt odd. M wondered if Laura was out back and couldn't hear the bell. Her car was in the drive.

"Laura, honey, it's me!" she called loudly through the door, knocking. She heard footsteps, and a moment later Laura opened the door. M stood there in shock. In all their years as friends, she had never seen Laura in such a state—dishevelled hair, ratty tracksuit pants, dark circles under her eyes as though she hadn't slept all night. Her face was filled with grief.

"Laura, what on earth … are you okay? What happened?" Her friend looked at her silently for a moment, then ushered her into the lounge. Laura sat on the sofa and M sat next to her.

"He's gone … he's left me," Laura said in a soft voice, the words barely audible.

"*What? How … why?* How did this happen?"

"I don't know ... he came home last night from work acting weird. He kept pacing the hall and he had this funny look on his face. Then he just blurted out that he couldn't do this anymore–he couldn't be married to me–and that he's leaving."

She began to sob uncontrollably. M held her tightly.

"How could this happen, Max? I did everything right. Everything! We were happy! There were no warning signs. No arguing. I don't even know if there is someone else."

"This is crazy, Laura. This isn't like James. What got into him? Bastard. He's just a miserable bastard ... how could he let go of something so good?"

"It happened yesterday afternoon. I couldn't even get out of bed after he left. I could barely text you guys." Fresh tears welled in Laura's eyes. "How could he do this to me, just pull the rug out from under me like that? He loved me! He always *said* he loved me. Now life as I know it is gone! Rubbish. Shot to shit. All because of him." She grabbed a pillow and threw it at their wedding picture on the mantel. It fell to the ground, the glass smashed. "Fuckin' *asshole* just ruined my life."

Elisha's face appeared in the window at the front door and there was a light knock.

"It's open, come on in," M called.

Elisha walked in and saw Laura curled into M's arms, with tear tracks running down her face.

"What's happened? What's wrong?"

"James left her," M said simply. Laura continued to wipe away tears. Elisha knelt down in front of her friend.

"Oh my God! Honey, I'm so, so sorry. How? Why? I mean, things were fine, weren't they?"

"I don't know. He just said he couldn't do it any more and he was leaving. No explanation. Then he just walked out," Laura replied.

"I don't know what to say. I'm just ... I'm *so* sorry." Elisha reached for Laura's hands and gripped them tightly. "You guys always seemed so in love. I'm shocked."

"What the hell happened to him?" M said shaking her head in dismay.

"He's a fucking *man*, that's what!" Elisha snapped angrily.

"Now listen," M told Laura. "You are not alone. We will help you. You *will* get through this."

"Thanks, guys. I guess at the moment it doesn't feel real ... that he really is gone. I still can't believe that this has happened. Hey, do you guys want some tea with me? I feel like tea."

"Sure," Elisha and M said together.

They stayed with Laura for a while and got her settled for the remainder of the day. Kathy phoned and said she was on her way and would stay the night. This was a relief to M and Elisha as they didn't want Laura–who was now tucked up on the couch, temporarily snoring lightly–to be alone.

As they heard Kathy drive up, M and Elisha walked out to the street.

"Oh my god, what a nightmare!" said Kathy.

"I can't believe it. Honestly, you wake up in the morning and you really don't know what is around the corner," Elisha said.

"I think in time, she will comprehend it better. But what a shock," M replied. "It just goes to show that you really don't know a person. Life can change in a flash."

"Yeah, nothing lasts forever," Elisha said.

"Maybe he did have someone else and he was too much of a coward to admit it. Asshole," said Kathy.

"Fuck knows. If he was in my face now, I would punch him so hard. Prick."

"Let's try to get her out of the house tomorrow," said M.

They all agreed and said their goodbyes before M and Elisha drove off in their separate directions, and Kathy headed down the driveway to be with Laura.

M felt wild mixed emotions. She was still a little up in the clouds over Adi, yet simultaneously so incredibly sad for her friend. And she felt confused, because she really did believe in love ... and Laura's marriage had been one she'd admired and hoped to emulate someday–obviously not any more. This was a real shock to her core beliefs. There really were no guarantees. What happens when love doesn't conquer all?

She began thinking about how Adi was to come over for dinner the following evening and what she'd cook. She felt a little guilty for feeling so good, given the circumstances, but considering her elation at seeing Adi again, she decided she'd go with it. M felt a pulse of excitement that nothing could bring down.

Adi arrived with a nice bottle of wine and some chocolates.

"Well, hello there, welcome to my house!" M said as she ushered him inside.

"Wow, this is lovely!" he said, glancing around, before giving her a quick peck on the cheek.

They went to the kitchen for wine glasses, then moved into the living room and sat down. It felt a little bizarre, as now there were no cobblestone streets or Vespas, but just the two of them relaxing in her home.

"So, have you settled back into everything?" he asked.

"Yes, all is well. The usual," she replied.

"Something smells great. I hope you didn't go to too much trouble for me. I would hate to think you slaved over a hot stove," he said sarcastically.

"Italian. And no, I didn't slave. I love cooking, so it was a pleasure." She twisted off the bottle top and poured the wine, handing him a glass. He looked as though he had something on his mind.

"Are you okay, you look a little worn out," M asked, concerned. It definitely wasn't the glow he was sporting when he was away, that was for sure.

"Oh … just a few things, you know how it is. I had to start back to work today, so I didn't get enough shut-eye. It sucks when you've just got back from an exotic adventure and you have to deal with what's happening in real life, hey?" he said as he swirled his wine and sniffed it. It was like he didn't want to say too much and change the subject. M dismissed her hunch and wanted to make a joke to change the topic somehow.

"Wow, very sophisticated, mister. You do that so well," M said cheekily, nodding towards his wine.

"I do, don't I? You should have got used to it in Prague, though," he winked at her and smiled.

Damn that smile, M thought. She was unsure if his cocky tone was playful sarcasm or arrogance, but she wanted to believe it was the former. There was just something about him that kept her guessing, made her unsure, left her clueless as to what he was thinking. It was that combination of his devilishly sexy bedroom eyes, coupled with his sweet schoolboy smile. Their banter felt good, though–real. Two friends (... *or lovers?*) talking away and drinking nice wine. Just friends. Yes, just quick-peck-on-the-cheek friends. They'd never discussed more. Prague was just a bit of holiday fun. Escapism. There was something a little liberating about acknowledging that, like releasing a pressure valve.

But was that what it was? Why did it feel like more? Did he feel it too? Was that magnetic pull only in her imagination? Prague was done, gone. Already in the past. Could the past equal the future? It was way too early to tell. But her hormones didn't think so.

They chatted and laughed easily over dinner as they exchanged funny anecdotes about life, travels, time at uni. Maxine enjoyed having an emotionally intelligent man's perspective on things. Shamus The Shit was a complainer and didn't have the confidence she really craved in a man. Maybe Adi was a little too confident? She thought about how different the dynamic was in having a guy as a friend, as opposed to the lover dynamic, or even the girlfriend dynamic. She observed how she felt comfortable talking to him about certain things that she wouldn't actually talk to her best girlfriends about, let alone Shamus The Shit. Weird but true, and this once again had her contemplating the nuts and bolts of their 'relationship' and if, in fact, this *was* a relationship ... or a friendship. *Ahh!* It was doing her head in. Somehow, though, not having any expectations made her feel more at ease.

After their lovely home-cooked Milanese feast, they decided to watch a film and wind down with a nightcap. She sat close to him on the couch, practically arm to arm, and didn't want to move. She figured it was *her couch and her* house. It was a big couch. *He* could move, if he wasn't comfortable. As it happened, he didn't move. This made her mind go into overdrive, as she suddenly felt awkward. Should *she* move? Was she too close? After all, this was reality now, not a holiday.

He looked at his phone when a message chimed and his facial expression, suddenly looking a little worried. M noticed this and figured it was maybe a work thing gone wrong. She didn't really know what to think.

"Is everything okay, Adi?" she asked, not wanting to invade his privacy, but feeling concerned about his change of expression.

He hesitated, like he wasn't sure what to say, but knew he had to be polite. "Sometimes I wish I could just hit the pause button on life," he said. "Like in Prague." It didn't really answer her question but she didn't want to stick her nose in any further so she just let it go.

He put his phone down and grabbed her arm, pulling her closer to him. "Let's watch that movie, hey? Let's relax."

"Sure ... okay," M replied. From his body language, it didn't seem like he'd be able to relax, but she was very happy to be with him all the same. She pressed play and the movie started, as she sat there a little neurotically, stiff as a board, his body so close that she could feel the static electricity off his arm hairs. *Why am I making such a big deal out of this?* her slightly high-strung internal voice squealed. It felt cosy and warm (*...just friends*).

The movie was slow and she was sleepy, but she didn't allude to the fact. She didn't want him to think he had to leave. Suddenly, his head dropped onto her shoulder. Her heart started hammering. She closed her eyes for a moment and rested her head on his. She felt so tranquil. Was it the wine? This felt nice. She would only close her eyes for a moment.

Then she felt his arm move closer. He gazed up at her. That look! It was the same look he gave her in Prague, that magnetic pull (*lovers?*). He moved in to kiss her. He begun to undo her top buttons. She, in turn, did the same. Was it really happening? Here, in broad 'real life'?

Then his phone chimed again with another text message, shattering the moment. He snatched it up and read the message, then instantly jumped up and pulled his shirt back on. "I'm really sorry, Max, I have to go."

What the ...?

"Is everything okay?"

"Yeah, fine, fine," said Adi, looking at his phone again, clearly distracted. "You're great," he said, kissing her forehead and she lifted herself up from the floor, suddenly very self-conscious of her half-nakedness.

I'm great?

"Let's catch up soon, okay?" he said and was nearly out the door when he suddenly did an about-face, walked back over to her, grabbed her around the waist and kissed her deeply, passionately, before clearly struggling to break away from her.

The front door closed and she stood alone, half naked on her shag pile, unsure if she should be concerned, elated ... or utterly insulted.

As the morning light streamed through her bedroom window, a surge of anxiety flooded through her as she recalled the events of the night before. A million thoughts ran through her mind: *Did he get turned off by me? Was there a work emergency? Does he have a girlfriend? Did he get spooked? Did he see a huntsman? What the hell?!*

She had to stop obsessing–it was doing her head in. She got out her vacuum cleaner and begun to do her floors. After that she begun to mop vigorously, corner by corner, inch by inch. Her bench tops, too, got polished within an inch of their lives. Cleaning house was her personal mind-clearer; her meditation.

Once she was done, she looked around her house–clean, perfect. Just as she wanted it. *Clean house and clear mind–Tick.*

She looked at the time and suddenly realised it had slipped away from her. *Oh shit! Work!* She jumped in the shower and got herself ready in record speed.

"Morning, Maxine," the receptionist said as she walked into the office foyer at 9.15. She was never late for work. This was a first. "You look good today ... have you done something to your hair?" *Good?* thought M, *I've barely slept a wink. It must be the increased blood flow–the glow of unrequited lust*, she thought sombrely, but forced a smile.

She stumbled to her desk and turned on her computer, scanning the paperwork piled up. Where to start? She sighed, putting down her takeaway coffee, and proceeding to straighten up the papers as she waited for her computer to boot. Yet as she reached over for a pen, she knocked over her coffee, spilling it across the table. "Shit! Shit!" She grabbed a handful of tissues and wiped up as much as she could, but coffee dripped to the carpet. She knelt down and blotted at it. "You're such a klutz, M," she grumbled to herself.

The rest of the day continued in much the say way—distracted, with her mind elsewhere, definitely not on her work. She thought about Adi constantly, and always with utter confusion. How could she be so crazy about a guy so quickly? Did he feel anything at all for her? What was last night all about? He seemed like he couldn't get out of there fast enough. But that *kiss*! What a rollercoaster! Was she really starting to fall for him, when their situation was so ambiguous?

Good ol' right-brain was telling her, *He's the one! He's your man!*, while lefty was running out of patience, saying, *Come back to earth, M. He ran away, you idiot.*

She hated that she was doing this to herself, all the analysing and dissecting, in her mind inflating each moment they shared to impossible heights. It was self-sabotage, pure and simple, as no man could ever live up to the He's The One label. If life had taught her anything it was that you should live in the moment, cherish the *now*, enjoy life for what it was, not load up experiences with unrealistic expectations.

She enjoyed the time they spent together. She liked the sense of intimacy she felt with him. It was the touch and connection that she appreciated. The hugs. The kind of affection that she considered real. *He's a decent guy*, she told herself. *Kind, respectful and funny.* What they had was beautiful. So he'd seduced her once again … then run away. She should just relax and see where it goes, not load it up with suffocating over-expectation. (*Here comes the bride!*, sang her right-brain. *Shut the hell up!* left-brain snapped). For Maxine, even gestures carried meaning, and she was grateful for them. So why was she dithering back and forth about it inside her head?

M needed advice. Girl-to-girl advice. She was bursting to share this and get it off her chest—talk it out with a girlfriend and hopefully get some wisdom. But with Laura's situation, she didn't want to bother her besties at this point in time. There was enough going on in everyone's heads, and they all had to be there for Laura. But M really needed a sounding board and some good advice.

Caroline was one of those friends who would drop anything for you. They'd met through a mutual school friend and had been as close as two peas in a pod all through university. They had loads in common, discovering that they were cut from the same cloth. They shared a love of music, shopping, food, wine and hobbies, as well as similar values, and quickly formed a bond. Caroline was an extrovert like her, so they had lots of fun together, and it was inevitable that their friendship became one of closeness, value and commitment. After uni, they had continued to stay as in-touch as they could, even though they were both busy with their lives. It was a relationship that they had always made time for and invested in. And Caroline had recently moved nearby, so now it was much easier for them to grab a quick coffee together in between other commitments. She had always told M that they would live within walking distance of each other so that when they were older, it would be easier to stroll together with their walking sticks. M was now happy that Caroline's little prophecy had come true.

It had been over a month since she'd seen her–not since M had helped her move into her new place–so a catch-up was definitely due. A lot had happened over the past weeks and M was craving one of their nice long chats. She also craved some cut-throat perspective on the Adi matter, and she knew Caroline was just the girl to dish it out, unsugar-coated.

She phoned Caroline to organise a coffee date. Caroline immediately said no to that. "Let's hit the day spa!" she enthused.

Oooh, what a treat! thought M. Frankly, with all the travelling and carrying luggage she'd recently done, it had taken a toll on her back and muscles, so this was a far superior idea to coffee. What better way to unwind and release. Just what the doctor ordered–not just for her body, but for her mind as well. "Hell yeah," said M.

They met at the front at the Dharma Spa Retreat down by the bay side of the city–a place they'd been a few times and enjoyed, but not for a while. They were well overdue and set to enjoy the day. After big hugs and check in, they made their way to the changing room, where they put their robes on. Emerging into the lounge, M felt her mind click over into that Zen place as she absorbed the background music, a calm and peaceful chant, the ambient dim lighting and the scented oils, which gave off an intoxicating floral aroma. It was a quiet afternoon for a weekend, there were only a few people around, as M and Caroline sat in a corner of the room sipping herbal tea.

"So, how was St Barts?" said M, realising they hadn't seen each other since she got back.

"Oh, amazing! The wedding was gorgeous."

"You lucky thing," said M. "We missed you at Sally's wedding though."

"Me too! I heard it was incredible. Sally sounds *so* happy!"

"Yeah, they make a beautiful couple. Speaking of which, how's Matthew?"

"Don't get me started," laughed Caroline, with a roll of her eyes. Caroline and Matthew had been together for a few years and, although they had a good relationship, they were a bit of an Odd Couple–to put it mildly. Every time she and M caught up, she had a good healthy vent to M about all those little things that drove her insane. It was the girlfriend code–if you can't talk to your friends about it, who can you talk to? After all, venting to each other was cheaper than psychotherapy!

"So anyway … with his late nights and my long days its feels like we're two robots on autopilot. I miss the 'us' time, you know. I thought I'd be proactive about it and spice things up in the bedroom. I'm reading this mummy-porn–*Jessica's Long Hard Ride*," she laughed. "Seriously, M, it's *filthy*. I'm loving it! I tell you, I wish I was getting half this stuff done to me," Caroline said, and they both broke into giggles.

"Oh, sweetie, everyone goes through a hard patch. You'll be fine. Maybe talk to him about it more. I don't know. You need to do what's right. But I would definitely talk to him and put it out there. Trust me. You don't want him to run off with another woman, like Shamus did. He doesn't have anything to do with his Accounts Department at his work, does he?" M asked, jokingly.

"No, he doesn't," she said, suddenly looking sad for her friend. "Oh, honey, how are you coping with all of that? Do you miss the shithead?"

M noted her compassion and instantly put her at ease. "Oh, no, I'm fine! Totally fine. She's welcome to him. Seriously," she smiled.

Caroline stared long and hard at her friend. "Honey, I may not be a mind reader, but I can see you've got something *big* ticking away in that pretty little head of yours. Spill it!"

"It's a man!" she blurted, and the dam burst as M took Caroline through her whole history with Adi–from Sally's wedding to the chance meeting in Prague to aperitifs by the riverside. She stopped short, however, of telling her about the non-stop European shag-fest, as she felt the need to test the water with Caroline first, before giving her the full X-rated version. "It's a weird feeling, Caroline," M explained. "I'm not sure why I feel it, but it's always there. Kind of like a tick," she laughed ruefully. "I know my head is in the clouds, but it's just really *nice*, you know?"

"Crikey, sounds like you're falling for him! Are you?"

"I don't know! Maybe!" said M. "I'm kind of afraid to let myself go there, you know? What if he doesn't feel the same?"

"You're allowed to feel these emotions, sweetie. You are a human being, not a log. You *feel* things. You've gotten to know someone. He makes you feel good. What's wrong with that? He sounds like a genuine kind of guy, and he wouldn't have spent all that time with you if he didn't like you too. Enjoy it and ride the wave. Take it and go with it, see what happens. Maybe Shamus left at the right time—he did you a favour as something so much better was on its way. Whether this is the beginning of a wonderful friendship or leads to something more, this sounds like a good thing for you." Caroline spoke with the certainty and conviction of a strong woman who had run into her fair share of obstacles over time.

M admired her and looked up to her, and understood that she knew what she was talking about. But she also knew that she had to spill the beans—*all* of the beans—if she really wanted her friend's fully-informed perspective. "Caz, we slept together!" said blurted, unable to hold it in any longer.

Caroline's eyes lit up. "Fuck me. How was it?"

"Passionate! Intense! Oh, man. It melted my insides. It was unbelievable."

"Hmm," said Caroline, with a smirk sprouting involuntarily across her face, excited to be living vicariously through M's torrid affair. "Well, okay, this changes everything. There is obviously an attraction there, that's for sure."

"There is, for sure," M nodded enthusiastically.

"So what are you worried about? Great friendship, great sex. This sounds like the start of something beautiful."

"Well, we're never actually talked about an 'us'. It all just kind of happened and now I'm worried that it may have been just a fling thing. If it was, that's one thing. But I can't get him out of my head. And I don't know how he feels. I don't know if this is something real for him. I don't want to let myself fall for him if it's not real. If it's just a fling for him, I need to take a step back now, as I know I'll end up broken hearted. And then, the other night, he came to my house and we drank some wine and kissed on the couch, and then … well, he suddenly jumped up and said he had to go! Oh God, I feel like I'm in way over my head already!"

"Oh honey," Caroline began cautiously. "So all the 'flinging' occurred when you were stranded in Prague?"

"Yep."

"And then it was all just kind of left up in the air?"

"Yep."

"Well, I don't want to be Little Miss Reality Check, but my advice to you would be to not over-invest emotionally, not until you see what shape it all takes here, back home," said Caroline. "People can do wild things on holiday."

"I know," said M, thinking about her own wild and reckless deeds with Adi between the sheets, and how liberating it had been to be away from all the usual white noise, and how she never would have let herself jump into it all so completely if it had occurred under real-life circumstances, back in Melbourne.

Caroline clocked M's slightly deflated expression and quickly added, "I'm not saying that it's not more. I'm just saying, you've come out of a two-year relationship. You've recently had your heart shattered into a million pieces. You don't need another man giving you the run-around. Just be cautious, take it one step at a time, don't hand him your heart on a silver platter. Because, honey, I hate to say it," Caroline added gently, "I've seen you do this before—give your heart away completely. Promise me you'll be careful. You deserve to be loved fully, the way *you* love."

"You're right," said M, appreciating her friend's honestly, but also feeling the sting of her words. This felt completely different to anything she'd ever felt before with a man, but Caroline was speaking the truth. She *did* have a history of jumping the gun, reading more into relationships than was actually there. "I'll keep myself in check."

"Enjoy it for what it is, honey, enjoy the moment. But don't get consumed by blurred lines. Not until you know how he feels or what his deal is," Caroline added, just as their names were called by a staff member from the treatment rooms. Their masseuses were ready for them. They gave each other a smile as they separated to head into their respective massage rooms.

M's room was dimly lit and filled with candles, which gave off heavenly scents of vanilla and sandalwood. She took off her robe and slipped under the large fluffy towel lying on the bed. Her body sank down gratefully into the softness. The therapist knocked gently on the door before entering and greeting M. Straight away, she selected an essential oil, rubbed it between her hands for a moment to warm it up and then expertly began to rub it into M's shoulders, pressing and kneading the tight muscles, working her way down her back. M took a deep breath and relaxed into the blissful feeling, before falling asleep to the melodic purr of waves crashing against the shore resonating through the surround sound.

Forty minutes later she awoke to the sensation of her entire body tingling with lifeforce. *This was so worth it*, she thought to herself as she dressed. As she waited for Caroline in the lounge area, she reflected on her friend's wisdom and her sturdy warning, thinking about how she was giving the situation with Adi way too much mental and emotional energy.

When Caroline emerged, a staff member brought in a steaming pot of wild orange blossom tea, and the two friends sipped and giggled as Caroline told her the filthy details of *Jessica's Long Hard Ride*, explaining how Jessica got away from the Mexican banditos, wearing nothing but a g-string. They roared with laughter, and between the heavenly massage, the frank conversation with Caroline and the tummy-aching laughter, M felt back in balance.

On the way home, she went to the grocery store to do a shop. As she made her way back to the car she had great difficulty finding her keys. As usual, the bigger the bag, the harder it was to find things. She sat on a nearby bench and began sifting through everything.

"We always put so much in our bags, don't we?" said an elderly voice.

M glanced up to see Soula, the old gypsy lady from Jimmy's Café, gingerly lowering herself down at the other end of the bench, with a trolley full of shopping by her side and a takeaway latte in her hand.

"Yes, we do," M said, smiling. "I think the bigger the bag, the more stuff we tend to cram in it."

Soula smiled. M noticed the lovely old crucifix around her neck, similar to a family heirloom she herself had.

"You must live locally, love? I see you all the time," said Soula.

"Yeah, not too far from here. But I've just come from a spa treatment with my girlfriend."

"Good for you, darling. Enjoy your youth. It comes and goes so fast, believe me. My husband and I used to do all these nice things together. We were married for forty-two years. It would have been fifty this year."

"Oh, Soula, I'm so sorry for your loss. How wonderful, though, to have spent so many precious years together. That's an inspiration to us all. I hope I find a connection like that someday. Not everyone finds that."

"Do you have a man in your life, love?" Soula asked.

M hesitated. This so-often-asked question that so often frustrated her had recently become a grey area and she wasn't even sure herself if she had a man in her life, not officially. She decided to downplay it. "No, not at the moment. I guess you could call it my search for the relationship Holy Grail," M said sadly as, embarrassingly, her eyes started to glaze up with emotion.

"Oh, darling," said Soula. "You seem stressed ... especially for someone who just came from a spa."

M laughed. "I guess I need to work on my transparency," she said. Looking into Soula's big compassionate eyes, M suddenly felt a strange urge to confide in the old woman, as though hungry for the wisdom of her years. With a forty-two-year marriage under her belt, she obviously new the key to a happy and lasting relationship.

"Well, I think I'm in the throes of some feelings for someone, actually. It's kind of a difficult situation. I have only known him for a short time and I think I threw myself in too deep, too fast.

He's kind of sending mixed messages, I guess. I'm not sure what is going to happen." M could hear the words tumbling from her mouth and knew that it was weird to be opening up to a semi-stranger like this, but it also felt oddly comforting.

Soula looked deep into her eyes. "What do you love about your life?" she asked.

"My *life*? Everything. My family, friends, work, social life. I've been lucky enough to have travelled a lot. I have freedom."

"So why let the question of a man be your defining point? Why let it override all the good that is around you? Feelings are meant to be felt, Maxine. You are human, a woman. We feel passion. Take your time and see. You really like this boy, huh?" she asked, her eyes sparkling.

"Yes … he is really nice. But I don't know how he feels. Men can be confusing."

"Oh, honey, that's true. Men are men. Who knows what drives them. But don't let your focus be entirely on romantic love. It is your love of family and friends and *life* that should be nurtured and grown. And, most importantly, the love you have for *yourself*. Embrace all that comes to you. Remember—the love of a man might last a few years, it might even last a few decades, but it's the love of *yourself* that will last a lifetime. That makes anything possible," Soula smiled.

Hearing the old lady's words were strangely therapeutic and they made M feel revitalised. It was just what she needed to hear. "Thank you for that dose of wisdom, Soula," she said gratefully.

"Be honest with yourself, Maxine. Know that whatever happens, this boy is part of your journey. Take that journey. If it doesn't work, that doesn't mean the journey was a failure. It could mean that it took you one step closer to your real destination. Don't take it all so seriously. That's life. Everything that happens to you is part of your destiny. You are always *one*, darling, even when you are part of two. You will always be you. Don't lose yourself."

M was shocked to hear that last bit, which sounded so similar to what she'd told the girls back at The Barkley that night. "You are very sweet to say those things," she said. "I appreciate it ... I still remember what you said at the coffee shop that day: 'Your one true love will come as two, but before he's yours, he'll be untrue.' These words still come to me. I don't really know what they could mean," M said, looking at her for guidance.

Soula smiled. "You are a beautiful girl. Just go on about your life and let it all unfold," Soula replied with kindness.

M felt her eyes tearing a little with emotion and optimism.

"And, remember," added Soula, "If he takes your affections but rejects your heart, he's an *asshole*."

M couldn't help but laugh.

9

"Daddy, Daddy," Adi heard faintly as he slowly opened one eye. As always when he stared at his son, he saw himself. A mirror image. Every time he looked at him he was surprised by how he could love something so much.

"Thomas, how are you, mate?" he responded, brushing his fingers through the toddler's hair before pulling him up onto his bed to give him a big hug. *If there is one only thing that I've done right in my life, it's him*, he thought to himself, giving his Tommy boy a big hug and walking them out to the lounge room.

"Gabba Gabba! Gabba Gabba!" Tom squawked gleefully, pointing to the television, as his dad fumbled for the remote control among the flotsam and jetsam of the coffee table–dirty plates, scrunched tissues, dog-eared magazines–before finally locating the device, then turning it to ABC for Tom. His boy instantly transfixed with giant dancing puppets on the screen, Adi looked the around the room. It was so piled high with unfolded laundry overflowing from baskets, Lego pieces, Spider-Mans, lidless Textas, coffee mugs and chip packets that it was hard to even see the carpet. The sound of the squealing kettle was emanating hysterically from the kitchen. This was the reality he awoke to, day after day. It sure wasn't Prague.

"Vege-bite toast, Daddy?" said little Thomas, a picture of pure innocence looking up at him.

Adi's heart melted. At just two years old, Adi was constantly taken aback by his boy's developing vocabulary; he seemed to accumulate more words every single day, collecting them like crayons. Even if they were often a little broken at first use. Adi always knew what he meant. He was so proud of his little boy and it filled him with sadness that he couldn't give him the perfect family life he deserved–a happy mum and dad, a home filled with love. A functional family. He hoped that one day he would be able to explain it all to Thomas and that he would be able to understand. And he prayed to God that his boy was too young to notice that mummy and daddy were constantly fighting. He didn't want to role model family life for his boy in this way.

Adi could hear Mary gossiping on the phone on the deck. It was a wonder she could hold a conversation with the kettle shrieking like a banshee. Annoyed, Adi went to the kitchen to tend to it.

"Vege-bite, Daddy?" Thomas said again.

"Yes, sweetie. Daddy will make your Vegemite toast," he said.

Gossiping on the phone for hours was a favourite pastime of Mary's and at first it hadn't bothered Adi. Nor the constant state of disarray she lived in, no matter how often he cleaned it all up. He had loved Mary in the beginning and she could do no wrong. Dark, wild and untamed, she was like no one he'd ever been with before. She juggled a number of casual jobs, quitting and applying for something new as the fancy took her—personal training, make-up artistry, bar work. Along with careers, she also seemed to have a never-ending stream of friends, but with whom—he discovered over time—she was equally barbarous, cutting them off completely over the smallest of disagreements, then becoming instant 'besties' with new people she met at parties and gigs. He had thought this demonstrated an unencumbered spirit; a devil-may-care attitude of a woman who truly took life by the balls and lived in on her own terms.

To say it was a shock when she got a positive result on a pregnancy test was to put it mildly. Although there was a certain controllable primal elation that came with discovering he was going to be a father with a woman he was crazy about, they'd been together only three months! (And who isn't crazy about their girl when you're only three months in?) Nevertheless, the discussion wasn't even open for debate as far as Mary was concerned. She instantly announced it to all and sundry, and just like that, he was on the fast track to fatherhood.

Once Mary moved in to Adi's house, and the novelty of the pregnancy wore off, she began to resent having to take things down a notch—wild nights at the Esplanade Hotel were replaced with warm milk and pregnancy vitamins. Yet it wasn't until Thomas arrived that the extent of their new reality hit her square in the face, as it does with most first-time parents. Adi embraced it. Night feeds, nappy changes, bath time; a side of him appeared overnight that he hadn't even known existed. He was exhausted. And he loved every second of it.

Mary's instincts, on the other hand, didn't kick in quite so seamlessly. The sleepless nights lead to escalating disarray and personal neglect, both of herself and their newborn. Financial strain meant that Adi needed to work longer hours, which lead to even more stress on the home front. He implored Mary to join a mother's group, or, better yet, to contact her own mother, ask her for help, perhaps assisting with the house or minding the baby from time to time so Mary could find her footing, catch up on some sleep–or even get out of the house and go on a date night. But she refused. Along with a trail of broken friendships behind her, she's completely cut her parents off when she was seventeen after she announced she'd dropped out of VCE and was heading off on a round-the-world trip with her then-boyfriend (a twenty-two-year-old wannabe rockstar) and they refused to fund it.

She would have murdered–literally *murdered*–Adi if she'd found out he'd been secretly emailing them photos of baby Thomas behind her back. To cut off family–*parents!*–was something he simply didn't have the capacity to understand. And they desperately wanted to be involved, to meet their grandson, to be a part of their lives. Yet every attempt Adi made to subtly broach the topic was stonewalled by Mary, and their world continued to crumble.

However, in all the chaos, the mounting lack of affection between them, the uncertainly about their roles in each other's lives, Thomas was their blessing in every way. Despite Mary's seeming lack of maternal instinct, she adored Tom, on her own terms, and would often extract riotous giggles from him as she blew endless raspberries on his chubby tummy.

Adi had expected Mary to withdraw a little after the baby was born—he'd read this was very common after childbirth, sometimes lasting months as the mother's hormones changed and she dealt with constant exhaustion and dramatic change of routine. It came as a great surprise, however, when she started partying. At first, it was catching up for a drink with the odd friend, which seemed perfectly fine—good for her, in fact, to get out of the house and unwind. But then there was gigs and parties, while Adi stayed home and looked after Thomas, and she'd return in the early hours, with that glow of wild, untamed recklessness on her face. The untethered Mary he had fallen in love with was now—as the neglectful mother of his child—a person he could barely stand the sight of.

When Adi moved into the spare room, Mary went ballistic. Had she not noticed his unhappiness in their relationship, or had she simply not cared? She begged and pleaded for him to come back to their bed, to not give up on them. And, at first, he conceded. Yet, once she had him safely back in her grasp, her reckless, neglectful behaviour instantly continued. Was she a person who simply wasn't capable of following through on commitments and responsibilities? The tragic part was, Adi had to acknowledge, Mary never pretended to be anything but what she was. She was this person all along. It was *Adi* who'd been fooling himself.

Yet, leaving was not an option. Even the very thought of not seeing Thomas every single day filled him with unspeakable sorrow.

As Adi waited for the toast to pop, he stared dreamily at the sunshine streaming through the kitchen window and his mind drifted uncontrollably to Maxine. Their time in Prague was the most insane coincidence, leading to the most unforgettable experience of his life. Then to have the airline strike was like an unexpected gift from the gods. She'd made him feel alive in a way that he hadn't felt in years. He couldn't get her out of his head—the smell of her skin, her silky hair, the dramatic curve of her breasts and hips as they plunged into her tiny waist...

Stop!

Smitten as he was, he knew he couldn't indulge in these thoughts. She was an amazing woman—smart, cultured, successful, totally together. She deserved so much more than the shambolic mess he'd made of his life and he simply couldn't drag her into his crap. *She must hate me now, anyway*, he thought to himself, *after I raced out on her the other night when he got Mary's text about Tom's fever. Or else think I'm a complete loser!* How do you even begin to explain that you have a son you never mentioned … and you live with your ex … and there's no escape …? Nope. His situation was just too complicated to pull Max and her tidy, perfect life into it.

Mary came back in the kitchen. "Oh, I see you're up. Did you have a good sleep in?"

He looked at her perplexed. "It's only quarter past seven."

"Yeah, well, we've been up since six."

"Thomas woke me. He was hungry. He's been up since six and you didn't give him breakfast?"

"Get off your high horse, Adi, you're his parent too."

"Of course I am, but I didn't get home from work until one a.m. last night."

"Yep, and I was up three times in the night dealing with Mister Night Terrors over there, so, again, get off your high horse."

The tension was so thick, it was almost suffocating.

"You've been on the phone for a while, I presume?" Adi replied.

"Oh, it wasn't long … Jeez," Mary said, as she made herself a cuppa.

"He was looking for you and couldn't find you. He was hungry. Maybe if you paid more attention instead of chatting," Adi replied to her in slight haste.

"Adi, I'm not neglecting my son, if that is what you are implying … Diane needed me she has some trouble at home with her man. I was being a good friend."

Be a good mother, he thought to himself, but he held it under his breath. His stomach knotted as the all-too-familiar rage mounted. But he had to let it go. He didn't want another argument and he certainly didn't want his son to hear them.

"Fine, Mary … Fine. I just think that sometimes, some things should be a priority and some things you can deal with later. But I'm not going to get into it now," Adi said.

"Good!" she cut him off abruptly.

"I have to get to work," he said curtly. "I have a meeting at eight."

Mary paused, her eyes softening, as she seemed to change course. "Today? Since when do you work on weekends? I thought we could spend the day together. As a family."

Adi knew this was nothing but a tactic, her trying to pull the guilt strings, to victimise herself … and Tom.

"I can't drop the ball on this deal, you know they're talking about restructuring," he said. "I have to go in today."

"We need time for *us*, Adi," she said, suddenly pressing up against him, looking up at him with melancholy eyes. "We need to work on it, so things will be how they were."

"It will never be how it was. We're holding on to … I don't know what … for Tom … but …" He broke off, choked up.

"There is still good stuff here. I know you love me. I love *you*, Adi," Mary said, her eyes pleading.

Again, it was a Jekyll-and-Hyde routine he was familiar with; she performed it many times before. She needed to have him wrapped around her little finger. Only then could she relax and return to her self-indulgent ways.

"Listen, I have to go," he said, walking to his room. "Try to clean up a bit today," he gestured to the lounge room. "For Tom. Don't worry about my laundry. Just leave it. I'll sort it out later."

He raced into the bathroom for a speedy shower as Mary stood outside the door.

"Do you have to go?" she whined, a last-ditch effort.

"I'll be home this afternoon," Adi replied, as he came out of the bathroom and went into the lounge room to say goodbye to his son. "Hey, buddy, Daddy just has to go to work for a bit, but I'll be back this afternoon and if it's not raining, I'll take you to the park."

"Okay, Daddy," he smiled, clearly not understanding such a long sentence, but responding to his daddy's warm attention. He was oblivious, an open heart of unconditional love.

Adi kissed his tiny forehead and felt pained. How he wished the situation were different. How he wished he could just take his son and go. But that wouldn't be fair on Tom. Despite Mary's ways, Tom loved his mum. And a child needed their mother.

Yet he couldn't bare to live apart from his angel.

10

"Hi Max, it's me," spoke the voicemail. "Call me when you get a chance."

Oh-em-gee! Handsome lover calling! M was beaming. She instantly dialled his number, feeling confident and excited, happy to have heard from him.

"Hey, it's me. How are you?" she said.

"Really well, thanks. It's just been so busy lately. Sorry I haven't been in touch. You have been on my mind."

On your mind? Really?! she thought to herself, practically taking flight with glee. "Yeah, me too. Flat out," she said calmly, trying to keep the exhilaration from her tone. What she really wanted to say was that he'd been on her mind, as well ... usually naked. Was that so wrong? She giggled to herself.

"Hey, Miss Gigglepuss," he interjected, "Guess what? I'm taking you out for a drink and a catch up tonight."

"Well, seeing as how you asked so politely," she teased. "Oh wait, I better check my diary. When did you say again? I might be busy ..." M trailed off, pretending to flick through an imaginary diary.

"Ha ha," laughed Adi. "Funny girl. I'm meeting you tonight at eight p.m. at La Luna. Be there ... or prepare to suffer the consequences," he added cheekily.

M felt a surprise volt of electricity zap through her body and her witty repartee suddenly escaped her. "Er ... I'll see you then," she choked out, before hanging up the phone, with a smile practically doing a three-sixty around her face.

As she applied a coat of 'Fat Lash' mascara in front of the mirror, her mind chattered away like a boat full of chipmunks. *I can't believe I'm seeing him tonight! I need to look hot. I need to be witty, charming, irresistible. I want him to enjoy my company. Does he think I'm smart? Funny? Is a 'catch up' another term for a 'date'? Am I waxed?! Yikes, yep, thank god. Are we lovers? Are we friends? Could this be more? What if it's all for nothing? Must defuse this negative self-talk ...*

M went to the cupboard and opened up a packet of macaroons, her go-to de-stressor, and indulged in delicious bites of salty caramel. Quickly her sugar hit worked its magic and calmed her slightly, and she to went to the closet to find the perfect dress. So many colours, so many cuts, so much fabric. She usually loved trying on a dozen dresses as part of the getting-reading-for-a-hot-date routine (*it is a date, right?*), but tonight she was just getting flustered. How could a woman have so many things to wear and yet have no idea *what* to wear? She eventually settled on a black backless dress, accessorised with some silver hoop earrings.

Back at the mirror and with the straightening iron heating up, M made a decision. She decided, once again, that she wouldn't tell the girls about this just yet. She wasn't sure why. Maybe it was to avoid hearing candid observations, no matter how well intentioned her friends were. What did that say about her? That she'd rather be in denial? Yet, if she started hearing a hundred different opinions from her friends, it would certainly confuse her—especially when they heard about his runner the other night—and she didn't need any more confusion. She was playing it safe in her own way, she decided. What was there to tell, anyway? But, then again, if it wasn't a big deal than why did she want to keep it from her girlfriends?

Sensing her contradictory thoughts, her 'brains' chimed in:

Why all the effort—what's the big deal? He is just a guy, said left-brain.

Right-brain, not to be steamrolled, butted in fiercely. *Oh, God, you look great, honey. Knock yourself out!*

Was this what it was coming down to? Her brain—or *brains*—needed a fucking holiday. M picked up her hairbrush and started stabbing it, Norman Bates style, at her reflection in the mirror. *Okay!* she screamed silently to herself, *everybody needs to shut up in there!* then laughed out loud.

La Luna was an inner-city bar with an extensive wine and cocktail list. As she was a few minutes late, Adi was leaned up against the brick wall outside as she approached, waiting for her, with a huge smirk on his face. His tussled hair, shag-me eyes and gorgeous grin conspired to take her breath away. *Do I leap into his arms? Or just wrap myself around his neck and snog his face off?* she wondered, excitement mounting. He beat her to the punch, with a quick (and ambiguous?) peck on the lips.

They were seated in a relatively quiet corner, where they could actually hear each other speak. As he ordered the wine for them, she appreciated that he was a classy man who knew his vine. What woman wouldn't be impressed? The mood felt intoxicating, the ambience exotic, and for some reason it felt like they were on holiday again tonight—not in their own home town. *Good company, good conversation, good wine*, thought M, as she took her first sip of Merlot. Even the way he looked at her, she noticed. It was the same lingering gaze he'd given her in Prague. It made her quiver, although she definitely wished it didn't. She wished she felt more in control, less at the whim of her hopeless-romantic self. Their 'status' was still so unclear to her, yet, at the same time, it didn't feel right to ask him directly at this point. They were still very much in the go-with-the-flow early stages of potential romance.

"It was a great time we had in Prague, hey, M?" he said suddenly. Was he reading her mind?

"Yeah, it sure was," she replied dreamily, trying not to drown in his eyes. "Although," she added with a laugh, struggling to break the spell, "all that food … I'm surprised we didn't come back as sumo wrestlers," she laughed.

"I did!" laughed Adi. "Actually, I have lost weight since I got back," he said. "The food here just can't compare."

"Yes, I noticed—you've lost your ass," M replied with a cheeky grin.

"Hey, watch yourself, girl. You know that's sexual harassment," he winked. "Why are you looking at my ass anyway?"

"Adi, I've been staring at your ass for a long while now. I just got up-close and personal for the first time on that trip."

"Ooh baby," he said, pretending to fan himself with a cocktail napkin. "That's reason enough for us to go back immediately."

M was aglow.

"Hey," he began, as a thought seemed to pop into his head, "maybe we can do Eastern Europe some time. Like a tour?" he suggested.

She smiled and froze, suddenly speechless. *Did he just say 'we'?* her mind raced. *Does this mean he sees an 'us'? He loves me, he loves me not, he loves me ... Am I on my way to being Mrs Adi?!*

"Sounds like a nice idea," she said calmly, impressed with the composed tone of her voice, while the butterflies in her stomach were singing 'Dancing on the Ceiling' by Lionel Ritchie. "Europe is always a 'yes' for me." Finally, the declaration she'd been waiting for. She wanted to grab him by the scruff of his neck and kiss him all over.

Declaration? she said to herself, abruptly applying the brakes. *Wait a minute. Calm the fuck down. Did he actually 'declare' anything? Or are you filling in the blanks with your own imagination? You've got to stop doing this to yourself, M.*

Suddenly she felt very exhausted with this emotional ping-pong game she was playing. Never in her life had she felt this way about a man before. Yet never in her life had she been so utterly, embarrassingly confounded as to whether he had the slightest romantic interest in her or not. Yes, they'd had a whirlwind affair to remember. But did he send her flowers, shower her with texts and phone calls afterwards? No. In fact, she was jumping for joy if he phoned her at all–tonight was a case in point. The haziness of it all suddenly infuriated her. She flat-out refused to be Little

Miss Desperado waiting around for some scraps of his affection, waiting for him to break out that Tom Cruise smile that would have her loins melting all over again ...

He beamed at her across the table, breaking out his big Tom Cruise smile, as he flicked the dark strands of hair from his eye ... and her loins started melting all over again.

Focus, dammit! she bellowed from somewhere deep inside, as he leaned in closer to her, deeply engaging her in eye-to-eye contact, and topped up her wine. She could feel herself losing the battle. Suddenly it felt like, for a moment, they were the only ones in the room. But she held on tight and played it cool. She had too. She may be almost powerless against his cup-runneth-over sex appeal, but experience had taught her that actions speak louder than words.

So just relax, she told herself. *Enjoy his company, enjoy the banter, enjoy the night ... have no expectations ... we'll eventually see where this leads. What will be will be.*

As the night progressed, they laughed and bounced witty anecdotes off each other, making headway into a second bottle of red. He had her in stitches and she had to admit, he truly was a funny guy. Sexual fantasies aside, she loved spending time with him, they just clicked, and she wanted more of it, that much she knew.

She also knew, through the grapevine, that she wasn't the only woman who'd been intoxicated by his smile–he had a few ladies interested. But he seemed to played Mr Hard-to-Get. She wasn't really sure how long he'd been single. He'd been vague about it in Prague, but had mentioned a significant other in his past. Was he a serious-relationship type of guy? Or a player? That thought made her a little uneasy, but it was a relief to know that he'd had at least one long-term relationship and he wasn't a blatant womaniser, bedding women casually, then vanishing into the night. Because with *his* smile, he'd certainly be able to.

He's a man who likes commitment, she thought, with a smile, and as though on cue, he randomly started another anecdote to prove it.

"There is something nice about this place. It kind of reminds me of my ex," he said, as he glanced around the room at the antique paintings and general décor.

What the fuck?

"When we used stay in B&Bs in the countryside, I mean. We would stay in houses and cottages with this kind of furniture and stuff."

And there's it was again—the ex factor. So unnecessary. Was he really likening the niceness of the restaurant to his time with his ex-girlfriend?!

In his defence, of course, he was clueless about the extent of her feelings for him and probably didn't realise that the mention of the words "my ex" where like fingernails down a blackboard to her. From his perspective, he was just making general chitchat about country furniture. Yet, on the other hand, M felt that it was rude to take a lady out to dinner and then talk about your ex, no matter what. She bounced off the topic to quickly change the subject.

"Hey, have you ever been on one of those wine-tasting tours?" she said, hoping he'd take the hint and suggest they go on one together.

"Sure, they're always fun," he replied.

Always? How many has he been on? she wondered. While she'd secretly been planting the seed of doing one of these tasting tours together, she suddenly wondered how many other women he'd whisked away to Red Hill for pinot noir, goat cheese tarts and Egyptian-cotton sheets in romantic B&Bs. Didn't he understand how mentioning an ex would inevitably sound to her? Uncontrollable jealousy bubbled just below the surface.

She quickly gave herself an internal slap across the face. He was just a guy, making conversation about wineries. He wouldn't be analysing what he was saying, she decided finally. He was just telling a story. She was being hypersensitive because she was swept away by him, and this, she reminded herself, was something she needed to get a hold of.

As Adi excused himself for the lavatory, she had a thought. How did someone discover who they were and what they wanted if they'd always been part of a 'one plus one' and never just a 'one'? M knew how to stand on her own and be comfortable. She understood that the most important relationship one would ever have was with oneself, even before Soula had reminded her. She learned that herself, the hard way. After her big break-up with Shamus The Shit and the crap she dealt with, she didn't want to compromise herself again for a man. She had done everything for him; it had all been about him, him, him. She got lost in a life that was all 'we' and never 'me', and had paid a high price for it. It stripped her of self-confidence and depleted her heart.

Being with Adi in Prague had somehow reignited her heart and she felt her confidence returning. But did that mean she wanted to leap into the whole shebang of a full-blown relationship again. Now that she had all the freedom that life could offer—plus the work, life, friend, family balance—did she just want to be a 'we' again, with Adi. Or should she just value that short amount of time they'd spent together and just be grateful that it was the catalyst that helped to thaw her out of her emotional coma? She had to ask herself, why was she—and every woman she knew, it seemed—always on the lookout for that the relationship Holy Grail?

With the way she'd squirmed when he talked about his ex, feeling jealous and possessive, she could see how she was already allowing her self-confidence to be compromised again for a man. Did she really want to do that to herself again? Here she was being jealous and possessive about a man whom she wasn't even sure was romantically interested in her. What did that say about her? Would she make the same mistake all over again—always putting him first and herself last? Do the lessons of the past go out the window when we get caught up in it again? Or perhaps she hadn't fully learned the lessons and was destined to relive the same experiences over again.

These questions hung over her head uncomfortably. Yet as Adi made his way back to the table, his smile beaming at her, her insides turned to liquid all over again. This was a man who had some strange power over her and she had to remind herself to tread carefully.

When they finished up and headed for her car, M decided she would absolutely not sleep with Adi tonight. Come hell or high water, she would stand her ground until he made his intentions clearer to her.

She offered to drive him home as he lived close by. As he directed her through the moonlit streets, Ed Sheeran sang seductively from the stereo. As she pulled into his driveway, she chanted in her firmly head, *Don't kiss me! Don't kiss me!*

He turned to her. "Thanks for a great night," he said, gazing into her eyes.

Oh God! There it was again. The racing heartbeat, the shallow breathing ... and the paralysing uncertainty.

"I had a lovely time, Adi," she said, quickly pulling out of his gaze, determined to hold her composure. Damned if she was going to stumble into another undefined night of passion with him. She liked him. And if he liked her too–*liked* liked her–he'd have to make an unambiguous move. No more hiding behind opportune circumstances.

He leaned in to her and involuntarily her lips puckered up! Her *Don't kiss me!* chant had turned into *Kiss me! Kiss me!*, as that familiar rush came over her and again she felt powerless against him once again.

Then, much to her surprise, he gave her a quick peck on the cheek and then *he* pulled away. "Bye," he said, opening the car door and climbing out.

Dazedly, she watched him walk to his front door and disappear into the house.

What the hell?

Her mind sped at a million miles a minute. Why didn't he ask her in? Even if it was just a fling for him, wouldn't he seize the moment and ask her in? Had she done something to turn him off? Why did he ask her to dinner? Was he no longer attracted to her? His long, lusty stares declared otherwise.

As she fell onto her bed shortly later, confused but abuzz, she had to laugh. What else could you do? This guy was an absolute enigma to her. She had no idea how he felt about her, which just drove home the fact that she should pull her head out of the clouds and stop yearning for some whimsical happily-ever-after. Prague was Prague. A sexy, intense, erotic fantasy. Nothing more.

Case closed.

I I

Over the next few months, M took her focus away from romance completely. She and Adi texted often and caught up for coffee regularly, but as far as she was concerned, he'd made his intentions crystal clear that night–that this was absolutely a friendship, nothing more–and while there was certainly an element of disappointment in this realisation, it was also somewhat liberating, as there's nothing more paralysing that uncertainty.

Nevertheless, she loved their talks and time the spent together. They bounced jokes off each other and genuinely enjoyed each other's company. Although it was undeniably different from the other platonic friendships in M's life. She felt like she was eighteen again–revived, alive and happy–and it was the one thing that kept her going and kept her anxiety about her job situation at bay. This elated feeling was a magic tonic that overrode all the other aspects of her life. While at work everyone walked on eggshells because of the restructure, she floated on air and didn't care. She felt safe and bulletproof. *What would be would be.* Romance or not, Adi ignited her soul and she gave herself permission to just live in the moment and enjoy it for what it was.

M's head was much clearer now that the question of *Will we shag or won't we?* was eliminated. Although, frankly, she had to admit that was something she missed! She'd never gone through so many packets of macaroons. Regardless, her relationship with Adi was finally defined and she was thoroughly enjoying getting to know him on a truly genuine level. As her comfort zone with him was widened, she slowly began to trust him as a person and a man—and, consequently, men in general—in a way that she didn't know she ever would again after the fallout of Shamus The Shit.

There was only one problem. She knew that deep down, she still thought about him on a level that she knew was dangerous. Like an addict, she feared that with the right circumstances, the right lighting, the right ambience, the right whispers in her ear, she might just slip back into his arms—even if only for one night— and she'd be right back to square one. The fact was, she was on an incredible high whenever they were together, and she felt low when she didn't see him. She was always looking forward to their next catch up. When she heard a funny joke or saw something she knew would interest him, she always felt an irresistible urge to call and tell him.

It bothered her that she was still so preoccupied by him.

"So what's new with you?" Laura asked, as the four of them dined at a swanky new eatery with views overlooking the bay, seated by the open area by the water. What a view. It was great to have Laura out with them again. She had been buried at home for weeks, but had finally realised that staying home was not going to help her. Being surrounded by love and support and positive energy was. Here she was, makeup on and strutting her stuff. It was good to see.

"Where do I start?" M sighed.

"What's happened, babe? Man troubles?" Kathy asked.

"Are there any other troubles?" Elisha said, and the all laughed.

"Well, yeah," began M. "I've been hanging out with Adi a lot since we got back from Prague."

"Oh my God, you go, girlfriend!" enthused Kathy, lifting a hand for a high five.

M laughed. "No, it's not like that. We're friends. In fact, we've become really good friends. I feel good around him. We've actually gotten to know each other pretty well."

"Well," began Laura cautiously, "that's great, right? He seems nice. So what's the trouble you speak of? A guy wouldn't be hanging around you if he didn't think you were pretty cool too."

"The truth is," continued M, "I think I like him as more than a friend. I think about him constantly. I shouldn't be thinking this way, as I know that he doesn't think of me in a romantic way. But, that being said, I feel so alive when I'm with him. It's like the world stops. I'm feeling kind of lost."

"You're falling for him hard, aren't you?" Elisha said as she put an arm around her shoulder.

M nodded and paused. "I *have* fallen for him, big time. He has all the features I want in a man. He says and does all the right things. I feel we really connect. And even though the friendship is purely platonic, I can't help but think that he feels the same way deep down. It's just a feeling I get," she explained.

"Hey, it's exciting when someone comes into your life in a certain way," Elisha said. "And it's great that you feel so comfortable around him. He obviously does, too. If he didn't, he wouldn't make time for you. It's okay, M. You are allowed to feel and enjoy. Go with the flow."

"Well … there is something you guys don't know," admitted M. *Drum roll*, she thought to herself, knowing she was about to drop the bomb on her besties. "We had a week-long shag fest in Prague and it was the most intense and erotic experience of my life."

"*WHAT THE FUCK?!*" the girls exclaimed simultaneously.

"Oh my God, you go, girlfriend!" said Kathy, for the second time.

"Right on, babe!" squealed Laura.

"*Now* you're talking!" chimed in Elisha.

"Easy now, ladies, it was only six days. We were stranded. I guess it was a holiday fling. I'm not sure that it actually meant anything to him," M replied, suddenly hoping they would change the subject. She'd said too much and now, as the girls would no doubt crack it open and analyse it, she felt uncomfortable.

"Wait a second … you guys are good friends, right?" Laura asked. "And you're hanging out, enjoying each other's company. I know you've mentioned dinners, wine, coffee. And now you're saying there was *sex*?"

"The most intense and erotic sex!" chimed in Elisha, smirking from ear to ear.

"Um …" continued Laura, "don't you think that maybe he might *like* like you?"

"I don't know … The feelings I have for him are like a force that consumes me. But the feelings he seems to have for me are blurry," M responded solemnly.

"Hey, you don't get intimate with a *mate*," said Elisha. "Hell, no. He is attracted to you, trust me."

"Guys, please don't say that. Please don't get carried away. I've gone over and over this in my mind. I can't do it any more. I'm not sure what's happening to me at the moment. It's confusing and I get really bad anxiety when I think about it, so can we please just drop it? I shouldn't have brought it up."

"Sweetie, we don't want you to get upset," Kathy said. "Just keep your wits about you. He may just be playing. With guys, you never know—even the nicest ones. So just enjoy yourself, but stay clearheaded. These Casanovas sometimes think they can have their cake and eat it, too. We just want you to be happy and not let anything stress you out. No more worries and no more thinking, okay. Just be."

M knew that this was true. But as the analytical part of her personality reared its head it began to analyse everything. *What if …? Will he …? Do I …?* M hated blurred lines—she liked clarity, tidy lines, order.

After her confession to the girls, she got home that night feeling flat, uneasy, conflicted, wrong. It's as though, so long as she'd kept her feelings secret, she was able to contain them, to pretend they weren't multiplying, to ignore the sleepless nights. But now they were loose, free-ranging, and she felt out of control.

She'd been able to keep her feelings in check by living in a state of denial, she realised. But now she'd accidentally cracked it open and she couldn't help but acknowledge the situation.

She knew there was something else going on with him, that it was more than friendship for him too. His actions went through the motions of a platonic relationship, but she could *feel* something deeper, a vibe. *Oh God, a vibe?! I'm such a flake*, she thought to herself. Sometimes it was in the way he stared at her, a little too long; the way he touched her arm and she felt a vibration. *Vibration?! Kill me now.* Sometimes she thought she felt him breathing in the smell of her hair when they stood too close. *Friends aren't supposed to sniff other friends!* she thought, laughingly, to herself.

But, regardless of all the ambiguity, why did *she* care so much about *him*? What was this power he seemed to have over her? And why did it bother her so much? She felt her normal enthusiasm and confidence gradually giving way to negative theories and endless worry. Considering their history and the fact that he hadn't acted on any romantic impulses since Prague—well, other than that 'almost' time at her house when he ended up running away and leaving her semi-naked and perplexed in the living room—she knew she enjoyed their time together and she should just enjoy it for what it was and stop loading it down with additional meaning that may or may not exist. But that was easier said than done.

M spent the better part of the next day relaxing with the unthinkable—a pile of girly magazines. She never read this stuff, but there were always stories and articles about men, women, relationships and sex, right? It was all in the name of research then, she reasoned.

The magazines reinforced the fact that there was still an undeniable stigma surrounding women being single, as opposed to men. Women were affected emotionally by whether or not they were in relationships, yet men were only emotional about the relationships they were currently in. Women were more likely to suffer deep despair when a relationship ended, M read. Did that mean they benefitted more by being in relationships? "But what if we are not? Does it mean we are doomed?" she said out loud. "Who writes this shit?"

One article concluded that it was better to be alone than in a difficult or bad relationship. "Hah! … Finally some truth," she said. She continued reading, wondering why women placed such weight on the labels 'single' and 'attached'. Why was it that when they got to a certain age this became such a chip on the shoulder? Was it because women had an innate urge to care and nurture?

There was a certain vulnerability attached to this, M reflected. In their late teens and twenties, women felt basically bulletproof. They knew there were plenty of fish in the sea, they were young and attractive enough to catch them, so they didn't sweat relationships. There was still heaps of time. But when they reached their thirties and things hadn't turned out like they thought they would, or the relationship they wanted hadn't come their way, they started to panic. Consciously or subconsciously, each woman started creating deadlines for herself.

Goals and milestone seemed to be important in most women's lives. By seventeen or eighteen, you'd finished high school. By twenty-four, you had your degree and had begun your career. By thirty, you'd travelled a bit and could buy a house. And not long after, you were possibly married with a child or two. While goals and desires were very important in life and they gave us purpose, M contemplated, what happened when some of those deadlines weren't met? What if by your mid-thirties you didn't have your house, your husband or your baby? What if that dream job with the company car and the travel hadn't come to fruition? Did you then deem yourself a failure and a disappointment?

And, conversely, what happened when all the deadlines *were* met–or well on track–but then breakup or unemployment occurred? Case in point: Maxine. First, Shamus The Shit disaster, then possible unemployment, and now never-ending anxiety over an ambiguous love interest that held her in a state of perpetual limbo. Life didn't hold out any guarantees, but anything was still possible. This was true.

What if you did have your house by thirty, travelled every few years and had a stable job that allowed you to live comfortably? Should you let the absence of a romantic relationship be the one thing that dampened an otherwise great life? Does the cherry really matter?

Well, yes, M confessed to herself.

Considering that, she began to seriously ponder if she should she tell Adi how she felt–just take a chance and set it free. Who said you can't have it all? She was scared, yes. But why? Was it solely because she wanted to avoid another Shamus The Shit situation? Would she really cash in a shot at true love and happiness because one relationship had bitten her on the ass? The absurdity of that rationale finally struck her. If she told Adi how she felt, it could turn out that he felt that same way and would sweep her off her feet. This was the hope she desperately held.

Yet she knew she couldn't tell him how she felt. It would mean risking everything and ending up losing the friendship altogether, which was an upsetting thought.

Either way, something had to change in order for her to move forward with her life. She had to be set her free from this prison of uncertainty. It was the unknowing that was causing the anxiety and sleeplessness in her life.

At that moment, a text came through:

Hey M. Just thinking about you. A

Adi and his timing. *Fuck*. Yet his spontaneous gesture made her smile. *He likes me ... even if only a little*, she thought.

12

The ringing phone startled her.

"Hello?" she said groggily, struggling for wakefulness.

"Max ... it's me."

"Laura? Is everything okay?" M asked, sitting up in bed.

"Yeah, sorry it's so early, but I just wanted to chat."

"Of course, honey, I'm here for you always. How are you?"

"Had better days. James is coming over later to get his things. I don't know if I should stay and talk to him or leave the house and let him come for his stuff while I'm not here."

"Well ... do you *want* to face him? Do you want to even see him?" M asked.

"Maybe I should, and just get it over with. I'm not sure. Maybe I need more time." Laura sounded shaky.

"Honey, you have to do what your instincts tell you. I know it's incredibly hard, but this is something you need to deal with and then slowly, slowly make peace with. It will take time."

"I still can't understand how this even *happened!*" Laura cried. "How can it be that this is where I find myself?"

"I wish I could take it all away from you, sweetie, but I can't. Look, why don't we go out, see a movie and just hang out for a while? You may not be ready to face him. You will know when you are. Do you want me to come and get you?"

There was a slight pause, then Laura sniffled. "Sure. That would be good, thanks."

"I'll be there as soon as I can."

M hung up, rose from the bed and stood pensively in front of her wardrobe. She thought about Laura and how, just a few months ago, she seemed to how it all, and felt devastated for her that she was now looking down the barrel of separation, grief, divorce, being single and alone once again. She also thought about how strange life was that two friends could be simultaneously going through such opposite extremes in their love lives. Laura was having all the love she'd once had for her partner sucked brutally from her heart. While M's heart was near exploding as the feelings she felt for Adi continued to multiple at an expediential rate. For both of them, however, the sensation filled them with horrendous angst.

Change happens whether we like it or not, she thought to herself, as she reached for a blouse. *We may never get answers, but we have to ride the wave of life. Take both the good and the bad.*

Whatever life held ahead, she knew that at least she had her crew. Helping Laura through this difficult time was a priority for her. She wanted to help Laura refocus on life. And, let's face it, although she hadn't had to face a marriage breaking, being heartbroken and newly single was something she *had* had some experience with and she hoped the lessons she'd learned were something she could share with her friend. She grabbed her keys and headed out the door.

By the time she'd arrived at Laura's, she'd had a brilliant idea. "Change of plans. Get your coat, we're going for a drive."

"What? Where are we going?"

"Off to the coast," said M, knowing that the fresh air and change of scenery would help her to get some perspective. Help them both, in fact. "It'll do us good. We haven't done a road trip for ages. We'll grab some coffee on the beach, watch the sunset and come back when we please."

"Sure," Laura smiled. "You always come up with the goods, M. You're a trooper, you know that?"

They cruised down the highway, windows down and music blaring. The sunshine and the coastal air made for a gorgeous drive.

"This is like a flashback," Laura said, as she turned down the music slightly so they could talk.

"Yeah, I know. The younger days, hey? We don't do this nearly as much as we should."

"Sometimes I wish we still as innocent and optimistic as were back then," Laura said wistfully.

"Clueless, you mean!" laughed M. "But I know. So do I. Things were—or at least they seemed—easier when we were younger. Simple. I guess maybe all the heavy stuff happens when we're older. Or maybe we just give it more weight. Who knows? All I know is that we are going to enjoy the day and relax, right?" M glanced over at Laura hoping for a smile or some positive reaction.

"Absolutely, my friend. Time to chill, I say," Laura replied.

Right on cue, a blast from 1995 came on the radio–'Gangsta's Paradise'–and the girls smiled at each other in delight as M turned up the volume. They bopped along to the beat, both in their own headspace.

M let the wind blow through her hair as she gazed at the passing scenery. She loved watching the land, the neighbouring suburbs and the trees and all that surrounded her. The sky was bright blue and the sun warmed her limbs, allowing her to let go and just breathe, mind-chatter free. She looked over and saw that Laura had closed her eyes. *Good*, she thought. *She needs rest.* M drove on, enjoying the ride. This route down the Mornington Peninsula was her favourite–a narrow strip of land jutting between the bays, with lush greenery all around, the hazy view of the Dandenong Ranges in the distance, and countless stunning beaches on both sides. At the tip, to the south, began the wild open ocean of Bass Strait. With burly winds and powerful waves, this is where you went to have your troubles literally blown away. *The perfect destination*, M thought.

After a while, Laura opened her eyes. "I just needed that moment, sorry," she said.

"Don't apologise. A cat nap does a world of good," M smiled, nurturingly.

"I don't know what tomorrow is going to bring. But right now I don't care. I just want to enjoy the coast and walk barefoot in the sand."

"None of us knows what tomorrow will bring. That's the thing about life. But enjoying the moment is the most important thing. If we continue to do that then we have passed the most important test. It's all about small steps. It's not a race. Things take time."

"Max, you're so great. You're a wonderful friend and you always go that extra mile. Please know that even though I'm the one going through a crisis now, I'm always here for you—all of you girls." Laura began to choke up as she spoke. "I'm not sure how I would be right now without you all."

"Hey, hey! No need for tears," M said encouragingly. "This is our drive. We have each other. Right now nothing else matters, yeah?"

"Right. Yes … yes," Laura said, audibly pulling herself together and looking around. "We aren't far from the ocean," she noted.

M smiled.

They continued to listen to the familiar tunes on the radio—they'd stumbled across a local oldies station—and even sang along with a few. Laura seemed more at ease, even smiling a bit now.

"Here it comes—ocean!" she said happily, pointing ahead as they rounded a curve in the road, between the grassy dunes.

M gazed in awe. Even though she had driven this stretch of coastline many times, it still managed to take her breath away every time, seeing the ocean stretch for miles out to the horizon. Today the deep blue sky, dotted with fluffy cumulus clouds, seemed to stretch into infinity. The sun reflected off the waves, which were speckled with surfers, created a dazzling display of diamond-like glimmers on the tip of each rolling swell. From afar you could see the staggering cliff faces, and the sand seemed to stretch out forever in both directions. It was a picture-perfect postcard.

"This place never ceases to amaze me. I love it here," M sighed, rolling the windows down to breathe the seaside air.

"It's so beautiful. Wouldn't it be good if we could retire here?" Laura said, laughing.

"Well, it is always an option. Who knows?" M replied with a giggle.

They found a parking spot near the foreshore and made their way down to the sand. M went to the kiosk to get the coffees and returned to find Laura barefoot, sitting pensively on a bench looking out across the water.

"Here we are. Two lattes."

"Thanks, darling."

They raised their takeaway cups ceremoniously.

"Here's to us," M pronounced. "To two great girls. May our stilettos keep us walking with heads held high, even if our feet get sore. To two fabulous girls, sans bullshit men."

"Cheers and amen to that," Laura said, as they tapped their cups and took frothy sips, then silently slipped into their own chains of though. M gazed out at the enormous sky and felt the warm sun on her face and arms as she considered how, in the grand scheme of things, there was no real reason to worry about anything. What will be will be, so why stress over it? Just having spent the time she had with Adi was something she should be grateful for. And, now, it felt good that she could just take off and be with her friend like this. After all, a bit of emotional confusion really didn't compare to having the rug pulled out from under you, like Laura had.

"Do you believe in second chances?" Laura asked suddenly.

"Well … I guess it all depends," M said thoughtfully. "Some people do deserve a second chance, but some don't. Why? Would you take James back if he came begging to you?"

"I don't know. Maybe. Even after what he did, I still love him. I hate him, but I love him. Part of me keeps saying that what he did deserves forgiveness. After all, we have so much history together, and sometimes people make mistakes and only realise it later. I keep going over and over it all in my head. What did I do? What could I have done differently?"

"Stop right there," M said firmly. "You did nothing wrong. *Nothing.* You can't blame yourself or drive yourself mad thinking about what could have been. He made a choice, a stupid one, and it's done. It is a bitter pill to swallow, I know, but *he did this to you.* Things may not have always been perfect—no relationship is—but you don't just up and leave a marriage, with no explanation. It hurts because you love him and you thought your life was going in the direction you wanted. You just need time to process your feelings. Get some distance and perspective. Slowly, though. Slowly."

"I know … I know. It's just so hard to take sometimes. There are good days and bad ones. Mostly bad ones," Laura admitted, sipping her coffee. M put an arm around her shoulders.

"Sweetie, we are women. We suffer for men. We just do. We put them before ourselves. I guess we kind of lose ourselves even though we don't want to, or don't realise it. But, in my opinion, there are two types of women: the ones who stay and struggle, and the ones who go make themselves a better life. For the ones who stay, maybe they think it will get better, or that he'll never do it again. Maybe they fear the unknown, or the financial implications of being on their own, or security. I don't know. What I *do* know is that the women who go, as difficult and core-breaking as that can be, don't do it light-heartedly. They do it out of a primal need for survival, because they know that it's for the best. They know that they deserve *better*. Women are survivors. Laura, please don't sit around waiting for him to run back into your arms. As much as you may think that's what you need right now–that perhaps you'll never find love again, or that you can't survive on your own–those feelings will change over time as you regain your balance. If it's meant to be, it will be. And if not, you'll be ready to let him go." M paused and looked directly into Laura's eyes. "This is a new chapter in your life, honey, a significant one. Either way, it means growth and change, and that can be scary. Maybe the universe has other plans and wants to give you even more. You have to do what's best for you, and no one knows what that is, except for you. Whatever you decide, we will be here for you. We love you."

Laura's eyes had begun to tear up, and M handed her a tissue.

"Thanks, M. Hearing you say all that means a lot. And you are absolutely right. I'm not going to put pressure on myself, and I need to forgive myself and take responsibility for the partnership we had. I punish myself by thinking what I did wrong or how I could have done it better. What's done is done. I'll be okay. I know

I will." Laura sniffled and dabbed at her eyes, before looking M directly in the eyes. "And the same goes for you, you know, M. Whatever happens for you or to you, don't let the situation define you. You strut your stuff and keep smiling. You have faith and be strong too. You're a great person," she smiled warmly. Then paused. "I hope he isn't leading you on. I'll smash him if he is," she laughed. "I hope he is genuine and sincere with you." Laura paused again to collect her thoughts. "But from what I can decipher, I think he has feelings for you as well. Life's short, M. Why don't you talk to him?"

"I know ... I know I should. I don't know. I'm scared, I guess. Scared of making myself vulnerable. Scared of losing the friendship. Scared mostly that he won't reciprocate and I'll be forced to give up the fantasy, once and for all, that he's going to sweep my off my feet. As long as I procrastinate, I can continue to believe there's a chance he loves me too. Sad, I know!" M said. "But, I'll see how I go. He hasn't exactly said anything either. He should be a man and step up, if he has feelings for me too," M said.

The fact that he hadn't stepped up made M suddenly feel solemn that those feelings, therefore, weren't in fact there at all. She suddenly thought about a book she'd read a few years back, *He's Just Not That Into You*, and a line that had resonated deeply with her, something along the lines of: If a guy's into you but he needs to take things slow, he'll definitely let you know so you don't get annoyed and leave. This certainly wasn't the case with Adi–he'd made no such declarations in order to ensure he didn't lose her.

M looked at the sky and sighed. She knew it was time to move it. As much as she loved the idea of being with Adi, she was wasting precious time with this emotional guessing game. She had to allow herself to be open to other options.

Laura intuited her friend's realisation. "Maybe he's sorting himself out too, men do things differently. He might be working through his own heart. Afraid to commit again. How do you know? But let yourself be open to possibilities. Do what you feel is right, but also put yourself first. That's all I'm saying."

"I will ... I will ... To be honest, I should be concentrating on my job and perhaps planning for another. Knowing my luck, I'll end up with no man *and* no job. I need to focus. Think of a plan B. Either that or I'll get diabetes from stress-eating too many macaroons!" They looked at each other and laughed. They were relaxed. They had each other.

"Now, miss, let's lighten up and watch the sunset before we drive home, hey?" M said with a soft smile.

"Sounds like a plan. Another step to a new beginning."

The sky turned shades of pink and yellow as the sun started to descend, looking larger as it approached the horizon. The clouds separated and formed patterns in the distance.

"How nice are sunsets," Laura mused. "We should make a pact to watch them more often."

"Yeah, let's do that. Wow, it's a piece of heaven on earth."

The sun came further down and the yellow and pink colours grew darker and more intense.

"Just look at that. Now that is creation. The possibility to all things," Laura said as she pointed to the sky and the universe beyond. God can move providence."

"True. Anything can happen, sweetie. We just have to believe it," M replied.

They watched as the last bit of sun slowly sunk into the horizon and vibrant hues of pink and yellow deepened and changed to other hues, all just as beautiful. Dusk turned to night, and the girls made their way back home.

13

The following day at work proved to be a busy one, with back-to-back meetings scheduled for M and her team. Mr Ferguson was away, so she and another colleague were responsible for the coordination of them all. M was a little nervous about this, but knew it had to be done and there was no time to wallow in panic.

"Stacey, have you got the McKenzie file?" she asked as she hurried by the assistant's desk. "I need to brief him on the ad space we got him and the budget for the ads."

"Yes, I have them here. I prepared it for you. All you need to do is present," Stacey replied, handing over a thick stack of papers.

"You're a star, thank you. I will let you know how I go," M said as she ducked back into her office to quickly review the file. Just as she was getting up again to head to the boardroom, her phone rang. She looked at the caller ID. Jack. *Jack!* It had been a while since she'd thought about sexy Man Boy from the bar. Her heart skipped a little beat. Deciding she could give him a moment and that it might actually ease her up a bit, she moved a little further away from her door and spoke in a soft tone, so as not to be overheard. "Hello?"

"Hey, Max, it's Jack. How are you?"

"I'm good. How are you going?" she said, feeling a huge grin spread across her face.

"I got sick of waiting to hear from you so I thought I'd take things into my own hands," he said.

"Oh, Jacky-Boy, I don't need to hear about what you do in the privacy of your own home!" she teased.

"You cheeky girl," he laughed. "Hey, I'm in the neighbourhood today, and I was wondering if you'd be home later this afternoon. I'd love to catch with a coffee."

She'd forgotten how deep and sexy his voice was. There was no denying that he was sweet, charming ... and quite hot. She remembered their sexy night of passion that had left her so satisfied, yet also wanting more. It had been a long time since she'd thought about another man in a sexual way–other than Adi, that was. All her thoughts had been so focused on him for so long that she forgot what it felt like to visualise uncomplicated lovin'. She reminded herself that she couldn't wait forever for Adi to make a move, that she had to get on with life and be open to other experiences.

"Sure, I'll be home around 4.30," she said, the butterflies taking flight in her stomach.

"Great, see you then," he said.

M was excited. Could Jack possibly yank her back to reality and make her forget the cat-and-mouse game going on in her head? She was hoping for it. This might be the welcome distraction she'd been needing.

Her meetings over and, she thought, successful, M left the office early, claiming she had forgotten a doctor's appointment. She'd barely arrived home, changed clothes and splashed on some perfume when the doorbell rang. Four-fifteen–he was early. Eager, perhaps?

"Hey, you, how are you?" M said as she opened the door to greet him.

"How are you, chicky?" Jack smiled, as he kissed her cheek.

There he was, Man Boy in a suit. *Wow.* What a spunk. She suddenly realised how aroused she was by the mere sight of him.

"Gee, you scrub up alright in a suit, hey? Come on in. Work been well?"

"Been busy, you know how it is."

They made their way to the kitchen and M began to prepare coffee. Jack eyed her speculatively.

"Have you lost weight?" he asked.

She knew he meant well so it didn't upset her, but M knew that the stress of the last few months with Adi had taken a toll. She'd noticed her pants getting looser. Evidently it was also obvious to others. "I've been at the gym and work has also been stressful, so I guess it shows. All good, though," she replied.

As they chatted over coffee, M realise that even though it had been a while since they had seen each other, the sexual chemistry was definitely still there. It was like an aura surrounding them. M enjoyed his charisma and welcomed their playful chitchat, as it was just what she needed right now. Some uncomplicated repartee. She noticed a gleam in his eye and decided to play on it to see what he would say in response.

"So … you had much action lately, or did I exhaust you that time?" she winked.

"Actually, you did exhaust me. But I liked it."

"I do aim to please," M smirked, feeling cheeky.

"Actually, I'm now managing a project in this area, so you might see me more often."

"Mmmm, that sounds like a plan," M replied with a grin.

"You know what? I think I owe you," he continued. "I should make *you* exhausted next time, don't you think?"

Before M had a chance to respond, he reached for her and kissed her passionately. She threw out all her inhibitions and met him full force, grabbing his shirt and pulling him even closer. They rose from their seats and came together as though their bodies were magnets. Slowly she unhooked his belt. He squeezed her buttocks in response, then went for the buttons on her blouse.

She pulled back and looked at him. "Let's go to the bedroom," she whispered.

And there they were again. Little Miss Confused about to embark on an escapade of hot sex with Mr Man Boy. While it felt strange to be with another man after all these months of thinking about Adi so obsessively, she realised it was definitely what she needed. All of her confusion dissolved in the moment, as her misery turned to ecstasy. He made sure of that. His touch ignited all her nerve endings. The longing and yearning were no more—it was all about this moment, *now*. She loved the feelings he gave her. She didn't care about the after.

They lay on the bed, he facing the ceiling with his hands behind his head, a smile on his face, and she looking at him.

"No spooning?" she asked, only half in jest.

He turned to her. "I've never really been the spooning type. I hope that doesn't bother you?"

"No, it's fine," said M. But suddenly it didn't seem that fine. While forty-five minutes ago she had been happy to engage in some afternoon delight with a handsome Man Boy, it now struck her how contradictory it was for two people to engage together in a moment of extreme intimacy, and then not feel compelled to wrap their arms around each other afterwards. Could men really separate the sex from the emotion so neatly? She had chosen to leap into this, eyes wide open, thinking she could go with the flow and not take it all too seriously, as before. But the feeling of void in the pit of her stomach told her something had changed.

This couldn't be further from an act of love, she thought to herself. *It's more like a love vacuum.*

She yearned for sex with real feelings, and all at once the idea of anything less seemed like it would never be enough. She wanted a real connection. Was it so wrong to want a little T-L-C to go with your S-E-X? She deserved that. She closed her eyes, consumed with the emptiness, and wondered how it was possible to sleep with someone and still feel so alone.

"Hey, you," Jack said, stroking her arm. "Are you okay? I hope I haven't made you feel bad?"

"It's not you," she said, knowing that *she* was more to blame for this than Jack. After all, his intentions had been crystal clear. There was no confusion there. It was M who had changed the script halfway through. "I just think maybe I'm getting too old for this," she said.

"There's nothing old about this gorgeous butt," he replied playfully, sliding his hand down to cup her cheek.

"Hey, buddy, stop right there," she smiled. "I'm serious. This was fun, *you* are fun. But I think I've just realised I need something *more*."

They lay sat silently for a moment, then Jack finally spoke. "Thanks for having me here, Max," and gently kissed her forehead before getting up.

"Anytime," M replied, even though they both knew there wouldn't be another time.

He pulled on his pants and buttoned his shirt, slinging his tie and jacket over his arm, then walked to the door. He paused for a second, then turned back to her. "For what it's worth, Maxine, a girl like you *deserves* more, if that's what you're ready for. Don't settle for less."

"Thank you, Jack," she smiled, as he closed the door behind him. And just like that, she knew she'd upped the ante on her romantic expectations and there was now no turning back.

M worked obsessively at her desk, completing a report that was due and doing the final preparations for a meeting with a potential client. Stressed to the gills (*all this hard work and I still might get the ass!*), the frenzy actually allowed for a welcome holiday from her obsessive thoughts about a certain person that she was trying to push out of her mind. She hadn't seen him in a couple of weeks and, although she missed him, it was a good thing to shift focus for now. And she had to admit, other than that, life was damn good. She was surrounded by friends, work was challenging but rewarding, her home was looking sensational …

and she'd just purchased a new pair of Louis Vuitton slingbacks at half price in an end-of-season sale.

An hour later, things were even better, as she reclined in her chair, basking in the afterglow of her meeting. It had gone down without a hitch—in fact, she thought she may even have kicked butt. But her quiet gloating was short-lived.

"Maxine, can you please come in for a moment," said Mr Ferguson, poking his head out of his office.

She felt her throat tighten. Was this it? Was she getting the axe? But her meeting had gone so well … perhaps he was going to complement her on the fine job she did on this latest project. Or maybe he just wanted a chitchat?

She entered slowly and smiled. He motioned for her to sit down.

"Hi!" she said, then wondered if that sounded a little overzealous. "Um, how are you?" she asked, trying to take the squeak out of her voice. She was hoping she wasn't as transparent as she felt—it wasn't like her to be this nervous.

"Good, Max, good. Listen, I just wanted to talk to you and give you an update on what is going on. Now, as you know there have been a few changes in various departments here. We spoke about a restructure and the possible downsizing," he explained, looking serious.

Stay calm, I'm not getting the axe, I'm not getting the axe, she chanted in her mind.

"Maxine, you have been invaluable to us here and we are like a family …"

Yay, I'm not getting the axe! I'm not getting the axe! her internal chant sang.

"… But a number of positions have been cut in your team and yours is unfortunately one of them."

Wait, wha?

"I tried to find another position for you, but I wasn't able to be. I'm sorry, Maxine. In four weeks your role will no longer exist," Mr Ferguson concluded, delivering the final thrust of his death blow.

Noooooo!

M's faced dropped and her heart pounded in her throat. She was speechless. The bomb had hit. Redundancy. That's extra salt on an open wound.

"I'm shocked," she finally croaked out. "I guess I never thought that it would be me. Although I knew the threat was there. But I didn't think it would be me. Shit." Her face was motionless.

"Maxine, don't think of this as the end. Think of it as a new beginning," Mr Ferguson said, trying to ease her pain. "I will give you the shiniest reference and you'll get a very decent redundancy package. I would highly recommend you to any firm. You will be okay … I know this will take time to sink in. It's not only you, there will be a few people getting this same message today."

No amount of consoling would help her at that moment. "I know this isn't your fault. I just need to get my head around it," M replied.

"Please take the rest of the day off. Come back tomorrow fresh," Mr Ferguson suggested. M smiled blankly, as she walked back to her desk, got her bag and walked out.

Who would have thought that her ludicrous little gag the other day would turn out to be correct. No man *and* no job. *I was only joking!* she wanted to scream at the universe, waving her fists about at the sky. *At least I didn't joke about losing my home as well*, she told herself mockingly.

She was plagued with frazzled nerves and wrought anxiety. How can life seem so breezy one moment and then, in a blink of an eye, change so much? She went from the known and familiar to the unknown and uncertainty. She felt low, unappreciated, dispensable. Talk about highs and lows.

Losing her job ripped a big gaping hole in her life and she didn't know *when, if* or *how long* it would take until she regained her security. *Here I am*, she thought to herself with self-pity, *thirty and jobless, with a case of crazy stupid love for a man who has no idea.* She reproached herself for not having grown the balls to tell him how she felt, as now—with unemployment on her personal profile—her sales pitch would be far less enticing.

At least there's one silver lining, thought M, sardonically. *My new Louis Vuitton slingbacks.* She considered donning the Vuittons for a much-needed power walk to burn off the excess anxiety that she was feeling, but instead opted for the more logical Nikes. She'd only been fired an hour ago. She wasn't going to go all *Gray Gardens* just yet.

She walked to the city's foreshore and the sun was shining, not a cloud in sight. The ocean water was crystal blue and the birds were singing. She spotted two people walked hand in hand down on the boardwalk, obviously deeply into each other. He was smiling and she was laughing. *Wow ... some people do have it all*, she thought, sourly, and kept walking.

Yet the fresh beach air was therapeutic and it didn't take much to rouse M out of her self-pity, forcing her to contemplate the bigger picture. Could, in fact, this all this be a sign? An opportunity for a clean slate? Clarity? Change happens whether we're ready for it or not, as she'd told Laura. Maybe this was M's time too.

And, let's face it, the past year had comprised one mini nightmare after another. Shamus The Shit and running off into the sunset with Tanya The Tramp, leaving her cuckolded. Falling head over heels for a man who remained so infuriatingly oblivious to her affections that it had her popping macaroons like beta blockers. And now the job thing. She'd worked ceaselessly crazy hours at the office—given her all to her work and put in so much—only to be the first one booted out the door. The mediocre workers got reshuffled into other departments, while she got the door slamming her on the ass. M sighed and just shook her head slightly and smiled. This was definitely a sign for change.

As she walked back to her car she stopped by a little café bar to grab a latte before she went home. Standing at the counter, waiting for her order, she heard a familiar voice and noticed a couple in the corner, talking closely. Then she did a double-take.

Adi.

She froze, paralysed. To see him with another woman made her heart leap into her throat. They looked relaxed … happy. All at once, she felt utterly betrayed. True, she and Adi were not a couple, nor had they ever discussed anything of the sort. True, she'd slept with Jack again, in her own attempt to move on (futile as it had been). So obviously he was a free agent—he could do what he wanted. Nevertheless, seeing him, the man she'd fallen head over heels for, with another woman was enough to make her burn with fury. Was she his girlfriend? Was she just a friend? The idea of her being *just a friend* somehow made M feel even more deceived, like he was having his cake and eating it too. A serial friendship monogammer on the prowl, seizing ambient opportunities to seduce his prey, make them fall in love with him, committing to no one, then moving on to the next coffee date.

Don't jump to conclusions! she reasoned with herself, feeling semi-hysterical. She knew she had no right to feel this way. But she couldn't help but feel jilted. Was he doing to this girl what he was doing to her? The thought made her stomach churn.

She didn't wait for her latte.

As soon as she got home she snapped on her rubber gloves and began scrubbing her bathroom–hard. She then proceeded to the kitchen where she emptied all the cupboards, scoured them with Ajax, then meticulously lined up her martini glasses and her champagne flutes. From there she attacked every nook and cranny of the couch with the vacuum tube, madly fluffy pillows as she went. She couldn't help but think how this would look to a fly on the wall ... like, a *psychiatrist* fly on the wall. She was well aware that it was a little nutty. But this was her therapy, and frankly it was cheaper than *actual* therapy. By cleansing her space, she cleansed her negative thoughts. It worked.

Once complete, her body was tired and her mind was a blissful void. Plus the house looked amazing! She went to the pantry and reached for the last macaroon, then bit into it with pleasure. *I really must stop eating macaroons*, she thought to herself. Then collapsed on the couch and fell asleep.

14

They walked together, hand in hand, on a secluded strip of blindingly white sand, surrounded by calm azure sea, as a string of palm trees danced in the balmy breeze. Their footprints left a double trail in the sand that stretched out behind them.

He turned to her and their eyes locked. "Maxine, you are a great girl," he said. "Always know that. I love spending time with you. There's something I've been wanting to tell you ..."

Her eyes widened in anticipation as he paused. Could this be the moment he tells her he loves her? She held her breath in suspense. Suddenly, clouds began to cover the sun and the sky turned grey, all within a matter of seconds. His face grew sombre.

"Max, I'm just not that into you."

Aaaaahhh!

M awoke suddenly in bed in a pool of sweat. She felt disorientated. "Fuck, it was only a dream," she murmured. It had felt so real. She tried to composed herself and took a sip of water before attempted to fall asleep again. But after what seemed like hours of tossing and turning, she got up before her alarm went off. Yet another restless night.

As she headed towards the shower, she realised that she felt like absolute shit. Between her horrendous nightmare and being hit by the retrenchment bus yesterday, she didn't know how she was going to face the day. She was depleted. She considered popping some Berocca, then washing it all down with a strong coffee, but then she got real. She rarely took a sick day, but she had to accept that she would be useless in the office today. Foggy, teary, tension headache, sore back from a restless night. She called in sick.

She was climbing back into bed when her iPhone chimed in a text message. Blurry-eyed, she picked up her phone to read it.

Hey, Max, how are you? Just getting myself ready for another business trip. I was wondering if you were free for a coffee. Can I swing by tomorrow evening? Adi x

Before she'd even processed the message, she tapped in "Sure xx" and hit reply.

Fuck.

All at once, her mind was a haze all over again. Did she reply too quickly? Did she sound too keen? Why did she type two x's when he only had one?! He hadn't contacted her for a while. Should she have playfully berated him for that?

Then a hot flush of jealousy rose to the surface as she recalled seeing him in the café with that woman. She wanted to hate him, or at least feel indifference. She wanted to switch off that crazy-lovesick-idiot button that was flashing madly inside of her. But she couldn't. Rather, a thousand tiny butterflies flapped their wings feverishly in unison in her belly, singing 'Because I'm happy!' in high-pitched Pharrell voices. She desperately yearned to see him. But the question was: why did he want to see her before his business trip when he hadn't contacted her in weeks?

M couldn't stop obsessing over it all day, like a scab that she couldn't stop picking, even though it was painful and festering. When it came to this man, she had lost all sense of control. It was bigger than her. She had never been in this predicament before or felt a connection this intense. She hated the fact that she was losing her power, and, even worse, that she was allowing him to take it away from her. Was this love or madness? Some would argue they're one and the same. She couldn't see through all the internal fog. By late afternoon, she felt like she was losing her mind. She needed some perspective.

"Hey, honey, how are you doing?" M said, when Laura answered the phone.

"Not a good day today, darling. I think I need some Belvedere time," Laura replied in a subdued voice.

"And here I thought you'd never ask! Come on over, girl," M said. "But before you do, let me ask you this. Why do men turn us into alcoholics?"

"Because being an alcoholic is the antidote to having an *assaholic* in your life!" Laura whipped back. "Sometimes I wonder how they get off so easily. Who knows, maybe we will have the last laugh."

"You think?" M asked.

"I hope so, because I'm not laughing now. I'll see you soon," Laura replied, then hung up.

'Belvedere time' was like a code red for the girls. Whenever one of them was in an intense situation and invoked it, whoever of the girls got the call would instantly come to the rescue … with the Belvedere Vodka. That was what was great about it. They were a team, with an unshakable bond between them–one that they knew would last a lifetime.

Laura arrived shortly after. M had prepared a feast–cheese platter, dips and rice balls. She had noticed that her appetite had been shrinking recently. The anxiety that gripped her was slowly taking away her basic ability to eat. She knew it was becoming a problem, but didn't want to let on to her friends.

"Okay, I know *I* called for the Belvederes, but I can see you're clearly struggling with something, M. Start from the beginning," Laura said as they settled on the couch. "Take a deep breath, take a sip of your medicine and relax," she said, nodding at M's freshly poured Belvedere and tonic. They both took a long sip.

"Laura, I'm losing it. I'm so consumed by thoughts of him … it scares me to death! I can't tell him how I feel, yet I can't stop feeling this way. I don't want to see him any more, yet I can't say no. He is coming over tomorrow for coffee. Why did I agree to that? I'm petrified. Do I talk to him? Do I tell him? I don't want to tell him. Yet I can't keep going like this. And I can't keep it in any longer! It's all been too fucking much. Him, losing my job, Shamus The Shit. Its been a crap year," M blurted, as tears welled up in her eyes. "Just look at me. And *you're* the one who called for the Belvederes." They both laughed and sipped again.

"Babe, I have watched you and I have seen the way you've been losing weight, the rings around your eyes. You're not acting like yourself. You have been like this for months and it's not good. Look at what it's doing to you. You have nothing to be distressed about. You are an amazing person. Don't let this get to you. You are better than this. You will get another job. And, as for him, *tell him* how you feel. And, guess what? If he can't see how great you are then he can *get fucked!*" Laura said, and once again they both laughed, now through a few stray tears.

They took another sip. Belvedere therapy.

"I don't know how I got to this place," said M. "I know it's not me. It's bigger than me, and it's not something I wanted to feel. I'm perfectly fine one second, then this wave of emotion comes over me. I could be at the shops or in the car or wherever. When it comes, I try to change my focus. It works for a while, but then it just comes back. Why the hell can't I stop thinking about him?"

"Okay, hold that thought. We need to turn up the IV drips. Let's have a shot before speaking any further," Laura said.

M got up for the shot glasses and the vodka, and Laura did the pouring, then they both slammed one back.

"Wow, that sure did it," M said, with an involuntary twitch.

"Wait–another, please," Laura replied, pouring them two more. Those were taken just as quickly.

"M, honey, you're lovesick. You can't get him out of your mind. Look at you: you're anxious, you can't eat properly, you can't sleep. Christ, I remember when I went through it! You got it bad, girlfriend … I mean, how often do we find a core-shaker? Maybe he's yours for now."

"Gee, if this *is* love, it kinda sucks," M replied moodily.

"Yep, it sure does. One minute you're all fine and love reigns supreme, the next it flies away into the arms of another woman."

"I hear ya," M saluted, and they clinked glasses and sipped their drinks again.

"I mean, for Christ's sake, she's twelve years his junior. How long is he possibly going to sustain that one for?" said Laura, letting loose. "It's all nice and fun now, but she will leave him for a younger guy once she discovers that he is old and she wants more. The prick will get what he deserves."

"What the hell?" said M, stunned. "You're saying there was another woman all along? That's why he left? Oh, honey." M put her arm around her friend.

"They're all fuckers," said Laura, as she poured the next round of shots. "I read his emails," she volunteered, reading M's expression. "That's how I found out. He didn't even have the decency to confess. And, *man*, does it all make sense now."

"I can't imagine what you're feeling right now, sweetheart. Well, actually I can. Although I know what I went through doesn't compare to a marriage breakdown. But what I can tell you is that once the fog clears, and it will, you'll be thankful you found out he's a cheater when you did. And once you're ready, you'll meet someone who truly and sincerely loves you and deserves. I know you don't see that now. But we have to take the cards life deals us. And in the meantime, you have us, you know that."

"I know, I know. And you're one to talk! You need to take a dose of your own advice, lady," she smirked momentarily, then her face dropped again. "Nights are hardest. The house is empty. I'm left to pick up the pieces and at first I didn't know where to start. I do still miss him. It makes no sense! I'm furious and could punch him for betraying our marriage." Laura grabbed a cracker and began to nibble.

"It does make sense. He was a big part of your life for so many years. I think you are brave and amazing. This too shall pass. You're doing the right thing. Small steps, sweetie. No rush. You have your independence back now and you can do what you want. Just think—you don't have to wash his dirty underwear."

"I'm living skiddy free!"

They both laughed and M poured them more Belvedere injections. They continued to chat, drink and eat, working their therapy on one another as only true friends can. At least they could forget about it all for a night. As they finished up their meal, M turned to Laura.

"So where to from here?"

"I have to admit to myself that it is really over. I have a new journey ahead. Even though I haven't figured it out yet. I guess for now I want to go with the flow," she said solemnly. Then she looked her friend deep in the eyes. "But as for you, I think you should take a chance and tell him how you feel, and then—whatever the outcome—accept the consequences. Be true to yourself. You will look back and regret it if you don't. If it doesn't work out, at least you can walk away knowing you did all that you could, with no 'what ifs'." Laura paused, as though weighing up her next sentence. "Maxine," she said, "what are you afraid of?"

M paused for a moment. "Of opening up again and letting my guard down … of exposing my heart. Could I go through it all again? Another heartbreak? Another betrayal? I'm not sure there is enough needle and thread to stitch that up again," she paused to reflex. "On the other hand, I could just totally embarrass the crap out of myself by confessing I'm in love with him!" she laughed. "Especially if he's actually seeing someone else."

"The heartbreak, I get. But does that mean we never take another chance?" said Laura. "Yet, embarrassment? Come on, Maxine, when have you ever been afraid to put yourself out there, especially when the rewards could be so great?"

"Okay, I guess you're right. I guess I could take it on the chin. But losing the friendship we've got—"

"What friendship?" she cut in. "You may hang out, but the dynamic you have, this constant torture of unrequited love, doesn't seem to even remotely resemble the comfort and honesty of friendship. It seems more like a prison." Laura was playing hardball.

"I know, I know," said M, starting to feel emotional. "But I'm afraid that once I tell him, it will pop the bubble to hear that he doesn't feel the same way."

"Isn't it better to know than to live in a state of suspended animation for the rest of your life? Is that what really scares you?"

Suddenly the floodgates opened and M crumbled over in tears. "I'm scared he'll love me! Truly love me! And I'll love him too ... then five years from now I'll discover a pair of knickers stuffed in his coat pocket and realise he's been screwing Angelina Jolie!"

As soon as the words popped out, they both burst into hysterical laughter. Laura wrapped her arms around her friend and they laughed and laughed, and cried and cried. "I get it. I do.

That Shamus The Shit really took a big dump on your heart. I get that. *Man*, do I get that. But we're stronger than that, right? Are we seriously going to let our lives come to a grinding halt because our shitty choices in men lead to lying, cheating assholes in our lives?"

"Assaholics!" giggled M. "Wait, if they're the assholes, does that mean that *we're* the assaholics?" They laughed again.

"Halleluiah to that, sister!" and they toasted another shot.

They both went quiet for a moment, then Laura sighed. "Maxine, be strong. Talk to him. Set yourself free."

Laura always knew the right thing to say. She cut to the bone but she spoke the truth and M felt reassured and comforted. "You're right, I have to get free again. I have to tell him the truth. It's the only way to put this thing to rest and move on. If he feels the same way, he'll say it. If not, well … then I will know. As much as it would kill me to know that all hope is gone. And if he *does* love me, if he *does* sweep me off my feet … then cheats on me–"

"Don't worry, honey," interjected Laura. "The girls and I will put in and we'll hire a fucking hit man!"

They both laughed again, as M's eyes welled up with a fresh round of tears. Laura held her. "But let's not jump ahead of ourselves, it may not come to murder," she smirked. "Talk to him. Then let's just wait and see what happens. Babe, these kinds of situations are never simple. Especially when it's a lover/friend thing, or should I say a friend *thang*," she winked. "Sometimes there are no winners. But don't hurt yourself any more. I think if he knew how this was hurting you and what it has done to you, he would be upset. He wouldn't want you to be in pain," Laura consoled.

"I'll do it," M said. "But not yet. I just need the right time."

"Look at what they do to us, M," Laura said, suddenly angry and a tad slurry. "I was *happy* with James. We did everything together! No one knows him like I do … Well, I thought I did, anyway. Of course we went through highs and lows, but every couple does, right? And then, snap! He just leaves. Lead by his dick. Did he even consider everything he was throwing away?"

"I know, sweetie, I know," said M, hearing the slight slur in her own voice and realising it was probably about time to put away the Belvedere.

"The thing is, Max," continued Laura, "you're worked up over some douchebag who's sending you mixed signal. What the fuck for? Men are all the same! My husband has *left* me, and here you have the hots for some guy but you're scared to tell him how you feel. That's high school crap! What James and I had was *real. A marriage*. He bloody well knew how I felt about him!"

M listened silently as Laura unleashed her emotions and let it all flow. She knew how important it was for her to let out all her anger and pain, even though some of it was the alcohol talking, and even though M had somehow ended up in the firing line. Still, Laura's comments upset her, as she knew there was an element of truth in there.

"I know, I know," said M, trying to be soothing, while also feeling the bite of her words. "You and James had a life commitment." She paused, suddenly feeling confused all over again. She was a thirty-year-old woman with a teenage crush.

But they'd both had too much to drink, and one more word along these lines could land them in an argument. So she announced jovially that it was time to call it a night. She was in no mood to argue, nor had any emotional energy for that matter. The last thing she wanted to do was attack Laura.

"Honey, I think you should stay here tonight and sleep it off. We are done with the boy talk for the night." M stood and held her hand out to her friend. Laura nodded and allowed herself to be led to the spare bedroom.

"Don't expect princes and white horses, M," Laura said in a more subdued manner. "If you tell him you love him and he doesn't say he loves you too, *leave immediately*. They're not worth hanging around for."

M took Laura's shoes off as she collapsed back onto the bed. She made sure she had some water and a bucket near the bedside, then shut the door with a sigh. She knew that Laura, as drunk as she was, was absolutely right.

15

M awoke, seemingly moments later, with a jackhammer in her head and her belt buckle pinching into her. She didn't even remember putting herself to bed, which had clearly involved collapsing in a heap, fully dressed. Her head thumped louder as she sat up. How many drinks had they had last night?

After a long shower and a double espresso, she felt a bit more human and ready to start the day. She looked at herself in the mirror. "I can handle this," she said to her reflection. "I'm a strong woman. I can take what comes my way. This too shall pass. Maxine, you are fabulous. If he can't see that, then fuck him. There *are* plenty of fish in the sea, and you are worthy of love. Don't settle for less."

"That's a pretty perky pep talk you just gave yourself there. Can I have one?" Laura said, leaning against M's bedroom door.

"Shit, you scared me! Good morning. I thought you would sleep in longer."

"No, I'm okay, actually. I have a headache, but nothing that eggs Florentine can't cure. Thanks for letting me stay. I really appreciate it, and I'm glad we got to hang out. You're really one of the best people I know. And I know that you will be fine and get through this, too. If not, we can just run away together. Live in an ashram in India."

"You know what? That doesn't sound bad at all. I've always wanted to move to Europe." They both laughed.

"Seriously though," continued M. "If Julia Roberts can do it, why can't we? Let's keep it as a thought. On our 'to do' list, maybe?"

M's focus improve as the day unfolded, although as the evening drew close, she grew nervous. She had never been so nervous about seeing Adi, while at the same time, she couldn't wait. She knew she would tell him tonight, if the right moment presented itself, and it filled her with both excitement and terror. She felt like a clock was ticking in the background.

"Hey ya," he smiled, when the moment finally arrived and he stepped through her front door.

"Well, hey yourself," she said. They kissed cheeks and she led him to the kitchen.

"Mmm, homemade pie! It looks delicious. Did you make it?"

"Well, I'm a domestic goddess, you know," she smirked.

It was nice to have her efforts noticed. She hoped it added a tick in his 'I love Maxine' file—if, indeed, he had one. The more she showcased her many talents, the more he would think she was wonderful, right? She cut them each a slice, then poured the coffee and sat down. He took a bite and leaned back, sighing.

"Oh, Max, this is brilliant stuff. You are a superstar."

She grinned. Surely the way to a man's heart was still through his stomach.

Adi told her about his upcoming trip and the stress he felt over some of his pending deadlines. He'd already told her that he was in transition at his job and was in a bit of a dilemma about what to do. Stay or go? She noticed that he seemed a little reserved and quite frankly a little down. It was as though there were something else on his mind and she wondered if work was the only thing troubling him. He was in a weird place, M could see, which made her think it wasn't the right time to confess her feelings to him tonight. It could ruin everything between them, simply because the timing was off. This made her feel both relieved and disappointed to acknowledge. However, she did at least feel she could offer him some sound advice about his work situation, an area she had far more confidence in.

"Just wait until this project is over. See it through until the end of the year. Then assess all your options, especially your finances. Speak to your boss, let him know how you feel and ask for a pay rise. Why shouldn't you? You work so hard. I hope he appreciates all you do for that company."

"You're so right. I guess I'm just at that uncertain stage, you know. Things are pretty good, but you want fulfilment and something more. You know sometimes when you are stuck between a rock and a hard place? Well, it's been like that for a while, I know what I can do but ... I guess maybe all of this is of my own making."

M felt hesitant and somewhat confused. Was he talking about work, or a personal situation? She really wanted to know who the girl was the other day when she was getting coffee. But she knew it was absolutely none of her business to ask, not to mention the fact that it would be somewhat embarrassing to confess that she'd seen him that day but hadn't said hello. "Always go within and listen to your gut. You will know what to do," M said giving some fresh perspective. She needed some herself.

"Thanks for understanding. I love how I can always talk to you." Then he paused, like there was something else he needed to tell her. He smiled nervously, making her heart beat faster, staring deeply into her eyes. Suddenly the world went silent as the moment seemed to stretch out, frozen in time.

Finally, Adi broke is gaze. "Well, time to fly, I'm afraid," he said, standing.

Fuck! thought M. *I should have told him. That was the moment.* But instead she said, "Thanks for stopping by," hearing the quiver in her voice. "We'll catch up when you get home," she said, walking him to the front door.

"Of course we will," he replied.

They embraced again. He smelled so good, she didn't want to let go.

And then something strange happened. She felt his face turning towards hers, the sensual rasp of his light stubble brush against her cheek, teasing out goosebumps uncontrollably to the surface of her skin, as his lips sought out hers and he kissed her— and not in a we're-just-mates way, either. Intensely, passionately, he seemed to drink her in and she could *feel* it ... she could *feel* his love for her.

As they gently released, he stared deeply into her eyes. "I will see you soon, yeah?"

"Of course," she whispered softly, utterly confounded. "Have a safe trip."

Once she closed the door behind him as he left, she wasn't sure if she was going to scream or melt into a puddle on the floorboards. *Why, why, why did he do that?* implored a voice in her head. She wasn't even entirely sure if she was elated or furious. Friends don't kiss like that. Did this mean she was more to him than that? The mixed messages he sent had created a molotov cocktail of emotion–which was ready to explode in her face at any second. "Oh Jesus, I'm in serious trouble!" she said out loud. The handsome bastard had her under his spell once again. That kiss– *that kiss!*–had totally screwed with her mind, and all the progress she felt she'd made flew right out the window. She was strong and empowered one minute, and then a limp rag the next.

Her confusion had leapt to new heights and, like it or not, she knew she had to have 'the conversation' with him when he got back. No question about it. It was better to try and fail than to live in this state of constant chaos and unknowing. His words and behaviour said two different things, which frustrated her beyond belief. He never alluded to the fact that there was more developing between them, but his actions sang another tune. Was it a game to him? Frustrated and angry, she muttered under her breath. "If this a game to you, I refuse to play."

Or maybe, just maybe, *he* was falling in love with *her* …

16

"So I'm lying here relaxing in the bath," said Laura, "and I'm reading something insightful that I just knew I should share with you."

"Oh? Do tell!" M said curiously. She'd just got home from a late meeting and was in the mood for a glass of wine and a juicy chat with a friend.

"Well, first I should fill you in a bit. I've been having anxiety attacks–you know, disorientation, tight chest, shallow breathing, jitters–the works. So I made an appointment and went in for a counselling session. It helped, I think. I saw a doctor who gave me a listening ear and some good advice. He says that emotional stress is taking a toll physically and mentally. He said that dealing with strong emotions is difficult, but that it will make me stronger in the end. He gave me a few tips and ideas on how to go about it."

"That's good advice. I'm really glad you took the initiative and went to see someone, hon. I'm proud of you for that. What else did he say?"

"That I should do things to clear my mind, relax and feel happy. So here I am in the bathtub following instructions," Laura chuckled. "And I'm reading this fascinating book. Did you know that when adrenaline is activated, it stimulates the desire for reward and intense pleasure? Apparently it's like cocaine."

"Um … very informative. I didn't know that. What on earth are you reading, Laura? *Fifty Shades of Grey?*"

"Not quite!" she laughed. "It's from a self-help book I picked up from the library the other day—stuff on love and stress and the whole shebang."

"Does that mean Adi is my cocaine? Is that why I'm addicted?" she couldn't resist asking.

"Pretty much," she replied, and M could feel her smiling down the phone line.

"So why the sudden reading binge?"

"I guess I'm just trying to stop asking myself all the 'whys' and the 'what ifs'. The books say there's a reason for it all. I'm trying understand it all … For instance, check this out," she said as she proceeded to read from the book. "A person can give special meaning. You focus your attention on this person and you have intense energy. You feel elation when things are good and despair when things aren't going good. Dependence is on this person. The motor in the brain cranks up. Romantic love isn't an emotion but a drive. It comes in the engine of the mind, specifically in the wanting and the craving part of the mind. It holds more power than sex drive," she read, flicking the page.

"There is a reason, Laura. For all of it. No one ever marries thinking they are going to break up, but look how many people it happens to. It's a bitter pill to swallow, that's for sure, but we have to have faith. It's hard, I know," M said, trying to comfort her friend, but aware that she hadn't been very good at practising what she preached—that is, telling a man how she feels and being able to cut ties emotionally.

"I think the help and advice will definitely be good for me. The pain just got to be too much," Laura said.

"That sucks to hear, but good for you for empowering yourself. I'm proud of you. That's what those books are there for—to help. You need to feel good and to put yourself first," M said.

"I'm going to continue to see a counsellor. I think it will be good for me," Laura continued.

"I'm glad you are taking this step. You will be surprised by how beneficial it will be to do that … you're going to be okay, you'll see. Be patient with yourself and kind," M said.

"And you? Have you heard from your cocaine?" Laura asked.

"No, not since he left for his business trip," said M. She'd spilled the beans to Laura about the whole confusing goodbye, leaving Laura just as confounded. "It'd be nice if he called so I'd have some clue as to what's going on. I feel like an idiot. What am I supposed to be feeling right now? Missing him? Looking forward do his return? Or was that a goodbye-forever kiss? I'm clueless! God, life seemed to friggen complicated when we were eighteen, but I reflect back on those years now and want to tell that naïve idiot, *Enjoy your stress-free life while you can, girlfriend! It only gets MORE complicated!* Anyway, enough of that shit. Why are we always obsessing about *them*?"

"I know, totally," said Laura. "I wish we could just take off and get out of here. Escape the dramas. New beginnings for both of us. But, hey, maybe that's just me. The jury is still out for you. You could be with your guy very soon. Watch this space."

"I don't know," M replied. "That first option doesn't sound bad at all, if you ask me. You know what, Laura? All we women do is bleed for love. We suffer for it. I know this sounds terrible, but in some ways maybe we really are the weaker sex ... well, at least emotionally."

"Enough!" Laura laughed. "Enough 'love' crap for one day. Deal? I'm going to continue my bath, and you continue being your fabulous self. Okay?"

"Deal. Enjoy it, my dear. I'll speak to you later on."

M hung up and, curious, did some research of her own. Googling, she discovered heaps of websites with information on the link between the brain, stress, love, the emotions and how our bodies function. Neurotransmitters in the brain activate adrenaline, she learned, make the heart beat faster (this sure sounded familiar!) and increased the cortisol level in your blood. Sure enough, she read: "Adrenaline stimulates desire by triggering an intense rush of pleasure, much like cocaine."

Interesting stuff, but nothing really struck a chord with her until she came upon the subject of attachment. *That* resonated. Apparently women in particular had the innate ability to become attached–specifically, during sexual intercourse and orgasm (*oh great*). A chemical called oxytocin releases during this time, which allows women to feel closer to their partners. So the more sex women had, the more oxytocin was released and the closer they felt. This, it seemed to M, explained why women became attached more easily than men did after intimacy, maybe even why women viewed sex as something more than the physical act itself. If this was part of women's biochemistry, no wonder they read more into things than men did.

She continued to scroll. Dopamine was another chemical that created an intense energy and motivation to win. It made you bold and willing to take risks–perhaps in love? That was why people talked about losing it when they fell in love. It made you willing to climb mountains or whatever it took.

"Fuck dopamine," M muttered at her computer screen. "It ain't helping."

At this point in time, scientific explanations didn't mean much anyway. She was lovesick, plain and simple, no matter what brain chemicals were causing it. Ruefully, she thought about all those misleading and deceptive movies that led women to believe in the fairytale ending with the knight in shining armour on the white horse (or Richard Gere in a white limousine) who would save the day and then ride off into the sunset with the beautiful princess. Yeah, maybe that was a way to escape the harsh realities of life for a while, but the movies didn't tell you what happened when the white knight didn't show up. Or showed up and then left with another princess. Or, case in point, showed up and swept the princess off her feet … then left her on her balcony feeling awkward as she waiting endlessly for the knight to call her for a coffee catch-up once he got back from his business trip.

Who didn't want their very own white knight to find them and tell them, "You're the one"? But what happened when love didn't conquer all? It appeared that you could blame, at least in part, biochemistry.

While this new understanding wasn't the magical antidote, it did bring M some clarity, and she actually started to feel better physically. This led to a rush of energy and the desire to go out and do something. She was determined to surround herself with positive things and good people, and she knew that friends and a bit of shopping would be the best medicine.

She had just grabbed her bag and keys when the phone rang. She glanced at the screen.

Adi!

"Hey, M, how are you?"

Her heart opened like a flower. "You're home? That's early," she said.

"Yeah, a few meetings were cancelled so there was no point in hanging around. I have so much work to do back here, so I got an earlier flight. Hey, listen. Is it okay if we catch up tomorrow for coffee? I need to talk to you."

Not another fucking coffee! After that kiss? Not dinner? Not fine wine? Not a weekend getaway to a B&B on the Great Ocean Road?

Involuntarily, her heart began to race. She supposed it was that rush of oxytocin or dopamine surging through her veins. It may as well have been crystal-fucking-meth for all the good it was doing her. Her head screamed, *Stop, stop, stop! For fuck's sake, just stop!* But her mouth said, "Sure, sounds good. Swing by around about eight tomorrow night, okay?"

"Great. See you then."

She hung up the phone and took a few deep breaths. This was it. It *had to be it*. *He* had asked to talk to *her* … could it be about 'them'? Although, his tone was weird, enigmatic more than optimistic. Yet if that wasn't why he wanted to talk, should *she talk to him?* Was it worth going in with guns blazing, telling him exactly how she felt and risking everything? To clear the air and start afresh? But, hell, what if that meant losing the great friendship they'd already built? Just the thought of not seeing his face and hearing his voice hurt. Not to mention being forced to give up the fantasy of the possibility. But she also had to be honest with herself. It wasn't just the fear of rejection that held her back. It was the fear of *acceptance*–falling in love again, opening herself up to possible betrayal. Either way, it had to be done. She had to tell him and set herself free for her own health and sanity.

M scooped up her bag again and headed for the door. She had to get out of the house, now more than before, and she'd arranged to meet Elisha. She needed the distraction, and if there was one thing that could take her mind off things, it was shopping. It ignited all her senses and definitely made her feel good. Well, maybe not so much her hip pocket, but nevertheless, it was one thing that would always get her out of a funk, so right now it was worth a little splurge. Besides, she reasoned, if she was about to have her heart broken, she should be looking fucking hot for the occasion. It would be her consolation prize. She'd prepare for the possible fallout with a cupboard full of macaroons, a bottle of vodka in the freezer and a sexy new pair of Manolo Blahniks. This handsome bastard had captured her heart, so if he was going to break it, he could at least see what he'd be missing.

"I just don't get it!" Elisha said, as they sat in the food court for a coffee break mid-shop. "Jackson and I have been going out for months now. Our dates are like ten hours long. We chat and laugh and have a really good time. Then kaput. Cold. No call back, no text. What the hell? What goes wrong? Prick."

"Maybe it's the commitment thing," M suggested. "He's scared to get too close and admit he has real feelings for you."

"But I *never* allude to all that stuff. We just go out and have a good time! I don't understand how you can just switch hot one second, then cold the next without explanation."

"Maybe it's *because* you don't mention it? Shit, I don't know, babe. We are like the blind leading the blind. I don't understand them, either. Men are fucked. Are you only just becoming aware of this now?" M teased gently. "I think they do taste tests. Maybe he's had a few dates on the side and thinks he's keeping his options open. Or maybe he keeps chickening out because he really likes you and doesn't know how to go about telling you. Men mature later than women, remember that."

"Yeah, tell me about it. Sometimes I think they never mature at all! Why can't he just be honest and tell me what's going on with him? It would save all the analysing and wondering. I tell you, I'm going to let him have a piece of my mind whenever he does ring next. I'm *so* over this."

Hearing Elisha spill her guts, M decided to come clean herself. "Adi wants to catch up tomorrow night. He says he needs to talk to me," she began.

"Really? That's great. I hope he gives you all the answers you need so you can lay this to rest, whatever the outcome. The stress of it all has already cost you."

"Yeah, maybe. I don't know. I shouldn't worry about it, but I am. Maybe it's partly the anticipation, too. What will be will be, though, right?"

"We are all behind you. We love you and support you. Let the universe do its job and just go with whatever it gives you. Whatever happens, it will be for the best." Elisha hugged her. That night M lay in bed, her mind awash with the fear of the confrontation. She tried to concentrate on Elisha's reassurances, but she was so afraid of what happened when you loved someone and they didn't love you back. Where did all that love go? She fell asleep praying for guidance, strength and peace.

17

M felt a mélange of emotions as she waited for Adi's visit: excited and nervous, frightened and elated, horny and furious—all at the same time! When the doorbell finally rang at eight p.m., she took a deep breath and opened the door.

"Hi, beautiful, how are ya?" he said. Damn he looked good. His smile was all teeth and boyish charm, and that alone swept her away. His strong arms wrapped around her firmly as they hugged hello.

"I'm good!" If only he knew. "Come on in." M offered him coffee, but he declined. That was a first. He looked tired and a bit preoccupied. They settled on the couch. "So, how was London?" she asked.

"Nice, but cold as usual, and the seminar was pretty intense. I was kind of glad when he meetings were cancelled. How has work been for you?"

She filled him in on a few projects, but avoiding telling him about the retrenchment. Now was not the time to open up that doozy—plus, she didn't want to risk distracting him from the point of his visit. He listened attentively, but she sensed that he was on edge. A little off, not his usual self. Maybe he was just jet-lagged from the trip.

"So, hey, at least you got to have a few pints at the local pub while you were gone, right? Surely you can't go to the UK and not have a drink or two at a pub," she teased, trying to take the edge off.

"Yeah. Yeah, I did … I caught up with my mate—you know, the friend whose wedding I went to? We caught up for a beer or two. But, other than that, I didn't get out much." He paused, seemingly searching for the right words. "M, there is something I have been meaning to talk to you about," he said abruptly.

There it was. The words she'd been both dreading and hoping for. The sentence that signals the beginning of The Chat.

"Sure, what about?" she replied, hoping to God she sounded more collected than she felt. Her heart was belting out a rumba in her chest.

"I just wanted to talk to you about how we have been hanging out and stuff. You're a good friend, yeah … I mean, it's a great friendship we've got going. I wanted to say, I'm sorry if I have given you the wrong impression, especially since we've been back from Prague, I mean with the kissing thing and how I have been acting towards you lately. I want you to know that I find you attractive and lovely and what we had going was amazing. But … well, I don't want to be the one that hurts you further down the line. I think we should just be friends. I'm sorry."

M's heart sank.

He was clearly struggling for words, and this was hard for him to say. But there it was, out in the open at last. It took all her restraint not to burst into tears.

"Adi, really … you don't need to worry. It's fine. It's okay. I mean, I totally get it. I enjoy your company and we should be able to hang out when we want," she began, trying to save him any discomfort. But then she reminded herself—he *had* made passionate love to her. Quite a number of times, in fact, in Prague. And then he'd proceeded to kiss her—*passionately*—on a couple of occasions back in Melbourne.

Suddenly she felt a little spark of fury.

"It's just that, I just … I think you probably shouldn't *sleep* with women or kiss them if you don't feel that way, you know. It just saves awkward conversations like this later," she managed to articulate.

"Um, yeah," he mumbled, at least having the manners to look a little ashamed. "You're great company and a great person, M, and I want to keep hanging out … I just didn't want you to think—"

"You don't need to explain yourself to me. I'm not stupid," she interrupted.

"I know you're not," he replied.

"What do you want, exactly?" M asked matter-of-factly. "From me?"

"I want us to enjoy each other's company and be as we are—as we have been. No worries about, you know … *stuff*."

"Okay," she agreed, stiffly, knowing she'd regret it later if she slammed the door in his face in a moment of enflamed disappointment. "Sounds like a plan. But don't think you can have your cake and eat it, too. It doesn't work like that. It's not fair to the other person," she said, trying to sound firm while her insides were exploding like a volcano.

"I would never do that to you, M. You don't deserve that," he said earnestly.

You have already done that to me! she wanted to scream.

But there it was—the very thing she hadn't wanted to hear had just been said to her. He was attracted to her, he loved hanging out with her ... but, apparently, just not enough to want a relationship with her. Then why *did* he want to be with her? Just for the female companionship until the next *real* girlfriend came along? And if that didn't work out, would he could come back and 'hang' with her again? Was she just a filler—someone to help him with his fashion choices and watch *Offspring* with—until the 'full package' came along for him? She was worth more than that.

Inwardly, she was crushed, but she worked to display an outward façade of nonchalance. The last thing she wanted was to be forced into admitting she'd had deeper feelings for him.

Lord help me! she thought in anxiety-riddled relief, *I was just about to declare my love to him!* She thanked the heavens that she hadn't. She refused to lose any more power to him, even though it tore her up inside.

As soon as Adi left, M collapsed onto the couch and let the tears streamed down her cheeks. *What was I thinking, anyway?* she thought to herself. *I'm such a fool.* She replayed every hug, every kiss, every meeting over and over in her mind, looking for clues as to how she could have deceived herself so badly. *Was it all in my own imagination?*

M wondered if she would actually be able to remain friends with him. Would she ever be able to brush her yearning and attraction for him aside and see him purely as a friend? It didn't seem likely. Yet if she didn't, it would mean never seeing him again, and the very thought brought fresh pangs of pain.

She cried so hard that her tears ran out, then a little voice spoke softly, but sincerely, deep inside of her.

Let go, M. Just ... let ... go.

She awoke with a crick in her neck from sleeping on the couch. As she came back into the living room, after splashing some cool water on her face, the phone rang. "Hello?" she said, her eyes not quite able to focus on the caller ID through puffy eyes.

"What happened, M? How did it go?"

It was Caroline. Ever since their catch up, M had kept her in the loop of the whole Adi saga. In yesterday's anticipation, she'd texted Caroline to let her know Adi was coming over with something pressing he needed to discuss.

"Well ... it was The Chat. It was the sorry-I-gave-you-the-wrong-impression-with-the-whole-kissing-and-shagging-thing chat. Blah, blah, fucking, blah. There you have it. It's done," M said flatly.

"I'm sorry, honey. I know you wanted and hoped for more. There's something better for you out there, you just wait."

"Well, what was I expecting anyway? I hate blurred lines. I guess now it's all crystal clear, hey? I'm such a dreamer."

"You are *not* a dreamer. At least not in a bad way. There is nothing wrong with having feelings and wanting intimacy and love from someone. We are human. We are women. We love and care and nurture–it's who we're designed to be. Don't beat yourself up for wanting something, sweetie. It wasn't meant to be with him. And now you're free to meet someone who will give you that all you desire, someone who truly wants to be with you, without these complications. You deserve that, and you *will* get it. This guy just missed a chance for something really great. His loss, not yours."

"Oh, Caz, thank you. That was a beautiful thing to say. I just have to push through this and nurture myself. I'll get there. I still care about him, of course, and since he still wants to be friends, I'll just enjoy that for what it is," M said, trying to sound convincing.

"Really?" said Caroline, sounding concerned. "Well, build that wall, M, and don't let him in. Keep the lines unblurred," Caroline said firmly. "Be cautious because I know it would be easy to keep living in that hope. But you have to protect your heart."

This was tough love, but M knew Caroline had a point. Besides, when someone offered you that kind of honesty, even when it hurt to hear it, you knew they really loved you. She felt Caroline's support around her like a blanket, which meant a lot to her.

"I will, I promise," she assured her friend.

In the wake of such a deep disappointment, M felt the walls she'd built to block out her past begin to crumble. She didn't go here often, but she allowed herself to remember Michael. He'd been her first big love, back when she was nineteen. They met through their network of friends. She remembered them waiting in line together at a popular club, holding hands and kissing. She'd felt so grown up–the world her oyster. They enjoyed nights out … and nights in, she thought, recalling her very first time. What a night. Having entered serious-relationship territory and encountered true love, it seemed that the sun was shining every day for them and nothing could go wrong. Then many months into their relationship, when she'd given him everything–her heart, her body, her soul–he told her he that he couldn't get 'too serious' as he was too young to be tied down. She was crushed.

It was the last time that she'd felt anything similar to the waves of sadness and disappointment that washed over her now.

After she finally got over Michael, things had seemed easier during her twenties. She stopped taking things so personally. She would date and try her luck with a guy, and if it didn't work out, the disappointment would dissipate quickly and she'd be into someone new. Were things so much easier then because she'd known she was young and it felt like she had all the time in the world? She tried to remember how she'd mentally gotten over each break-up and carried on meeting other guys and dating. Did women take things more personally as they got older? Was rejection simply more painful?

M decided suddenly that she needed to get away–perhaps go to one of those health club retreats that everyone raved about. Every magazine had articles on them. How you loose pounds, learn new chill-out techniques and eat nourishing superfoods. Maybe this was what she needed to reboot her life and do something for herself, to patch up the holes in her soul that had been ripped open when the man of her dreams–the man she had made crazy, mad, passionate love with–told her he just wants to be *friends*.

Douchebag.

She looked up some websites and begun to investigate. With so many incredible options–organic fruit detoxes in Thailand, hot-rock chakra realignments in Noosa, yoga and meditation retreats among the rice paddies of Bali, private mineral baths and seaweed body wraps in Daylesford–the next challenge was in deciding where to go. Although the options looked luxurious, she told herself she should be cash conscious, since, to be frank, she'd just lost her job.

She'd heard about a silent meditation workshop an hour away that was purely donation-based. The timetable boasted four a.m. gong wake-up calls for the dawn meditation, a vegan semi-fasting menu of breakfast and lunch, with nothing but hot lemon water after noon, lights out at nine p.m, and strictly no talking for the entire duration. *This*, she thought to herself, *looks like the kind of spiritual escape I need to totally reboot my system.*

Until, that was, she clapped eyes on an award-winning pampering Sunrise Spa Retreat located in the Byron Bay Hinterlands and thought, *Silent mediation and fasting? What the hell was I thinking?!* Voted one of the best retreats in Australia, it also had one of the heftiest price tags, but it didn't take much arm twisting for M to quickly reason with herself that with her hefty retrenchment package, there was absolutely no reason why she shouldn't splash out. *Like I haven't suffered enough lately?!*, she thought to herself as she clicked out of the silent meditation site.

If ever there'd been a time that she needed to fully invest in her physical–and emotional–health, now was the time.

She was ready to escape it all, if only for a week. But it would be a week, according to the website spiel, of pure bliss. As she clicked 'book', she felt a surge of excitement. A whole week of no phone, no friends ... and no obsessing about Adi. Disturbingly, there was also no coffee, which she thought was going to be the hardest thing to conquer. But this was all about conquering. The thought of detaching from coffee left a lot to be desired but she figured that if she could do that then she could really do anything. There would be no time for thinking, no stressing; it would be time, purely, to invest in herself and just let go.

It was time to have her *Eat, Pray, Love* moment. She would definitely eat (the vegetarian buffet looked incredible); she would definitely pray (the retreat had six a.m. meditation sessions every morning).

But, she thought gloomily to herself, *when will I love?*

18

Adi had imagined that after talking to Max, after telling her that he was sorry about what had happened, he'd feel better; relieved. But what he felt was the opposite.

The talk hadn't gone well–for either of them. He was gut-wrenched that he'd ultimately closed the door on an amazing thing, an amazing woman. But he knew he had to. His feelings for her were becoming unbearable, and when he started to realise that she had strong feelings for him too–more than just a flirtation–he knew he couldn't keep her hanging on, living in a state of confusion, waiting for him to get his crap together and be with her the way she deserve. She was worth so much more than that.

But, worst of all, he'd upset her, and each time he thought of it, of M's face as she spoke to him, on the verge of tears, telling him he shouldn't have led her on, he felt a stab in his chest. His behaviour towards her–sleeping with her when he knew it could go nowhere–was reprehensible. He'd allowed himself to be swept up in the moment–the food, the wine, the cobblestones … the smell of her skin–and then let it continue for a week when he should have given more thought to her feelings and how it may have impacted on her to know that it was a romance that was destined to go nowhere. He should have at least let her know, right from the start. He had warranted so much worse than the berating she had given him.

He'd confronted her because he wanted to tell her the truth. He knew he owed her that much. But, since the conversation, a hollow echo resonated. The fact was, he hadn't given her the truth, not even remotely. If he were any kind of man, any kind of *friend* even, he would have been honest with her–about his son, about Mary, about the fact that he'd twisted his life into such a tangled mess that he couldn't get out of it. Yet he hadn't offered her *any* of that–instead he'd hid under the cowardly let's 'just be friends' pretence.

Friends?! How *that* was even possible, he didn't know. Yet to cut the ties completely would have killed him. Spending time with her, hearing her laugh, seeing her smile, this was often the only thing that got him through the week.

And Thomas, of course.

Adi looked down at Tom fast asleep in his cot. His face was a picture of purity. The love he felt for his little boy was all consuming. Yet, the void he felt in his heart, the absence of romantic love, was something he couldn't deny. What a contradiction! To be so filled up with love, while simultaneously so devoid of it, was like an icy wind that never stopped howling through his soul.

He thought about the conversation he'd had with his sister the other day. In hopeless desperation he'd asked her to meet him for a coffee and a chat. She'd told him to follow his heart. He'd left the café feeling no less confused, as his heart screamed two things: Tom *and* Max.

He realised how very different the two forms of 'love' actually were. While the purity of the love he felt for his son was something that seemed to flow from an internal well—a well that could never dry up, something that his soul regenerated itself on an ongoing basis—he realised that the love he felt for Max came from a very different place, as though pouring out of the universe itself—and it was something a rare and powerful gift, something a person could either choose to accept or reject.

At that moment it all suddenly became crystal clear. He simply couldn't go on living this half life. Terrifying as the thought was of not seeing Thomas every single day, he knew that if he didn't make a change in his life, it would destroy him. And what kind of father and role model would he be for his son, anyway, if he continued to live this way?

"Adi, are you okay?" asked Mary, who'd appeared at the door and noticed him lingering over the baby in sombre contemplation.

He glanced up at her, then turned away. He remained silent for a long time, staring at Thomas, before finally speaking. "No," he said. "I can't do this any more."

19

"You guys! What a surprise!" M squealed, feeling the love from her besties who were waiting out the front of her house as she drove up in a taxi. "I didn't know you would all be here!"

"Oh my God, you're glowing!" shrieked Elisha.

M beamed at her girlfriends as she got out of the car. *Seven days of organic vegetarian food, filtered water, dawn yoga, meditation, Turkish steam rooms, mineral hot springs and detoxifying massages will do that to you*, she thought to herself, although she knew it had also been hard work and she deserved the healthy glow–and clearheadedness–that she now had.

"You guys are too sweet. I'm so lucky," M replied, feeling overwhelmingly fortunate to have such a beautiful group of friends. Despite now being officially jobless, she would always have her friends. She hugged them one by one, then opened her front door.

"I bet you could do with a caffeine hit!" said Laura, as the walked into M's house.

"Actually," said M, surprising even herself, "I think I'll have a herbal tea."

"What?!" laughed Kathy. "That retreat really *did* change you!"

The girls gathered in the kitchen, boiling the kettle and arranging the nibbles they'd brought over onto a platter as M put her bags in her room. She listened to their cheery banter in the other room and really felt so incredibly grateful to have so much genuine love in her life. One week in Byron Bay had made her so much more focussed, wiser and feeling more empowered. It's as though that short break from reality was all it took to make the penny drop for her about her whole situation, and life felt so much clearer. Life is all about the *moment*, she's realised. It's not what happens to you but what you do with it. No longer would she let a situation define her (a.k.a. *Adi!*), but rather she'd use it to do better, learn from it and make better decisions. Being back in her home, she really understood how much she had learned and looked forward to applying it to life.

Right now, however, she just wanted to be with her BFFs–the people that mattered most to her. She joined the laughter in the kitchen. "I soooooo missed you guys," M chuckled, as she took her first sip of tangerine and frangipani tea–just one of the many blends she'd purchased from the gift shop at the retreat before she flew home.

"We've missed you!" said Elisha. "So, tell us all! How was the whole experience?"

"It was a great step," she began. "Some bits were hard–we had team-building exercises, such as tree surfing and kayaking in rapids. Scary! But I met some really nice people during them.

And the weather was gorgeous, so I managed to catch up on a bit of reading by the pool."

"And clearly work on your tan!" said Laura. "Where do I sign up?!"

"It was incredible, Laura. You should totally do it if you ever get a chance," she replied. "Each day began with yoga and meditation, followed by a nature walk. The breakfast buffet was incredible! Brown rice porridge with caramelised dates, organic yoghurt, nuts, seeds, shredded coconut, tropical fruits, freshly baked gluten-free bread, freshly squeezed juices ..."

"Stop it!" interjected Kathy. "You're just trying to torture us!" They laughed.

"The life-coaching sessions were confronting. It wasn't easy talking about my stuff. But I learned some great things. I honestly feel better about myself. It's like I'm happy with or without a man in my life. I just put it away in a box, you know. Just released it all ... well, the prospect of having him in that way, I guess. I have to be happy and love myself regardless of what happens. You just have to be happy with yourself."

"Wow," said Elisha. "I really can see you're in a different place. I'm so proud of you."

M was proud of herself too. She knew that just taking the step to go there was courageous for her, which made her proud she was strong enough to do it. To seek assistance wasn't easy, yet she'd done it as she knew it would make her become emotionally and spiritually attuned. She knew that it would help her to heal—and it had. Her heart had been broken and she had been sad—really, really sad—but the retreat had worked like magic. She'd returned with a whole new take on life. It was now time to reclaim her life.

"I'm going to ask an unpleasant question now," Elisha said. "How do you feel about the whole Adi thing now?"

"You know, I'm honestly okay about it," M replied. "There is nothing I can do about it. You can't change a man or make him love you. Love should be free and come willing. I shouldn't have to beg for it. I still feel for him, if that what you are asking," she said, honestly. She wasn't going to sugar coat it. "But I'm not pining any more."

"That's fantastic, sweetie," said Kathy. "And that sounds perfectly reasonable. Feelings don't just disappear magically overnight. It all takes time. But it's clear that you're in a better place, and that's what matters."

"Yeah, I do have a better outlook about it all. After all, when push comes to shove, they're just boys right?" M said.

"Yep, and boys will be boys," Laura added smiling at her friend. "If you don't mind me stealing a bit of your thunder, I have a little announcement myself," she smirked.

"Oh my, what is it?" M asked.

"Since you left, M, I felt inspired by your little escape. With everything that's happened in my life these past months, I've been feeling I need my own change of perspective for a while. So I'm leaving for New York. I'm going for a month … or three months … or six months … I don't know. I'll play it by ear. I just need an adventure. My cousin lives in Staten Island so she can line me up some work when I get there. She knows a few people. I'll see how it pans out. I think I need to get some distance from it all. Then I can sort things step by step when I get home."

"Laura that is wonderful! I'm so happy that you. I think it's great," M said as she hugged her friend with joy.

"Good for you, darling," said Kathy. "I think this is just what you need. When are you leaving?"

"Well, as soon as possible, really. As soon as I sort out some odds and end."

"Cheers to both of you!" said Elisha, lifting her mug to the toast. "You've both come so far, considering the crap your men have put you through."

"Girl power!" the girls toasted in unison.

M had just started lowering herself into her steaming hot coconut and vanilla bean bath (another well-deserved splurge from the Sunrise Spa Retreat gift shop) when her phone began to ring, startling her—she wasn't quite used to being back in the digital age. *Can't a girl have a moment of peace in the bathroom?*, she thought, as she leaned over to check the screen. And then her heart suddenly skipped a beat.

Adi.

Just when you think you have it all under control and you're ready to conquer the world, the universe tests you.

"You are kidding me," M said out aloud, but then picked up the phone to answer. She knew she could handle this. She felt in a very different place than she'd been a week ago, and had totally accepted the fact that they were *friends* … She just had to forget about the whole Prague thing, and what a sexy bastard he was.

"Hello," she said in a casual, I-don't-give-a-rats-about-you tone of voice.

"Hey, Max, it's me," he said.

"Hi," M replied. She remained strong. She didn't do all that work in order for him to come in and ruin it for her.

"Um, I just wanted to say hi," said Adi. "How are you going?"

"Great, actually, really good. I've been away," M replied, wanting him to hurry up. She didn't want to falter.

"Oh really?" he said. "Where have you been? Actually, don't answer. You can tell me in person. I'd love to catch up—that is, if you don't hate me now. Would you like to? To be honest, I have been thinking about you a lot. I hope it's okay for us to still hang out?" Adi sounded a little hesitant and awkward, nervous even, almost like he was scared to ask her.

M paused as she thought about it. Could she handle this? "Okay," she said at last. She could handle this.

20

M got to the foreshore early as she wanted to get some fresh air to calm her nerves before he arrived as, despite her steely resolve, she had to admit she was a little nervous at the prospect of seeing Adi for the first time since The Chat. Yes, she'd returned from her retreat armed with some Zen new tools, but ultimately she was an emotional person who loved deeply and passionately and was still slightly gutted about the 'friend speech', after all the intimacy they had shared.

She was breathing in the beach air and watching the waves crash onto the shore when she heard her name.

"Maxine."

As she turned and saw Adi standing there, she felt a warm glow that she simply couldn't control. She was happy to see him, with every cell of her being. He looked more handsome than ever and it made her feel giddy. *Oh God, have I made a mistake coming here?*, she thought.

Adi's smile spread from ear to ear as he leaned in and kissed her on the cheek. "How are you going?" he asked, kind of awkwardly.

"Good," she replied, just as awkward. *Dear God, please send a tsunami!* M pleaded silently in her head.

"You're looking … amazing," said Adi, unexpectedly, looking her up and down.

"Oh, well, thanks. As I mentioned, I've been away."

"Yeah, you said. Where did you go?"

"Byron Bay," she said with a slightly forced smile. *I went to a retreat so I could sort myself out because of you, douche*, M thought, her calm momentarily escaping her. What happened to Zen? Once again, she wondered if this had been a bad idea meeting up with Adi, like a recently sober alcoholic going to a wine bar. What the hell was she thinking?

"Byron? Nice. Tell me all about it," he said.

M was happy for the invitation to talk, as, if there was one thing she could do, it was *talk*, and as long as she could babble away about something it would mean she could escape her neurotic thoughts and the awkwardness of being there, next to him … and his sexy smile … and honey skin … and thick kissable lips. As they walked along the boardwalk, she told him about the zumba classes and the tai chi, the roasted pumpkin and cous cous salads, and the deep-cleaning eucalyptus-infused steam room.

"Holy cow," he said, finally getting a word in, "no wonder you look like a million bucks."

M laughed, and they both went silent.

"Listen, M," said Adi, changing tone as he finally cut to the chase. "I have been meaning to speak to you. I don't feel good about where we left thing the last time we spoke."

You and me both, buddy, thought M.

"I wasn't entirely honest with you."

M looked at him curiously. What could he possibly have to say? Did it really matter? She was in a better place and she really didn't want to crack open all the ambiguity all over again.

"Adi, really, you don't need to—"

"No, I really do," said Adi, cutting her off.

Oh God. What could be so important? He's married? He's gay? He has herpes? Her mind raced.

"I'm in a predicament," he said with clear difficulty. "I have been for a while now and it has been a hard one. I'm not sure I've made all the right choices, but I haven't really known how to handle it. It's the reason why I've been acting the way I have."

M's mind ticked over. She was absolutely clueless as to what he could possibly have to say. What could be so bad that could explain his, frankly, prick-like behaviour that impelled him to make mad passionate love to her for six days straight, then later tell her he wants to 'just be friends'? She was starting to feel uncomfortable.

"What is it?" M finally asked, after the pause seemed to stretch out forever.

"I have a two-year-old son," he finally said, with clear relief on his face as soon as the words came out. "His name is Thomas. I'm not in a relationship with his mother anymore, but we do live together." He stopped talking there to gauge her response. She stared at him blankly, so he continued. "We *were* together, of course, but it was only a few months into the relationship when we found out she was pregnant. Things had already become tense, I'm not sure we would have lasted much longer, but, you know, she was *pregnant*. We had to try. Things got *really* difficult from there. We tried to make it work for a while but it all just became too hard, especially after Tom was born. We've stayed under the same roof, but only for the sake of Tom."

M was speechless; there was so much to process—girlfriend, pregnancy, baby, one household.

Adi continued. "I want you to know, when I met you in Prague, you were like this breath of fresh air. So vibrant, funny, beautiful. I knew you'd just come out of a hard relationship so I wasn't expecting it to be more than a fling for you. But when we got back to Melbourne, I felt more drawn to you than ever. Only, by then, I felt like I'd totally deceived you. I know it was misleading on my part. And I should have had this conversation with you ages ago. I'm sorry. I really am. Please don't hate me. It's been tearing me up, it really has." Adi finally took a breath and waited for her reply.

M stood, stunned. A son. This was big. Not what she expected. "Wow, I don't know what to say. Why didn't you tell me earlier? It would have saved so much angst. For both of us."

"I know. I'm sorry. I thought about it so many times. I just couldn't bring myself to say it. It was hard. Not only did I feel like I'd totally misled you, the more I thought about it—you, me, Thomas ... Mary!—the more embarrassed and confused I became. I didn't want to drag you into it, even for a second. I had to work my shit out. I still do."

"Well, thank you for telling me. I'm sorry that it's been tough for you."

It was all too much to absorb. M wanted to run away back to Byron Bay … or maybe even to New York with Laura.

"I want you to know, I'm moving out. I just can't do it any more. I'll get my own place and we'll share custody of Tom," Adi explained.

"Well, you have to do what's right for you," said M, too overwhelmed to really process it all, too burdened with deception, no matter how unintentional it had been. "I'm sure you'll be okay. And so will your son." She didn't know what to feel.

"Are we still okay, Max? Can we still be friends? I'm so sorry I misled you. But I didn't want to drag you into my mess," Adi said.

"Yes, we can be friends," M said, after a considered pause, although she felt somewhat numb. Then, for a crazy moment, she thought about coming clean, spilling her guts and admitting she had feelings for him. But a little voice inside her told her that was madness. She'd done so much work to lift herself out of her lovesick funk and she didn't want to find herself sliding back into it. Adi's life was complicated and the bottom-line was, he needed to sort it out.

As they walked back to the car, she thought about how different everything felt now. She was emotionally stronger and had worked so hard at acceptance and peace. He had taken a huge leap of faith in confession his situation to her. He had exposed himself and finally let her in. She felt strange. Part of her wanted to run, to bury her head in the sand and forget she'd ever laid eyes on Adi. Yet another part of her wanted to embrace him and make all his pain go away. However, she knew that was irrational. He wasn't in the right headspace for anything but being a dad and setting up a new home for himself and room for his son; sorting out all the tangled threads of his life.

When they got to the car park, he turned and stared deep into her eyes, just like in Prague. "Well, thanks for listening and understanding. I really do love spending time with you, Max," he said.

"You will be okay, Adi. You just need time. It will all work out for you. And your son will be fine too. Kids are tough," M replied.

Adi smiled, then leaned in and embraced her in a tender hug. Instantly, it made her, for that split second, feel warm, secure and whole–just like he always made her feel. But she quickly reminded herself that it was just a hug, nothing more.

"Take care, Adi," M said, and then she got in her car and drove away.

As M lay in bed that night, thoughts of the afternoon raced through her head. She was still coming to terms with what he said. A son. That changed the whole story. Maybe if he had come clean in the beginning, things would have been different. It certainly would have spared her all her tormented emotions. On the other hand, she knew it was her fault too. She should have told him how she felt, not tried to play it so cool; not been so afraid of love … or rejection … or whatever it was that held her back. But it was what it was, and she had learned from it.

She sympathised for Adi, but she didn't want to think too hard about it or she'd feel too sorry for him … and if she felt too sorry for him, she'd want to help him … and if she helped him, she would fall in love with him all over again. Besides which, as the life coach had talked about at the retreat, people make their own beds. Adi certainly had. He was on his own journey.

On top of which, with her Zen new change in perspective, there was no way she was going back to her old ways. The truth was, if a man really wanted to be with her, he would fight for her, go to the moon and back–secret son or no son.

As she switched off the light on her bedside table to try to sleep, a thought suddenly occurred to her that made her heart leap with surprise. 'Your one true love will come as two, but before he's yours, he'll be untrue.' Soula's prediction.

No way! thought M. *No fucking way! That's exactly what happened. Adi's not one, he had a son–he's two! Does that mean he's my one true love? Does that mean we're destined to together?*

But before she let her thoughts take off like a runaway freight train, with Zen-like poise, she pulled them back in. She knew they were just words, silly words from a silly old lady, and they could probably be interpreted a million different ways. They really didn't mean anything at all.

"No more what-ifs and maybes … I'm a new M and I'm ready for a new start," she said to the dark, before rolling over to go to sleep.

21

M was lying in yet another delicious essence-infused salt bath and listening to meditation music when Caroline called.

"Heya, how are you?" Caz said.

"Good, baby, just in the bath chilling out. I'm not going to let my hard work go to waste," M replied.

"Well done, darling. I think you are doing a great job. You keep it up," Caroline replied with enthusiasm. "Just one question and I will move on to more delightful things … have you heard from douchebag?"

"Well … actually, yeah. Boy, do I have news, Caz," M replied with a smile.

"What? Tell me! Are you okay?"

"Yeah, yeah, I'm totally fine. It's just that there turns out there's more to Adi than meets the eye … Caz, he has a son!" M blurted out.

"*What!* Are you kidding? A secret son! What's the story?" Caroline spluttered, not knowing where to begin as she was stunned by her friend's revelation.

"Well, a few years ago he was in the throws of a new relationship when his girlfriend fell pregnant by accident, like a few months in. It went pear shaped from there and they tried to keep it together for the sake of the baby, but it didn't work. So they've tried to just live under the same roof, in separate rooms, but it's been a disaster. When we met in Prague, that was his situation. He said he was into me, but he thought I was rebounding from Shamus The Shit and that things wouldn't go anywhere between us, so he decided not to mention his home life. Then when we got back and it seemed like there was something more between us, he felt like he'd betrayed me, kept this kind of huge lie. He was embarrassed ... and confused. Apparently he wanted to tell me, said it was killing him, but he didn't have the balls."

"Oh my God, M. Talk about *The Bold and the Beautiful*," said Caz, clearly astounded.

"He says he can't do it any more, though, and that he's moving out and will do the shared-custody thing," added M.

"I'm speechless, Max. Who would have thought. Gee. It must have been hard for him, I guess. Still, it doesn't excuse his behaviour with you. Not really. I mean, why wouldn't he just tell you in the first place?"

"I know, exactly, right? But, anyway, it is what it is. Or *was what it was*. I'm in a better place and have moved on. But we plan to stay in touch," M said.

"Hey," began Caroline cautiously. "Do you think that maybe he's moving out of there because of *you*?"

"What the ... *no!* Of course not ..."

"It's just," Caz continued, "maybe he has stronger feelings for you than what he's letting on …"

"No, not at all. He says I was a 'breath of fresh air' in Prague. That's all. I think the whole fling just kind of rattled his cage, got him thinking, you know?"

"Hmm," Caz smirked down the phoneline, "Yes, thinking about *you* is my theory. I think he's downplaying his feelings for you because he doesn't want to drag you into his shit. Do you think that's why he gave you the friends talk?" Caroline asked in curiosity. "He doesn't want to stuff you around … yet he also doesn't want to let you go." That's the thing about Caroline—she always cut to the chase, no matter how crazy it might seem.

"*No!* Don't be stupid. He said what he said and that's it. Caz, please, I don't want to do this. I've spent too much time, energy and essential oils trying to move passed this. I can't let myself slip back into that does-he-love-me-or-doesn't-he frame of mind. I need closure."

"Okay, okay, I'm sorry. Just thought I'd mention it," she said with a wink in her tone. "Anyway, I'll see you on Saturday at your place for movie night!"

After they said their goodbyes and hung up, M sunk down deep into her ylang-ylang and geranium bath, allowing all tension to melt away in the delicious steam. Yet one troubling thought refused to evaporate.

Could Adi actually be in love with me too?

22

Adi's new bachelor pad wasn't exactly the Playboy Mansion, but it was nice of his brother and sister-in-law to put him up while his real-estate agent found a more suitable place for him in the city, with an extra room for Tom. Nevertheless, now that he'd finally cut away from the prison of his old life, he felt an overwhelming sense of liberation.

He missed not seeing Thomas every single day, but he and Mary had come to an agreement about custody, and Adi looked forward to the days that he got to collect his boy and see the look of glee on his face as he leapt into his arms. Yes, it was a juggle, but worth it. He certainly felt he could handle the new adjustment–in fact, it was working well for all of them. Mary had taken on some bar work a few days a week and Thomas got to play with his cousins on the days he stayed with his dad.

Adi sat on the deck with a cold beer as his spaghetti sauce bubbled away on the stovetop of his tiny kitchenette and thought of all that was going on and that had happened. He missed Max.

He pictured her there with him, making dinner together, having a drink, laughing.

But he knew he had to stop entertaining such thoughts–it would be totally unfair of him to string her along with the promise of a full-blown relationship at this time in his life. Everything was in such a state of uncertainty and he knew that, until he got his shit together, he had to keep things uncomplicated, in every facet of his life. He was sleeping on a fold-out sofa in his brother's spider-infested backyard bungalow, for Christ's sake! Maxine deserved the red-carpet treatment and she deserved a man who could give her that–and more.

He simply couldn't bare the thought of not having her in his life, though, and he'd do everything in his power to continue to see her, under the banner of 'friendship' … even if it took all his willpower to not try and touch her every second he was around her. He picked up his phone and began to text:

Hi Max, hot summer Friday night forecasted for tomorrow. Meet me on the boardwalk and I'll shout takeaway? A xx

23

Deliciously balmy, it was the perfect night to be outside. M had slipped into a lime-green maxi dress with studded sandals and twisted her hair up into a bun to show off her new gold hoop earrings. *It feels like holidays all over again*, she thought to herself, as she drove to St Kilda with the windows down and the humid air caressing her skin. She thought about how she'd been previously on occasions when she was on her way to see Adi and it felt good knowing that now she was in a different headspace. She was so much more at ease now that she'd laid the relationship to bed—so to speak. Nevertheless, she did still enjoy being with him and, at always, loved the opportunity to see him, if only for takeaway on the beach.

She found a parking spot then adjusted the rear-view mirror to adjust her wind-tussled hair. Applying a touch of lippy, she thought about what Caroline had insinuated the other night, about the possibility of Adi having embarked on his recent changes because he had feelings for her. But then she quickly brushed it off. *He's hanging out with me because he likes my company as a friend*, she said, *plain and simple*. Besides which, he was so busy sorting his life out that he could use a true friend. *A friend with NO benefits*, she laughed to herself, thinking about how much more at ease she felt with no overhanging ambiguity, no what-ifs. Clearly, she still had her defences up a little, but she refused to let the self-talk negate her as it had before.

"That pizza smells good!" said Adi, as they greeted on the boardwalk and he planted a kiss on her cheek in greeting.

"It does," said M and they set off, by silent agreement, towards the kiosk for some gourmet pizza and drinks. There was a long line, as most people had the same idea—hot night, hot house, go to the beach.

"Thank God there is a nice breeze here, hey?" he said, as the queue shuffled forward.

"Yeah, tell me about it. The beach is the only place to be on a night like this."

They reached the front of the line and placed their order as Adi reached for his wallet. "This one's on me."

"Are you sure? I can get drinks—"

"No, no, I got it," he insisted. She smiled.

They headed down to the sand and walked along the beach to find a semi-quiet spot. The sand was soft and warm from the sun. They sat and clicked open their cans of Coca-Cola. As M sipped, she drizzled a little by accident and a drop started running down the side of her mouth.

Adi leaned over and caught the drip before it stained her dress. "Oops, almost spilled," he said, as his finger brushed across her lower lip.

She looked at him with a racing heart. Even after The Chat and the never-ending analysis in her head and all the conversations with the girls, and the retreat … just the touch of his hand made the hairs on her skin stand up on end all over again. She couldn't afford for him to do those things. Not even a brief touch, as she'd just discovered. Was all that work for nothing? Not if they were going to remain 'just friends'. "Um, thanks," she said softly, pulling away.

"This is nice … look at those colours. I love sunsets," he said as he bit into his pizza.

"The breeze is what I'm loving right now," M countered. "Maybe I should sleep on the beach tonight."

"Sounds like a good idea. Have you ever done that?" he asked.

"I was joking," she laughed. "I can't do that. I'm scared of creepy crawlies."

"Like this?" he asked, making crawly spider motions up her leg with one hand.

"Stop it! I'm ticklish," she said, quickly moving his hand away.

He laughed and moved closer to her. "Mmm. Love this. Love the beach on a hot summer night," he sighed happily.

"Yes," she replied simply, taking a deep breath and relaxing. She wanted to press pause so that time would stand still. She may never have another moment like this with him.

Wait. What's happening?! she thought, with alarm.

In that instant, it seemed her inner Zen had taken flight like a seagull. She had a weird sensation in the pit of her stomach and something suddenly became crystal clear. The warm sand, the delicious pizza, the balmy breeze … all of that was magical, but what she realised, what she suddenly knew for certain was: she really did love him. This wasn't just a post-Prague crush. This hit her with such clarity that she *knew*, despite their friend agreement, that she owed it to him–and more importantly to her herself–to tell him. Being Zen was important, but more important was being true to ones self, regardless of the consequences.

The sun dropped down into the bay and, all at once, it was night.

"Ooh, that breeze just got cooler," she said, as goosebumps puckered over her skin.

"Yeah, I'm getting chilly too, all of a sudden." He reached over and put his arm around her shoulder and began rubbing her arms up and down to warm her up.

That was the last straw. Although she was irritated with herself for suddenly falling back into this state of mind, after working so hard to move on, she knew she simply couldn't ignore it. There was no denying it. After tonight, she would have to find the guts to confess to him–sooner rather than later–or else it would tear her up. She couldn't just be friends. And if being more was not an option, than as much as it killed her, she'd have to cut the ties completely.

But could she really find the courage to tell him? It would take real gusto to do it. It's not every day you tell a man–a man who says he wants to be 'friends'–point blank that you're in love with him. It wasn't like when she was considering telling him before. Before it was an expression of interest, a hope that he'd want to take things further with her. This time it was bigger than her. And she knew with absolute certainty that it was love. She was willing to take the risk. The price would become too high in the long run otherwise. Three words, eight letters, and it would be done.

But, she decided, just for tonight, she'd enjoy his arm around her and the smell of his skin as he sat so close, and block out the nerve-wracking conversation that lay ahead of her. Just for tonight, she'd pretend they *were* just two friends, just hanging out, as she knew that once she confess her true feelings, there'd be no turning back. *I'll tell him next time*, she promised herself. And maybe, just maybe, Caroline was right and he did have feelings for her too.

Later that night, M fell into restless slumber, knowing that the wheels of dharma had already begun to turn and that–for better or for worse–her life was about to change dramatically.

24

The sound of the phone ringing startled M into wakefulness, even though it was well after eleven in the morning. It had taken her forever to get to sleep the night before. "Hello?" she said huskily into the receiver.

"Maxine? It's Christen from Mr Ferguson's office. He'd like to speak with you as soon as possible."

"Oh," said M, wondering what he could possibly want so urgently on a Saturday. *Maybe he will tell me the firm can't run without me and will beg me to come back*, M thought with a giggle.

"How's one p.m. today?" asked Christen.

"No problem," M replied.

She hung up feeling somewhat pensive. *Could it actually be possible that he may have another position for me in the company?* she thought, although she didn't want to get her hopes up too high. However, with her Zen new attitude post-retreat, she did feel she was pumping out positive new vibes into the universe. She jumped in the shower and got herself ready.

Decked out in her black power suit and six-inch Manolos, she strutted in Mr Ferguson's office just like it was still her turf and she'd never left. It was a good feeling and it made her remember just how much she missed this place.

"Mr Ferguson?" she said, with a smile, as she knocked lightly on her ex-boss's open office door.

"Well, hello stranger!" Mr Ferguson beamed, giving her a hug, then motioning for her to sit down. "Thank you for coming, M. I'm glad you could do it on such short notice."

"I'm intrigued," she replied. "It feels nice to be back, I must admit. I've missed the office environment."

"I'm glad to hear it, as I have a proposition for you," said Mr Ferguson, cutting straight to the chase. "Our Sydney office has a maternity-leave position that they desperately need filled. It's a project management role and apparently the original replacement, which they lined up months ago, just backed out this morning–can you believe it?–for a full-time offer elsewhere, so they need someone to start, well, pretty much immediately. I know it's not ideal, being temporary at this stage, with option to extend–not to mention interstate–but it's a six-figure salary and being in management, it would be a big step up in your career. Of course, it's your call, but I want you to know, you were the first person that came to mind when they phoned me. I wanted to talk to you first, obviously, before I suggested you. But if you decide to take it, it's in the bag. I know it would be a juggle to relocate by next week, but they're offering a decent moving allowance and have a furnished executive apartment in the CBD that you could take up immediately. To be honest," he added with a chuckle, "I'd take it myself if I could!"

M was floored and sat there in stunned silent. What an offer. She remembered her life coach on the retreat saying that when one door closes, another one opens. She hadn't imagined that meant with Harbour views and a six-figure salary!

"Wow," she finally croaked out. "This is an incredible opportunity. I don't know what to say."

"Look, you don't have to accept it on the spot. It's a lot to think about, a big move, so think it over. I'll email you the job description and all the details. Read it over and get back by first thing Monday," Mr Ferguson said, rising from his chair to shake her hand.

"I will, and thank you so much for thinking of me," M said.

"I've had my ear to the ground, Maxine. You were an asset here and I'd hate for the firm to lose you," he replied.

"Thank you for looking out for me," she smiled.

As she drove home, M's mind was racing at a million miles a second. She felt elated, yet it also felt very surreal. Could she pull this off? A new job, a new city, a new life. She though about the girls and how much she would desperately miss them. But how could she pass up such an opportunity?

Then she thought of Adi. She thought about her feelings for him and her plans to tell him how she felt. Was this offer to move to Sydney throwing a spanner in the works, or was it, in fact, simplifying things. A timely escape hatch? If she told Adi how she felt, there was a chance that he'd reciprocate. But, really, only a slight chance. He had been the one, after all, to give her the 'just be friends' speech. Had anything actually changed since then? Wouldn't it be easier just to take off, leave the complications behind and start over?

No, stated a firm voice in her head. If the retreat had taught her one thing it was that it was essential to listen to her inner voice; her truth. She had to be true to herself. An amazing job offer was one thing, but did it really compare with true love? There was no escaping it. She had to tell Adi how she felt about him or else she'd regret it forever. If he turned her down, well, she knew the first phone call she'd be making would be to Mr Ferguson. A decent consolation prize, but the real jackpot, she knew with absolute certainty, would be hearing Adi tell her that he loves her too.

She had to give Mr Ferguson her decision by Monday morning. Therefore, time was of the essence. Her heart raced in panic and exhilaration as she picked up the phone and texted Adi:

Can you meet me in an hour? I need to talk to you.

The beach had become their favourite meeting spot over the summer. As M sat in her car, waiting for him to arrive, she took deep breathes, trying to work through the anxiety in her gut. She was glad she'd raced home and slipped into a summery dress–she was already sweating up a storm. She started to berate herself for worrying so much about talking to Adi, but then thought about how this *was* a big deal. It was reasonable to be nervous and she shouldn't feel she has to be ashamed of her feelings any more. How often do these moments occur, when someone comes along and rocks your world so profoundly? This was her time.

She thought about all the great love poems and songs and stories of the centuries–the lengths that people went to for this powerful emotion. Love was all around; it had been happening since time begun. She comprehended now how it's a bigger force than the mere individual. It's a gift from the universe. And whether it's reciprocated or not, she knew that expressing those feelings was in itself an act of love and gratitude to the invisible force that it hails from. Once again, the principals of her Zen learnings were turning out to be very helpful in this matter.

"Hi!" Adi said, through her car window, making her jump out of her skin.

"Oh! Hi, yourself," she said, practically in cardiac arrest. She got out of the car and gave him an awkward kiss on the cheek. Dressed in board shorts and a singlet top that showed off his brawny arms, she momentarily wondered why *every* woman wasn't in love with him!

This is it, she thought. *After today, good or bad, everything will be different.* I was time to jump straight to the chase. "So, listen, there's something I need to tell you. Something that I've had on my mind for a while," she began clumsily. She couldn't even make eye contact with him. She stared at the trees, the passing rollerbladers, the seagulls. Anything but his eyes. She feared she would lose her nerve.

"Sure, Max, what is it?" he asked curiously.

"Well, it's just that I've–"

Suddenly they were interrupted by the sound of his mobile phone ringing.

Don't answer! she silently pleaded.

He looked at his phone. "Sorry, Max, I have to take this." He began talking into the receiver as he walked a few steps away to focus on the call.

M stood there with her heart beating like a jungle drum. Her palms sweated and her stomach churned. She was going to be sick. Suddenly, the impulse to flee was overwhelming. *I can't do this!* Before she knew was she was doing, she was back in her car and turning the ignition.

Adi turned around, still on the call, and raised his eyebrows in a 'What the …?' gesture.

She burst into tears and drove away. She sobbed the whole way home. *This is ridiculous*, she thought to herself. When was it ever a good time to come out and tell someone you loved them? She felt like a chicken–a loser. She had built herself up for the big moment and then couldn't follow through.

His call came through as she pulled into her drive. She'd been expecting it, of course. Her heart raced.

"Hello," she said quietly.

"Hey, what happened? Where did you go?"

"I'm sorry, I had to leave. There was something I had to say, but you got distracted and I couldn't … um … it's …"

"What is it, Max? Has something happened?" he asked with concern.

"Oh, it's nothing bad. It's just that I have to be honest with you and there is something that you need to know about me. I … I …" Her words refused to come out.

"Maxine, are you okay? Talk to me, Max."

"I just want to know that spending time with you has been, well, amazing, and I'm really grateful for all of it. I know this is not something you want to hear but I just want you to know that I feel very strongly for you," she blurted out in a rush. "The thing is, it's just that, well, um, it's that I have fallen in love with you," she finally spat out. "I didn't mean to, but I have. I know this changes everything, but I just wanted you to know that I … I … I love you …" M trailed off, tears streaming down her face.

"Maxine, I–" he began.

"Please … don't. You don't have to say anything," she cut in, suddenly deflated and certain he was going to reject her. "I have to go," she said, and hung up quickly.

She stayed in her car for half an hour, with tears pouring endlessly down her cheeks. Each time Adi tried to ring, M pressed the 'decline' button on her phone. When the sobbing finally subsided, she dialled Louis Advertising.

"Hello, Mr Ferguson. It's Maxine. My answer is yes. I'll take it." After she hung up, she felt numb. It was done. Consolation prize it was. She'd just set a new course in motion. She felt sadness mixed with a deep sense of relief.

So her confession hadn't gone to plan. But, then again, she really hadn't had a plan! She'd spent so much time building up her nerve to confront him that she realised she hadn't spent any time at all preparing herself for his reaction. Nevertheless, it was done. She'd finally confessed. As she moved into her new life, there'd be no regrets.

As M got in the door and made a beeline for the bottle of vodka she knew she had stashed in the back of the freezer, a text chimed on her phone. Adi wrote:

> Hey M, since you won't answer my calls, perhaps you'll read
> this. I'm moved by what you said. I had no idea that's what you

felt. Thank you for your honesty. I want to talk to you about it–but first I need to sort some things out xx

At least he acknowledged it, she thought. But beyond that, what he thought, what he felt, M had no clue. The message gave very little away. Yet clearly her feelings weren't reciprocated as that would have been the easiest reply in the world. Nevertheless, she felt a strange sense of calm; a liberation. She'd needed to tell him, and she had. Now ... what would be would be. Until they spoke, she'd stay busy and try not to think too hard about it.

Regardless, she had bigger things on her plate now: the big move ... and saying goodbye to her best friends.

Speaking of which, the timing was perfect as the girls would be heading over shortly for movie night, including Caroline. It was just the distraction she needed–several bottles of red, popcorn and chips, a soppy love story–because, *my God!*, so much had happened over the last twenty-four hours.

"Gee, how appropriate," M said, when she saw the cover of *An Affair To Remember* as Kathy walked in the door.

"Hell, why not?" Kathy replied. "It's romance and tragedy and happy-ever-after all in one. Plus I love the Empire State Building thing, you know." She'd made her famous sponge cake and went straight to the coffee table to start slicing it up to pass around.

"Ooh! Cake!" said M.

"Nothing like cake to soothe the soul," Laura said.

"Plus, we're celebrating tonight," M said.

"Celebrating what?" Kathy asked, through a mouthful of sweetness.

"Us. Women. Laura moving to New York. And me being offered a job in Sydney and accepting," she said. "Oh, and finally telling Adi that I love him," M added with a smirk, waiting for the hysteria to begin.

"What?!" exclaimed Elisha and Laura in unison.

"You told him?!" squealed Caroline.

"Sydney?!" shrieked Kathy.

"Where to begin?" laughed M. "Yes, it's been a big day …"

By the time they'd polished off the first bottle of wine and half the cake, M had brought them up to speed with the afternoon's events. "I still can't believe it, girls. I'm going to miss you guys so much!" she said, getting teary eyed.

"Oh stop it," said Kathy. "With you *and* Laura leaving, you'll have me sobbing on the floor!"

"I'm so proud of you, M," said Caroline. "You told him how you felt. You faced it head on. And, like you said, what will be will be."

"Do you think he'll call?" asked Elisha.

"I don't know," said M. "But either way, it's like a huge weight is lifted."

"You have to do what's best for you," Laura said. "And Sydney's not far away–"

"Unlike New York," interjected Kathy.

"Hey, you'll just have to come visit!" said Laura.

"And visit me too," chimed in M. "I'm getting an executive apartment as part of the package."

"Bitch!" shrieked Caroline, and they all laughed.

"I can't believe you're leaving next week," said Elisha. "How on earth will you be ready in time?"

"The firm organises a packing service, so it's really just a matter of tying up some loose ends," M replied.

"Like Adi," said Elisha. "Be proud, M, you ticked a huge 'loose end' off your list."

"Here here!" said Laura. "We're always putting ourselves on the line and going out on a limb for men. Well done. Pat yourself on the back, darling."

"You did so great, sweetheart," Kathy added, as she opened the second bottle of wine. "You finally put it out there. If you don't take chances in life, you're not really living."

The wine was poured and they all lifted their glasses.

"To Laura's adventures!" toasted M.

"And to our gorgeous Maxine," said Kathy. "An inspiration to us all."

The girls clanked their glasses and M felt a wave of love and peace, surrounded as she was by the people who cared about her and loved her the most. At that moment, that was all that mattered. The future was uncertain, but she had her friends. And whatever happened, they would always be there for each other.

25

As planned, M arrived at Laura's house the next morning for their outing. Determined to keep busy, M had suggested a 'girly' day—museum, lunch, perhaps a movie later on. With her new job starting in Sydney, she knew visiting Laura in New York simply wouldn't be an option any time soon, so she wanted to make the most of the time they had left. She arrived to find the gate open, so she went in and around to the back door.

"Laura, are you ready? I'm here," she called loudly. When there was no response, she stepped inside and found Laura lying motionless on the couch in her pyjamas.

"Hey! What's wrong?" she asked, startled.

Laura peeled herself off the couch enough to point to the envelope lying on the coffee table. "I got it hand delivered this morning. I guess this is it."

M looked down at the official-looking unopened envelope on the table and didn't need to be a psychic to realise that it was divorce papers. "Oh, honey, I don't know what to say. Really, I'm so sorry," M said genuinely saddened.

"The last few months of going to counselling was starting to help, slowly. I was starting to understand and come to grips with reality, with the fact that James is not coming back. He's moved on, and how I have to do the same. But this? This is a bitter pill to swallow. It's so *final*."

Laura looked around the family room and M's eyes followed her movement. Photos of James and Laura had been replaced with images of other family and friends. James's fifty-inch plasma television screen had gone and been replaced by a thirty-two-inch one, thanks to a friend who was upgrading and insisted that Laura have it.

Laura rose and M followed her. They walked by the spare room, and M noticed the open wardrobe, which had been cleaned out—no more fishing gear, no snow equipment. Now it appeared to be filled with all of Laura's storage items—photo boxes, winter boots and coats, books.

"Yep, it's all mine now," Laura said, seeing where M was looking. "James has left the building. I thought I'd be out of here and in some tiny little apartment, but for some reason I can stay here for now. Maybe he got a last-minute conscience. You know, my counsellor reminded me of the 'out with the old, in with the new' theory the other day. He told me that cleaning out one's closet is like cleansing one's soul and spirit. Change is ever-present in life, and we have to roll with it. So I took him literally."

"I totally agree," said M, thinking of her own cleaning fetish, which had long been her crutch in times of crisis. "I guess in life, the one thing that remains constant is change. Nothing is ever meant to stay the same." M felt a sense of loss herself and she understood this theory and believed it to be true. But, for Laura, she knew that this was a defining moment—to learn to live the way she wanted to, on her terms. Her friend's next words confirmed this.

"I'd been thinking about renovating the house. Once all is finalised, you know, to really make it *me*, to represent my new life," Laura said. She sighed deeply. "And now I guess I can."

"That sounds great. Keep that as a goal and a focus," M said encouragingly.

That particularly sombre Sunday, they sat around Laura's almost empty house, the museum and movie no longer mattering. Now it was all about processing the inevitable and accepting reality. Planning a new beginning.

Laura knew she had to deal with that envelope on the coffee table eventually and that she'd rather do it while M was there to support her, so she made them both a vodka and tonic, then sat down before it. Sure enough, it was a petition to file for divorce. M sat quietly next to her on the sofa as she read through the documents.

"I guess I'll need to call my solicitor tomorrow to make an appointment," she finally said, when suddenly there was a knock at the door. Laura stood, walked to the front door and looked through the peephole. The next thing M heard was her friend's shocked gasp.

"*Oh, my God. What is he* doing here?" Laura whispered.

"Is it …?" M half-asked.

Laura nodded from the door, eyes wide.

"Are you fucking *kidding* me?" M burst out. "You want me to tell him to go?"

"No, it's okay. I have to face him sooner or later. Just wait in the spare room. I'll be okay. Really."

M walked into the other room and shut the door most of the way, standing behind it and listening avidly. She heard the front door open and James step inside.

"What are you doing here?" she heard Laura ask angrily.

"Look, I'm sorry to bother you. I just wanted to talk to you, in person."

"You could have called rather than just popping in. I wasn't prepared for this."

"I wanted to see if you were okay. I think you would have got the papers?" James asked in a low voice.

"Yeah … yeah, I got them alright. Thanks. Really appreciated it. Now if you could just–"

"Laura, wait. I never meant to hurt you. You have to believe me. I can't change the way I feel. I know what I did it was wrong, but I couldn't–"

"No worries, James. You ran into the arms of another woman without thought, respect or explanation. You made me feel worthless, you asshole. I hope she gives you all you are looking for."

"Worthless? You're anything but. You are a wonderful person. I just couldn't do it any more–try to be that person you wanted me to be. I was lying to myself."

M rolled her eyes, glad to hear how uncomfortable James sounded, and silently cheering on her friend.

"Is she that good, James?" Laura snapped. "Is she? Did she have you at hello? I can't see you any more. It makes me sick just thinking about it. I hope you are very happy together. I will be in touch through my lawyer. Let me just say that *I* will play fair. I don't want to fight like a predator. But do *not* come to this door. Ever. Again."

M heard the door slam so hard, it rocked the house. She waited a moment, then came around the door and back into the family room to find Laura sobbing on the couch.

"Oh my God, honey, you handled that *so* well. I'm so damn proud of you, Laura." She sat down next to her friend.

Laura threw her arms around her. "Thanks, M. Thanks so much for being here. I'm sorry you had to be here for that. But I'm also really glad you were."

"I can stay for as long as you like," M said.

"No, that's okay. I'll be fine. I think I need to be alone now. You go and enjoy the rest of the day. Really, I'm fine. The worst is over now. I will call you if there is anything, I promise."

"Okay, sweetie. As long as you're sure. Let me know if you need anything–anything at all. I'm so proud of what you just did, kiddo," M replied, smiling. She hugged her friend and then left her to her healing process.

M stopped at Jerry's on the way home. She needed a coffee after what she had just witnessed ... not to mention the fact that Adi still hadn't made contact. Almost twenty-four hours had gone by since she'd spilled her guts to him. What exactly was it that he needed to 'sort out' before he could speak to her? She knew she was indulging in unhealthy self-pity, but she couldn't help but let it make her feel like a loser. Quickly, though, she gave her internal self a slap across the face. *He's the loser!* she said to herself. *It's his loss.* She'd tried to be the bigger person when he came clean about his son, but now, with his insulting silence, she was reaching the point where she didn't care anymore.

"Hello, beautiful girl!" Jerry yelled from across the room. "How are you? The usual, love?"

"Hi Jerry! Yes, please ... actually, no, wait, make that a doppio." The owner nodded. Just then she spotted Soula at an outside table. She smiled and went and sat with her.

"How is everything, darling?" Soula asked. "Are you okay?"

"Well, my career is about to soar to new heights as I got a new job so I'm moving. I'm going to miss this place," M replied. She couldn't believe that she was being so candid with Soula, once again, but she figured her advice last time had been so spot on. Old Greek women were so switched on.

"That is great news! But ... I detect something else ... This problem is with a boy, yes?"

"Of course–isn't that what I'm always complaining about?" M said, trying to make a joke of it. Soula smiled gently.

"What's happened?"

"Well, that man I told you about, the one I thought I had feelings for ... I told him how I feel. Yet, he didn't really reply and it's been a whole day and he hasn't really said anything to me," she said. She could hear the disappointment in her own voice and tried to change tune. "I'm proud of myself for doing it; I need to tell him, move forward, you know. Hell, there are plenty of fish in the sea, eh?" she added, trying to lighten the mood.

"My dear girl. You are a beautiful person. If this boy is too blind to see that, then he is lost. It is hard because love is a very powerful thing. You stay strong and have faith always. Remember to always open your heart. I see someone coming for you … but he comes in two."

"That's what you said before," said M.

"Ah, I did? Well, yes, I still see that. He is coming. But, in the meantime, enjoy your life and be happy."

M heaved a sigh and smiled at the older woman. It seemed like wise advice; simple. She was baffled by the comment, though. 'Comes in two'–could it be Adi and his son she's referring too? Or was that just wishful thinking? What else could it mean?

"Thank you so much for your kind words. You've made me feel better about things," said M. Despite everything else, she knew she should take the 'just chill' advice totally on board–wise advice for anyone.

They sat together in silence as they finished their coffee, enjoying the sunshine. Then M got up to leave, but before she did, she leaned down and gave the lovely Soula a warm hug.

26

The girls met on Tuesday night for Laura's send-off at an old English pub that had been renovated into a modern Art Deco eatery with an exceedingly well-stocked bar, large dining area and rooftop lounge, which had quickly become a local hotspot. She'd insisted they say goodbye to her over drinks, as doing it at the airport would be too sad.

One by one, the girls arrived and were directed to their reserved table on the rooftop. Kathy had got there first and taken the liberty of ordering two jugs of sangria, as the girls came in one by one. M poured herself a glass of cool, fruity deliciousness and sighed with pleasure after her first sip.

"We're going to want updates on all the hotties and the adventures," Elisha admonished with a grin.

"Imagine that huge island with all those eligible men. Makes me want to pack my bags too," Elisha said.

"I would like to propose a toast," Kathy said. They all raised their glasses. "To friendship and good times ahead. To Laura."

"And Maxine!" chimed in Elisha.

"No way," said Kathy. "She doesn't leave until the day after tomorrow—I refuse to say goodbye now!"

"Cheers. To Laura!" they said in unison, as they clinked glasses.

"It's going to be far too quiet around here without you guys," Kathy continued. "Yeah, can you believe it? No more drama," Laura laughed.

"Oh, as if," Elisha replied, rolling her eyes. "I've still got Jackson!" They all chuckled.

Friend are the best medicine, M thought to herself. It was nice to be able to laugh and just relax. What will be will be, but for now she knew that she was the master of her own fate.

They talked and laughed for a couple of hours, enjoying their last night as a foursome for the foreseeable future. Finally the time came to say goodbye, and the girls all hugged Laura tightly one by one. It was a nice moment, M thought. After all, it wasn't goodbye—it was 'see you later'.

27

With Laura's departing, it was the final countdown for M's own. She couldn't believe how quickly things could change—he entire world had been turned upside-down in less than a week!

It was five days post-confession and she still hadn't heard from Adi. As each day passed, it got a little easier as she convinced herself a little bit more to just let it go, release, trust in the universe, move on. Everything was happening for a reason.

She looked at a photo on her bedside table. It was a picture of her and the girls, taken a year ago at Kathy's thirtieth birthday at a fancy Japanese restaurant. She remembered the laughs that night like it was yesterday, with a smile on her face. She couldn't believe all that could transpire within a year. Talk about life-changing! She took the frame and put it in her suitcase—at least the girls would be there with her in spirit. And they really were only a short plane ride away.

Kathy and Elisha had offered to manage the leasing of her house, which was a big load off her mind. She really didn't know how she could have survived without her friends. Caroline had been phoning every day to check in on her–never once mentioning the 'A' word … which M was so appreciative of.

Tomorrow was D-Day–the landing in Normandy. *Or*, M thought with a smirk, *the landing in Sydney, to be exact.* As she zipped up her suitcase, the phone rang. She looked at the number. She didn't recognise it. Could it be Adi? Maybe he was calling to finally confess his real feelings. She took a breath and picked up the phone.

"Hello?" she said.

"Hello, Maxine, it's Paul Ferguson. How are you?"

M was stunned and surprised to hear from Mr Ferguson. "I'm well, thank you. How are you?" she replied, a little taken aback.

"Good, good. Listen, as you're leaving tomorrow and I just wanted to wish you luck. I think you'll be a great asset to the Sydney team. They're lucky to have you," he said enthusiastically.

"Thank you so much, Mr Ferguson. It really means a lot that you called," she said. "I really appreciate you finding this position for me and recommending me. I think its come at a good time," she said.

Mr Ferguson picked up on this immediately. "Maxine, I don't know what's happened in your personal life as of late. But I've seen you've been going through a hard time. I just want you to know, I have full confidence in you and your abilities, and whatever has happened, a change of scene is always a good thing. I think this job is just what you need. I'm not far away if you ever need anything," he said compassionately.

M felt a wave of emotion. "Thank you for that, Mr Ferguson. And thank you for all your support," M replied, trying to be professional in order to mask her emotion.

"Remember, Maxine: grab life by the helm. Don't be scared to try. Take care."

"You too, Mr Ferguson," M said before hanging up.

Suddenly she couldn't hold it together any longer and she burst into tears and blubbered like a baby. *Good Lord*, she thought to herself, *am I crying about Mr Ferguson?!* The thought made her instantly laugh at the ridiculousness, as she knew, of course, that it was another man that was causing the tears to flow. The flood of tears streamed down her face. She cried and cried and felt the release. It was cathartic. She knew she was saying goodbye to everything, the world she'd built for herself, and also to the man that had been in her heart for so long. With every tear she shed, she felt the weight lift.

M zipped up her suitcase, finally ready for the next chapter.

28

"M, relax! You've checked everything four times already," Elisha said, smiling.

"Yeah, I know. That's just me, I guess. Type A personality," she laughed.

"Have you got everything, darling? Documents, magazines, phone, lipstick, passport?" Kathy asked.

"Ha, ha! Yes, I have. I know they're strict with the passport control in the Sydney domestic arrivals." They laughed.

The girls had come to bid her farewell. They'd watched suffer over the past months, but seeing her happy now and embarking on a new chapter in her life filled them all with joy. They group-hugged.

"I'm going to miss you guys," M said as she was swept with a wave of emotion.

"Us too, sweetie," Elisha said, starting to cry.

"Don't cry because then we'll *all* start," Kathy said, surreptitiously dabbing at the corner of her eye.

"Thank you for all you've done for me, both of you. I love you very much," M said.

"We love you, too. You go and have a great time. Don't worry about the house, we'll advertise it on Airbnb. We have it covered." Elisha said.

With that, they hugged one last time and M was off in the taxi. As she sped towards the airport, she thought she'd make one last-ditch attempt to close the book with Adi. Since he hadn't contacted her, she decided she'd end it nicely with him. It was the adult thing to do. She tapped into her iMessages:

> Couldn't leave without telling you, I'm leaving for Sydney, flight leaves at 3. Unexpected promotion in the Paddington office. New job, new city, next chapter. Wanted to tell you in person. In fact, so much to say. Where to begin. I'm sorry if I rattled you. But it needed to be said. I wanted you to feel the same. But I'm okay that you don't. Love is too big to not be reciprocated completely. It's all or nothing. I realise that now. But I hope you don't mind if I keep a little piece of you in my heart forever. And, remember, we'll always have Prague XX (#bogartandbergman #casablanca #yesIknowI'mlame)

As she hit 'send', she felt a weight lifted off her shoulders.

29

"Congratulation, Adi!" said the estate agent, shaking his hand. "I'm sure you and your son will be very happy in your new home!"

Adi beamed. To say it was a relief to have found a new house was to put it mildly. And located so close to work, and so close to Thomas' daycare centre, it felt like a huge box finally ticked. A new chapter. Although the three-month settlement date was still a while away, but at least he could start planning–buying furniture, contacting utilities companies, start to build a new life. And, most importantly, finally be able to confess to Max that he loved her too. He hoped to God he hadn't blown it and that she'd still want him.

At last his life felt like it was coming out of the doldrums that he'd existed in for so long. He so looked forward to the future ahead. He'd felt terrible about not calling Max, but with the house settlement so close, he didn't want to talk to her until the offer was accepted and the papers were signed. He wanted to wait until he was actually in a position to start building a future with someone, as he knew that, until he got himself sorted, he simply wasn't the man she deserved. As much as he wanted her, he didn't want to even try to start something with her while he felt like a loser, sleeping on a fold-out sofa, living a half life!

But all of that was now behind him … well, at least in thirty days it would be.

As he left the real estate's office, the first thing he did was get out his phone to call M. Just at that moment, speak of the devil, his phone chimed, as he received her text.

Oh fuck! He looked at his watch. *There was still time*, he thought to himself, thanking God his real estate agent office was so close to the airport.

30

M relaxed in the passenger lounge with a magazine and a bottle of water, waiting for her boarding call. As she reached into her bag to check her phone for any last-minute messages, she found a mysterious envelope tucked inside, which she pulled out with curiosity. It contained a photo–which, no doubt, Kathy had slipped into her purse when she wasn't looking–of all of them, all the girls, dressed as cartoon characters at a fancy-dress party they had years ago. On the back there was a caption: 'Life is what you make it. Always make sure you laugh'. Tears streaming uncontrollable down M's face. She felt such gratitude. She took a few deep breaths and a sip of water, just as the boarding announcement commenced.

As she gathered her travel documents and stood, she noticed several people, obviously running late, walking briskly toward the gate. One of them, a man, seemed to be coming straight for her. As he came closer, her heart sank to the pit of her stomach. She felt paralysed. The one person she thought she would never bump into was walking toward her.

Adi.

He stopped in front of her. There was an awkward pause as they both stood there, staring at one another, until finally he spoke. "I got your message. I couldn't let you just disappear without seeing you again."

M took a deep breath. "I'm not sure why you are here, but I'm leaving, so–"

"Sydney, eh?" he cut in, his eyes glassy. "I suck at timing."

"Yes, you certainly do," she laughed.

"I'm sorry for all the pain I've caused you. I didn't want that … ever. I've been an idiot. I hope you can forgive me, M," he said, looking deep into her eyes, clearly overwhelmed with emotion. "My God," he said. "I'll miss you like crazy. I can't believe the time I've wasted. I needed to sort my shit out. Max, I just bought a house! But now I'm too fucking late. I'm an idiot. A lovesick idiot. I love you, Maxine."

"Yes, you *are* an idiot," she smiled, gleaming. "But you're not too late. I love you too, Adi."

He grabbed her arms and pulled her close. Their lips locked in a passionate kiss.

"When will you be back?" he whispered huskily into her neck.

"Actually," she said smiling, "I get a flight home per month. It's part of my package."

At this, he couldn't even pretend to contain his smile. "And how do you feel about long-distance romances?" he said.

"Optimistic," she replied.

"Late-night phone calls?"

"Can do."

"Skype?"

"My best friend."

"Phone sex?" he winked.

"Hey, buddy, don't push your luck," she said, winking back.

As the final announcement was made, they kissed again, until, reluctantly, M pulled away from his embrace began walking towards the awaiting flight attendant at the exit.

"Hey, I know someone who might be interesting in renting out your house for the next few months–my settlement's not until June," he called out to her. "And my brother's bungalow smells like spiders!"

"Oh, sure!" she called back. "But don't you dare bring any of those spiders with you. And, um … if your settlement's delayed, you'll still have to be out by June," she quickly threw in, smirking to herself.

"Okay. Why?" he asked, suddenly very curious.

"This job's only a three-month maternity-leave position, you lovesick idiot," she said, as she blew him a kiss and headed off down the boarding ramp, leaving him standing there in the terminal, grinning like the Cheshire Cat.

END

Acknowledgements

To ALL of my friends who have supported me and been there for me. You are invaluable. To my mother for all her love. To Julie and the team at OpenBook Creative, thank you for making my dream a reality. To Bree thank you for your ideas and thoughts - you allowed the words to manifest.

About the Author

Once Bitten Twice Shy is the debut novel of Marisa Ferraro. A huge fan of tv shows and books that resonate with professional single women and their quest for love, she is a great observer of her own, and friends, relationship experiences. Marisa finally put pen to paper to deliver a book about love, life and the meaning of it all. Marisa lives in inner city Melbourne. She is often out with her friends, enjoying wining and dining and taking in all of what the city has to offer. She is usually spotted in heels and her signature RayBans.

CPSIA information can be obtained
at www.ICGtesting.com
Printed in the USA
BVOW09s1348201117
500905BV00001B/88/P